Jack-In-The-Box

Mark T. Bacome

RedVette Media Productions— Silverdale, WA
ISBN: 978-0-9852360-7-6
eBook ISBN: 978-0-9852360-6-9
Library of Congress Control Number: 2023915066
Title: *Jack-In-The-Box*
Author: Mark T. Bacome
Digital distribution | 2023
Paperback | 2023

Edited by Jennifer Grace

Dedication

I would like to dedicate this book to my loving wife Jacquie and daughter Amberlyn for their inspiration of this story while playing to a simple nursery rhyme "Jack-in-the-Box" many years ago. As I overheard them playing, the rhyme sounded to me more like a synopsis from a Steven King horror novel. We laughed about what I thought I was hearing in the simple rhyme that day, then Jacquie strongly encouraged me to write the story. Jack-in-the-Box is that story after nearly twenty years of "thinking about it."

Thank you Jacquie and Amberlyn, I love you both.

Prologue

Sunday, November 11th, 1956

Jack pressed his hand high above his head against the cold pane of window glass at the front of the large building as he watched his mother winding her way down the path to the cab they had arrived in moments earlier. He wanted to be sure she could see him waving good-bye. Her heels clicked on the hard pavement down the second and third set of steps while her yellow hair, topped in a red bandanna, glowed in the sunlight as she stepped from the shade of the large building. Her long heavy brown winter coat reached almost down the full length of her dark red dress well below her knees. She paused each time at the top of the next set of steps, taking care while stepping down to the next level. She stepped into the cab and closed the door. He did not dare breathe or blink in fear he might miss her glance. He could see her through the back car window as the bright yellow car drove away. He waited for her to turn. He waited as the car slowed at the corner then turned up the side street and disappeared from view. He waited, but she never looked back.

Jack's heavy sigh of disappointment fogged the dirty glass and he wiped the trace of the tear on his cheek as he turned to see his little sister, Jillie, sitting on the edge of a wooden bench in the long wide hall. She was attempting to be brave and fight back her own tears, as she clutched Mr. Carrots, a small floppy patchwork rabbit doll. Jack would need to step up and help his little sister. He turned six years old today; Jillie was still only four and she did not understand why Mommy had to leave.

Jack brushed the dirt from the window sill off his Sunday coat, adjusted his white-collared shirt and bow-tie, and placed their suitcase on the bench behind Jillie so they both could sit more comfortably.

Jillie wore her favorite blue dress with white dots, her nice white coat, little white gloves, white Sunday hat over her shoulder-cut blonde hair with a blue ribbon that matched her eyes, white knee-high socks and shiny black-buckled shoes. Jack wiped at a small scuff mark on her shoe. Mommy would be upset to see Jillie had already scuffed her shoes. He took a quick glance at his own dress black shoes to be sure they were unmarred.

Mommy had told them to wait on the bench and someone would be there soon to take care of them, so they waited. Jillie held tight to Jack's arm while snuggling Mr. Carrots. A real nice nurse-lady at the hospital had given Jillie Mr. Carrots last year when Mommy had gotten mad at her for knocking over a glass of Mommy's special night drink. The nice nurse-lady said Mr. Carrots would help take the pain away from around Jillie's bruised eye. Jillie had not let go of Mr. Carrots since. Jack could not forgive himself for not watching Jillie closer that night, keeping her away from the glass sitting on the edge of the table. He loved Mommy so much, and never liked to see Mommy upset.

The large building seemed very old, and although the air was warmer inside from the cold November chill outside, there was still a draft of cool air that Jack could feel across his legs. The draft brought along an awful smell like the dirty bucket of water the cleaning-man always seemed to have at the hotel where they lived. Jillie smelled it too. She buried her face into the arm of his coat.

The double wooden door where they had entered had two large windows on each side and opened up to a long wide hall. Across from the lone wooden bench where they sat, was a door with a built-in glazed window and some writing. Jack was learning his letters and read them to himself: O. F. F. I. C. E. He pondered what those letters spelled as they continued to sit and wait.

"I'm hungry," Jillie said muffled through Jack's coat sleeve.

Jack nodded and slid off the front of the bench and searched through his pockets. He pulled out a candy bar and tore the wrapper open half way down, broke the bar in half and handed a piece to his sister.

Jillie scowled, "But that's your birthday canny bar."

"I know," Jack shrugged. "And I can do with it what I want. I want to share it with you."

Jillie smiled, first pretended to feed Mr. Carrots a bite, then nibbling a bit for herself. Jack wrapped his half and shoved it into his pocket. He noticed the wallpaper behind Jillie was dirty and torn, showing brick underneath. Further down that wall were another set of double doors and at the end of the wide hall another set of double doors across from what looked like a crossing hallway. Out of the corner of his eye, Jack thought he saw someone peeking from around the corner but there was no one there.

The whole building seemed to be alive with various sounds radiating from all directions. Some sounds seemed like muffled mechanical noises just like their hotel. Then there were the other noises, like children, but far off in the distance. The sound of adults talking grew louder and finally a woman stepped out from the door with the letters, giggling and clutching at her blouse. Her skirt was tight, just like Mommy wore. She stopped short when she saw the two children by the bench.

"Oh, hello," she said. Jack could feel his cheeks flush when he noticed bare skin through the opening in the young woman's blouse. The young woman attempted to close her top. "Who are you?"

An older balding man stepped out, wearing suit-pants, and a white-collared shirt and vest like the businessmen in the big city. He was not as tall as the young woman but was much heavier and stumbled behind the woman as she had stopped right in his path.

"My name is Jack Thompson and this is my sister, Jillie. I'm six years old and my sister is four. My Mommy brought us here to stay the night. My Mommy says she is going to become a movie star and will be back for us when she is done. She says that I am old enough to start school now and she promised she will be back to take me to my new school," Jack had memorized what Mommy had told him to say.

"Oh, honey," the young woman said, shaking her head in dismay.

"Helen. Umm Miss Ward, I've told you before. Do not interact with them."

"But that is just sad—"

"They're all just sad. You cannot be involved or get attached."

The double doors at the far end of the hall opened and a man carrying a bucket and mop stepped out. The man in the vest waved him down. "Ruphord, come here."

"Yes sir, Mr. Farwether." The man wore overalls over a dirty white undershirt and an unbuttoned plaid shirt over with his sleeves rolled up to his elbows. Jack thought his overalls were too short, not quite reaching the tops of his dirty and worn-out ankle-high boots.

Ruphord stopped by another door just a few feet away from the office door and set the mop and bucket down.

Ruphord gave Miss Ward a long glance, combed his straggled greasy-black hair back with the fingers of his right hand and wiped at his stubble-covered chin with the back of his other. "Mrs. Farwether and the girls here today?" Ruphord asked with a smirk. Miss Ward cringed at the sight of Ruphord's single mangled upper tooth.

"Ruphord, you know my family never miss Sunday church. Now Miss Ward and I will be in a—business meeting—for a few hours. Miss Ward, if you would please. I'll meet you shortly." Mr. Farwether gestured toward the far end of the hall.

"Of course," Helen answered, attempting to sound professional. She clutched at her blouse with both hands, uncomfortable with the look Ruphord was giving her as she walked away. The two men waited and watched her all the way to the end of the hall, until she was out of sight around the corner. The sound of her heels clicking on the hard black tiled floor echoed back from around the corner along with the sound of a door squeaking open, then closing.

Jack thought about a time he had asked his Mommy about church. She told him churches were not a place for mothers with children and no father. Too snooty, she said. Jack helped Jillie down from the bench, and she clung tight to his arm with one hand and Mr. Carrots with her other. He was not certain what was happening but wanted to be patient and act appropriate. He wanted his Mommy to be proud.

"As you can see we've had two more arrivals today," Mr. Farwether said, keeping his voice low.

"Registered?"

"On a Sunday? Of course not. Just another drop-off."

"That makes six over the last three weeks," Ruphord said and turned his attention to the two children. Jack did not feel comfortable with the look the strange man was giving them. Mr. Farwether refused to even glance in their direction.

"You know the routine. Just take care of it, and keep them quiet. I don't want to be disturbed."

"Yes sir, Mr. Farwether."

"One more thing—"

"Yes sir, Mr. Farwether?"

"We had that awful smell from the furnace again this last week."

"Yes sir, Mr. Farwether. I think another raccoon got into the furnace."

"Well, I have no idea why that keeps happening, but I want you to figure out a way to get that stopped."

"Yes sir, Mr. Farwether, I'll do my best." Ruphord knelt down next to the children then turned to watch Mr. Farwether walk all the way to the end of the hall and round the corner. He waited until he could hear the door open then close. He even waited for the sound of the door lock turning that echoed back up the long wide hall.

When Ruphord turned back toward Jack and Jillie, Jack noticed Ruphords' contorted smile with his single upper tooth. "My name is Jack and this is my sister Jillie—"

"Jack and Jill went up the hill," Ruphord interrupted with a sing-song tone, and turned his direct attention to Jillie, holding tight to her brother's arm. Ruphord leaned in and pulled her closer as he put his face into the back of her neck and took in a deep breath. Jillie tried to pull away and whimpered her displeasure into Jack's jacket sleeve from the man's actions and abhorrent breath.

"You are not a nice man," Jack announced.

"You smell just like your momma, sweet as apple pie," Ruphord said. "I just might have to have me some sweet apple pie today."

"My Momma—"

"Your momma nothing boy! What have we here?" Ruphord grabbed at Mr. Carrots, catching Jillie off-guard, as he snatched the doll from her without warning. Jillie started to cry out. "Hush now, ya' hear. If you want this back you'll be real quiet now." Ruphord hissed shoving the doll into his overalls. "You heard Mr. Farwether. He don't want to be disturbed while he an' Miss Helen are meetin'."

"You give that back to my sister," Jack demanded.

"I said quiet, and I mean both of y'all." Ruphord took Jillie by the arm. His vice-like grip hurt Jillie even through her coat-sleeve and she reacted by biting at the mean man's hand. Jack took the opportunity and kicked at Ruphord as well.

"Fighters! I like me some fighters." Ruphord took Jack by the arm and he now felt the pain of the man's strong grip as well. Keeping their arms stretched out too high to bite at, Ruphord drug the children toward the double doors just a few feet away along the wall. He pushed through the unlatched doors and onto a landing of stairs that went both up and down, and started down.

"Let go of us," Jack yelled as Jillie kicked and screeched and cried in pain. The mechanical noises became louder as they continued down the stairs to a lower level.

"You can scream all ya' want now. Ain't no body gonna care. Even ol'man Farwether boning Miss Helen won't be hearing ya'll down here," Ruphord continued, dragging Jack and Jillie along a dark corridor into a hot dark room full of pipes and tools.

"Let us go! You give Mr. Carrots back to Jillie!" Jack yelled as loud as he could.

Ruphord flung Jillie toward a stack of crates next to a table. She bounced off the crates and slumped to the dirty floor with a stunned whimper. Ruphord held Jack high enough his feet dangled above the ground. "Jack an' Jill, went up the hill," Ruphord versed then stopped. "I've got one even better. You can be my Jack-in-the-box."

"Jillie, Jillie!" Jack called to his sister over and over, but she just continued to whimper.

Ruphord walked over to a large iron box next to the brick wall not far from a furnace, raised the lid up with a chain-hoist and dropped Jack down inside. "Jack-in-the-box, shut up tight. Down in the dark, without any light. Jack-in-the-box, oh so still. Won't you come out? By my will." Ruphord repeated the verse over and over, as he closed the heavy lid.

Jack peeked through a small hole in the side of the iron box toward the furnace, "JILLIE!"

***

Chapter 1
Urban Legends

Monday, May 13th, 2019

Gillian set the small cardboard box on the edge of her desk and pulled out a few things to make her new office feel more at home. Like the pen set she received as a parting gift from her last job at the Frederick Maryland Police Department, Domestic Crimes Investigative Division. After seventeen years moving up through the ranks, she decided on a change of pace, and the Port Latch P.D. Investigations Division in a much smaller town on a completely different coast seemed like the perfect move.

The office was not much larger than her desk and a guest chair, with a bookshelf and a window behind her. At least there was a view of the bay. The town of Port Latch sat on low hills overlooking an inlet of Puget Sound across from the Bremerton Naval Shipyard. After a few more knickknacks she unpacked a picture of her late husband and deceased daughter—the one thing she had trouble displaying, although a good friend, and psychology major would be proud of her for the attempt. "Fourteen years," Gillian sighed as she traced their outlines inside the silver frame. The picture was taken on a vacation to Virginia Beach. Six months later a woman two times over the legal alcohol limit and on amphetamines ran a stop sign along Gambrill Park Road not far from their home. Gillian woke up three days later to find out she and the drunk driver were the only two survivors of the crash that took four lives that night.

Gillian refocused her glance on her own reflection on the picture glass, fidgeted with her new bobbed haircut and straightened her blazer jacket. A whole new look for a whole new job, but some things just don't change. "Not yet," Gillian answered the unasked question, and slid the picture frame face-down to a corner of the desk.

"Knock-knock, Detective McClary?" a voice called out.

Gillian looked up and recognized the man's face from the photos in the front office. "Mayor Drafice." He appeared a few years older, a little shorter and balding with slacks, suit vest and a bolo tie. She wasn't sure, but would guess he was wearing golf shoes.

"I'm not interrupting am I?"

"Oh, no-no. Just getting settled. It's so nice to finally meet you in person after all the long-distance phone interviews and such."

"Likewise, and please, Alfred or Bud. Especially when we're out of the public eye. I hate all the formality."

"Okay, Alfred."

"Bud, please," Bud stepped into the small office and reached out a hand to formalize their greeting.

"Bud, it is," Gillian chuckled, "And Gillian is fine for me too, when not in the public eye."

"Okay. Now that we have that all out of the way, if there's anything you need, Darla, out at the front desk, is really the backbone of this whole operation."

"We've met already and I'm all set for now."

"Knock-knock," another voice called out at the door.

"Chief Johnson, come in," Gillian offered. She had briefly met the Chief of Police over the weekend when she arrived in town to scope out the station offices. Somehow he appeared taller in his uniform. In his civvies he had a more pronounced Native American appearance, with high cheek bones, dark wavy hair and hazel eyes. Funny how a ball-cap, jeans and leather sport jacket can accent one's appearance. The uniform seemed to wash his heritage away.

"Getting all settled in okay?" the Chief asked.

"We've just gone over all that ,Trent. Gillian is good to go," Bud nodded and winked toward Gillian.

"Yeah, we're all pretty informal around here, you can just call me Trent."

"Except when in the public eye," Gillian added.

"Exactly," Trent said, not sure he was getting the joke everyone else was chuckling about. "Well I just hope this little ole town of Port Latch is going to be exciting enough for you, after workin' in the big city of Frederick, Maryland."

"Don't you worry about that. I'm looking forward to being a part of the team."

"Well that's what I like to hear," Bud praised.

Darla stepped up to the crowded office door. "Chief, can I have a moment."

"Certainly, what's up?" Trent asked.

"Uh-oh, sounds like work is calling. My queue to leave," Bud said, as he squeezed his way out.

"We had a call earlier this morning that we've been checking out. A Mr. and Mrs. Meyers reported their daughter Stacy went with some friends to the Stilles Asylum over the weekend, and now claim their daughter hasn't been seen since. Deputy Burelli took statements from the girls' friends at the school this morning. Their stories are all over the place, probably trying to keep from getting into trouble for trespassing," Darla reported, checking her notes on a pad.

"Okay. We'll need to go check it out, make sure no one got hurt or lost in there. Call station 35, let's have them send the EMT unit and meet us there just in case. Deputy Pierce can handle that prisoner transfer to Tacoma scheduled today by himself, so let Deputy Burelli know to meet me at the Stilles Asylum as well. Lots of places to hide there if you want."

"Roger that." Darla scribbled some more notes and darted off.

"Sounds like you could use a hand," Gillian offered.

"I certainly won't turn down an offer. Come on."

Gillian followed Trent out the back of the small police station to the Chief's PLPD SUV. "Stilles Asylum? Why does that sound familiar?"

"Unfortunately that's where that Internet investigator got himself killed a few years back," Trent said as they both buckled up. "I would be surprised if you hadn't heard about that. That story went viral."

"Oh right. I think I remember now. A ghost hunter."

"Actually a ghost de-bunker. Jeffrie Trace was famous for his provocative, hostile methods and taking down fakers in the paranormal world." Trent flipped the lights on the roof rack and headed out.

"I don't remember hearing if anyone was ever charged for his murder," Gillian said.

"Nope. Never found anyone. That's our only cold case at Port Latch, for this century," Trent said with a hint of pride.

"Not a whole lot of traffic on the streets for a weekday," Gillian noted.

"Yeah, but the population nearly doubles on the weekends during the farmers' markets down town." Trent turned down an alley and followed it for a long way, finally leaving the old housing neighborhood into a wooded area where the road turned to gravel. They passed a couple of old small, single-story brick buildings with the windows boarded up, then the road opened up to a large open grassy knoll surrounded by tall cedars and maple trees. On the far end stood a large granite-block building four stories tall, a couple hundred feet wide and about a hundred feet deep. Gillian could see that the architecture was definitely early 20th century or older.

The gravel road led to a large old concrete surface where Trent parked. The EMT unit came up the hill from the opposite side followed by Deputy Burelli in another PLPD SUV who parked alongside Trent. They both rolled their windows down.

"Chief, the girls' stories are all over the place. Some admit they went in, others insist nobody went in," Deputy Burelli said before he noticed the Chief had a passenger. "Oh hey—you must be the new Detective? I'm Deputy Burelli."

Gillian noted that the Deputy seemed very young with a military 'high-n-tight' haircut, and expected this might be his first job in civilian law enforcement since he seemed a little 'green.' "Gillian McClary, nice to meet you."

"Likewise."

The EMT driver stepped up between the SUVs. "Hey, Chief, are you guys going in?"

"Yeah, Pete, we've got reports a young girl may have gone inside and possibly not come out."

"You don't need us to go in too, do you?"

"I'm always taking volunteers, Pete."

"Great, well, we'll just monitor from out here, standing by on channel 8. Okay, let us know if you need anything," Pete hurried back to his EMT van. Trent rolled his eyes and shook his head.

"Chief, you can't blame them. You know this place gives me the creeps too. Christ this place gives everybody the creeps," the Deputy complained.

"Because people think this place is haunted?" Gillian asked.

"Oh this place is haunted. Despite Jeffrie Trace's assertion—" Trent said.

"That got him killed," the Deputy interrupted.

"Okay, let's not get ourselves all worked up. Let's go check the perimeter fence and grounds first, maybe she's not even inside," Trent suggested as he got out of the SUV. "Burelli, you take the west side and head north out to the front of the building, we'll check out this backside and around to the east and meet you out front. Stay on your radio if you see anything."

"Roger that," Burelli acknowledged and headed out on foot.

"I see you've got the place fenced off, is it falling apart inside?" Gillian asked as they walked up to the free-standing temporary chain-link fence surrounding the building. There were sections that had been pulled apart with room for someone to crawl through.

"The fence was put up after the murder. The community demanded it. But as for the interior, it really isn't that bad. The bones of this place are still very strong. Before the murder, the city was making good money providing permits for ghost hunter groups to go inside and investigate. A couple of T.V. shows filmed episodes right here."

"Early 1900s?"

"Built in 1888, started out as an Army Garrison, named after Major General James Abernathy Stilles the third, a veteran of the Civil War—fought for the North."

"Wow you know your town history," Gillian praised.

"Grew up here," Trent checked the chain on the gate which was cut and wrapped to appear locked. "Damn, cut again."

"Happen often?"

"Seems like every few weeks." Trent went on and pushed the gate open, holding it for Gillian.

"So the Army is haunting this place?" Gillian gave the building a good long overall examination. The building and the grounds were quite stunning. Although the grass needed to be cut, she could easily see the area being used as a park or picnic grounds, particularly on a day like today with the sun out and spring very much on the way. The grounds were large and the beautiful trees were easily a hundred to a hundred-fifty yards away, lining the property and leaving plenty of area to soak up some sunshine.

"Yes, but that's not where the legend starts."

"Legend?"

"The urban legend that brought ghost hunters here and what brought Jeffrie Trace."

5

"I'm not familiar," Gillian said taking her visual attention to an odd structure along the backside of the building at ground level. Something about that caught her eye, but she was not quite able to put a finger on it.

"'The Jack-in-the-Box' legend," Trent said following Gillian's lead.

"Jack-in-the-Box?"

"After World War I, the Army abandoned the building and the state of Washington took possession and called it the Stilles Asylum for Disabled Children."

"Oh, that just sounds bad."

"It gets worse. The story goes that back in the 50's a small boy named Jack was dropped off here and was tortured by the building caretaker by being put into an iron box in the basement. In 1966, after several years of the abuse and torture, the boy took his revenge and hacked the caretaker into pieces. The place has been closed since."

"Sorry to interrupt but what is this?" Gillian pointed to a large box-like structure with a locked opening on top up against the back east corner of the building.

"I believe that's the old coal chute. Coal for the furnace was delivered to the chute that leads to the basement and furnace area."

"Okay, that's part of the original structure then. So… that's the urban legend?"

"Oh, no. The official urban legend is that if you go inside the building and say the verses of the 'Jack-in-the-Box nursery rhyme' Jack will come out and chop you to pieces."

"Well, that would seem unlikely wouldn't it? Jack would be nearly—what—seventy years old by now?"

"Unless Jack is a ghost," Trent suggested as they continued around the east side of the building, checking for signs of forced entry.

"If you believe in ghosts," Gillian added.

"Oh a skeptic? You don't believe in ghosts?"

"Now I wouldn't say that so much. I like to think there is some kind of life after death. I'm just not fond of the idea of a person's spirit being stuck where they die. That bothers me."

Gillian and Trent rounded the corner and met up with Burelli at the original front entrance.

Deputy Burelli was checking the metal bar bolted across the doors. "Good and tight, nobody's getting through there. Same with the two side doors on the west side," he reported.

Gillian was once again taken aback by the beauty of the property, even with the amount of restoration the old building needed, the grounds were really quite stunning. There was a grand walkway leading down from the building to the street by three separate sets of steps. One could just make out the view through the trees to the inlet and marina.

"Okay let's go around to the back; I have the key for the padlock on the back door, we'll make a quick sweep inside just to make sure we haven't missed anything," Trent said, leading the way back around. He walked up the steps to reach the padlock on the chain at the double metal door at the back, but the chain fell down. "Damn. Cut too."

"Do you have issues with squatters?" Gillian asked, looking up at all the windows on the back of the building. She wasn't sure if her eyes were playing tricks, but she thought she'd seen movement in a couple of the windows on the top floor.

"They did years ago, but mostly now they're just thrill seekers looking to get a scare." Trent finished pulling the cut chain from the holes in the door, then pulled them both open. "The power was cut from the building decades ago, but since we're here during the day, we should be able to see well enough. Hold on before anyone enters though—" Trent pulled some face masks from his jacket pocket. "This place is full of asbestos."

"Will these be enough?" Gillian asked.

"As long as we're not tearing anything out, or creating large clouds of dust, we should be fine," Trent explained. As they all entered, Burelli followed behind, and Gillian sensed he would have rather stayed outside.

The graffiti on the walls started very modern, but the further in they walked the styles changed like passing back in time. The first dark room on the left was an electrical closet. Trent pulled out a tactical LED light and shined inside. "Stacy? Stacy, are you in here? Port Latch Police, you need to come out now."

"Stacy, you're not in trouble. You can come out now, if you're in here," Gillian affirmed. The next openings on the right appeared to be large storage rooms, cluttered with wall shelving and trash.

Gillian took out her own small LED pen light and tried to illuminate the room.

Trent pulled out another small tactical LED, lit up the entire space, then handed it to Gillian. "Here. I keep spares."

"Thanks." Gillian scanned the storage room once more and listened. "Hold on everyone, I keep hearing something." Everyone froze.

"Did you hear something?" Trent asked.

"Yes, I also thought I saw some movement in the windows of the top floor while I was outside, but again, I'm just not sure."

"Welcome to Stilles Asylum for Disabled Children," Burelli said.

After a few more moments they continued on into the building, passing the large kitchen and a laundry room with several deep sinks. Everything was covered in layers of dust and various decade-ages of trash.

"Stacy? Stacy?" Trent called and everyone stopped to listen.

"Hear that? Sounds like footsteps," Gillian said. They turned to focus their hearing.

"Yeah. Sounds like it's coming from the central hall," Burelli answered.

"I thought it sounded like it was coming from behind us," Trent countered.

Gillian listened. "Stacy! If that is you, please come out of hiding. The dust in this building could make you sick. You're not in trouble, you just need to come out with us now please." Gillian's voice reverberated into the guts of the building.

"Burelli, take point and check the stairwell. See if you pick up any signs of her or any recent activity. Gillian and I will continue checking this main level."

"Roger," Burelli answered, attempting to stay focused and professional, even though he really just wanted out of the building. He headed further inside to the main corridors to locate the stairwell.

Both the kitchen and laundry area were dark without access to outside windows, but the next room down the hall reached across to the outside wall and was well lit from the large ground floor windows. Gillian and Trent entered to investigate.

"I just heard something again," Trent reported, then spun to his left around a corner.

"What did you—"

8

"Shh!" Trent held a hand up, staring into the space. Although well-lit from outside, there were many doors leading to dark spaces along the wall opposite the windows. Trent took another step in and Gillian followed close behind. "I just saw movement," he whispered.

"I'm hearing noises from over there," Gillian whispered back.

"I'll check this way, you go that way. If this isn't Stacy we're probably looking at some squatters so be careful."

"Roger that," Gillian answered and turned to go back in the opposite direction. "Stacy? Is that you? My name is Gillian. You really need to come out now," Gillian called out. She could hear Trent opening doors as he was calling out Stacy's name then listening for any responses as well. His voice seemed to be reverberating in all directions.

"Jillie—"

"What?" Gillian answered back over her shoulder.

"Jillie—"

"What? Trent did you find her?" Gillian returned to the other room.

"Did you find anything?" Trent asked.

"No. And I realize this sounds a little petty, but the only two people that ever called me Jillie were my husband and his grandfather, so it's a little awkward for me. That's why I prefer Gillian."

Trent felt a little confused, but nodded his head. "Okay."

"So did you find something?"

"I was calling for Stacy."

"Yes but I distinctly heard my name, Jillie…twice."

Trent scowled and shook his head. Gillian felt the hairs on the back of her head standing straight up as well as goosebumps on her arm. "I know what I—" Gillian stopped, as she saw a dark shadow dart inhumanly fast from one open door behind Trent to another.

Trent saw Gillian's eyes go wide and was certain he heard a noise. He spun quickly around. "Was that Stacy?"

"No. It's broad day light in here, and that dark shape was too small and fast."

"Damn it. I think we're literally chasing ghosts here."

Gillian was starting to feel uneasy, her heart was pumping hard and felt like it was in her throat. "Shake it off Gillian, shake it off," she said to herself. They heard footsteps approaching from down the hall.

"Hear that?" Trent asked.

"Stacy is that you?" Gillian called as the sound of steps got louder and seemed to be coming from all directions. Gillian felt as though static electricity was dancing over her body, sending a chill down her spine. She looked at Trent and could see he felt it too.

A loud clank of something metallic falling on the floor behind them made them jump back.

"What the hell!" Trent spouted.

"I don't remember that being on the floor, do you?" Gillian pointed to an empty paint can in the middle of the floor where they had just walked.

Trent shook his head, as he pointed with his tactical light toward the hall. "The footsteps are sounding louder," he said in a hush.

Gillian turned to concentrate her hearing as well. She felt a cool draft pass her face and the hint of something very unpleasant like the smell of death and decay.

"The stairwells to the upper floors are clear and completely covered in dust and debris. I don't think anybody has used them in years. No foot prints, hand prints, nothing." Burelli stepped around the corner from the hall, causing both Trent and Gillian to jump and gasp at once.

Trent gave Gillian a look of relief and shook his head. "I hate this place."

"Did you call my name?" Gillian asked the deputy.

Burelli furrowed his brow confused by the question. "No, ma'am."

They stood in silence until Trent pointed up. They heard rustling noises from above and all around them.

"Could be raccoons or rats, mice, cats, you name it," Burelli said, keeping his voice low.

"Or a little girl?" Gillian added.

"With all the noises and shadows we've been seeing. We have to check the all the floors just to be sure," Trent announced. "I'm just not comfortable calling it until we do."

"Agreed," Gillian replied.

Burelli shook his head. "As much as I hate this place, I know you're right, but I think we should stick together if for no other reason than safety."

Trent nodded. "Agreed. Let's just knock this out, so we can check this place off the list."

"Chief, this is dispatch," the Chief's radio crackled loud enough to make everyone jump and gasp.

"Dispatch, this is Chief. Whatcha got, Darla?"

"Mr. Meyers just called. They found Stacy over at a friend's house out in Belfare. She was hiding in their friends' RV. She's home now, okay, but pretty shook up."

Deputy Burelli let go with a long hard sigh, and Gillian could see the looks in both Trent and his eyes of extreme relief, but she wasn't sure if it was because the little girl was found safe, or because they were all done searching the building.

"Get. Out."

"No argument from me," Burelli said.

"I agree," Gillian answered.

"About what?" Trent asked.

"You said we need to get out," the deputy replied. Trent gave his deputy a confused look and shook his head.

Gillian noticed that the room, although still well-lit from outside sunlight, seemed darker and the air was harder to breathe. She pulled her mask down to try and take a deeper breath. A foul odor was drifting in from somewhere she could not pinpoint and it seemed the walls were closing in around them. There was a static charge in the air once again. "I heard it too," she said.

"Well I didn't say anything but I think we've spent enough time in here for one day," Trent offered. All three let his comment hang, as they listened to what sounded like someone running barefoot across the broken tile flooring right between them. Gillian even felt a breeze.

Deputy Burelli turned for the hall and the exit, "I'm out!"

"Yep. Let's go," Trent followed close behind. "Gillian, let's go."

Gillian was frozen in place. She thought she heard the sound of several children whispering as a sense of loneliness and sadness washed over her.

"Gillian," Trent called out again from down the hall.

"Uh, yes. Right there," she said, and caught up with them at the back door. The sun was shining bright through the doors, but was swallowed up by a darkness inside the hall. Gillian turned and shined her flashlight back as she stepped out the door. Down at the end of the hallway, beyond where they had been exploring, the hall seemed even darker than before, and something shook her to her core.

"Are you all right?" Trent asked and peeked back down the hall before closing the doors. "Did you see something?"

Gillian took a second to catch her breath. She wasn't sure what she had seen, or how to even begin to describe it, "I don't know...just my eyes playing tricks I think."

"I know what you mean," Trent said.

"Welcome to the Stilles Asylum," Deputy Burelli said in a heavy breath of relief.

***

Mr. Meyers was already on his front porch waiting as Trent and Gillian got out of the SUV. "Hello, Chief Johnson, your office called and said you would be on your way. I am so sorry for all this trouble." He waved them up to the single-story ranch house. Gillian noted this was one of the newer neighborhoods compared to older homes closer to downtown Port Latch.

"This is Detective McClary," Trent introduced.

"Detective." Mr. Meyers nodded. "Please, come in."

"Mr. Meyers," Gillian greeted as she stepped inside after Trent.

"This is my wife, Sharon," Mr. Meyers said.

"Please sit down. We're so sorry for all this trouble, Detective. Can I get you anything?" Mrs. Meyers asked.

"No thank you, we're not trying to alarm anyone, Mr. and Mrs. Meyers. We're just looking to get a few more details as to what happened. Detective McClary is just here to help," Trent explained.

"I used to work in domestic family investigations in Maryland and dealt with traumatized children so—"

"I assure you, Detective, we are a very happy family," Mrs. Meyers assured.

"Yes, nothing like this has ever happened before," Mr. Meyers added.

"We understand. Again, we just need to get some more details. Can we talk with Stacy?" Trent asked.

"Of course, she's in her room, let me go get her," Mrs. Meyers said as she got up from the couch and walked down the hall. "Stacy, please come out."

After a few moments, the young girl stepped out from the hall, wiping tears from her cheeks. She was just a little shorter than her mother with long dirty blond shoulder length hair and blue eyes. Gillian noted that she looked very much like a cross of her mother and father. She sat down between her parents on the couch and stared down, not making eye contact with anyone.

"Stacy, I'm Chief Trent Johnson and this is Detective Gillian McClary, we just want to ask you a few questions regarding what happened. You gave us all a pretty good scare."

"Your friends told us a few things about what happened a couple nights ago, but they're having some trouble getting their stories straight. We're hoping you can help us with that. Can you do that for us?" Gillian asked. Stacy nodded and wiped at her cheek again without looking up.

"Can you tell us what happened?" Trent asked.

Stacy glanced up at Trent and Gillian, then back down. "We all had gone to the movies at Mile Hill Drive Cineplex Saturday night."

"I had given her permission to stay at her friend Janine's house for the weekend," Mrs. Meyer interjected.

"After the movie we all walked down the road that goes toward the Stilles, and Christine mentioned that she had heard the chains were all cut again, and the building was open," Stacy continued.

"Did she say who cut the chains?" Trent asked.

Stacy shook her head. "I didn't want to go, but everyone else wanted to go see the building and see if anyone would go inside."

That's a pretty dark road to be walking on at night," Trent mentioned. "There's only a couple street lights the whole length of that road."

"We had our flashlights to walk back to Janine's house after the movie. So we took the trail through the woods that leads to the backside of the Stilles. Christine was right, the chains had been cut and all the girls started teasing that someone should go inside."

"And you decided to go?" her mother asked.

Stacy shook her head, "No, Momma, I didn't want to go in, but they all dared me, said they couldn't stay friends with me if I didn't go inside. I had to prove I wasn't too scared."

"So you went inside?" Gillian prodded.

Stacy tucked her chin lower and nodded, tears streaming down her cheeks. "I stepped in and they closed the doors behind me. I had to go to the end of the hall and shout the nursery rhyme loud enough they could hear me before they would open the door again."

Mrs. Meyers held her hand to her mouth in disbelief.

"So you said the rhyme?" Gillian asked.

Stacy shook her head hard, "No, I, I—" she began sobbing, then burst from the couch heading back to her room. "NO ONE WILL BELIEVE ME!"

"Stacy!" Her mother stood to follow her.

"Do we really need to go through all this?" Mr. Meyers asked.

"Mr. and Mrs. Meyers, please. May I go talk with her…alone?" Gillian asked, giving Trent a glance for support.

"Detective McClary is a trained professional and has dealt with young adults and extreme stress," Trent said, trying to reassure the girl's parents.

Mrs. Meyers gave her husband and glance of approval, and he nodded to Gillian. "First door on the right."

"Thank you," Gillian said as she walked down the hall. The door was obvious with artwork of pink hearts, glitter decorated rainbows and hand drawn ponies. Gillian could hear the young girl crying inside and gave the door a soft knock. "Stacy? It's Gillian. I'd like very much to come in and just sit and talk. I know you're very upset, but I may be able to help."

"You'll just think I'm crazy," Stacy answered through sobs.

"Stacy, I promise I won't think you're crazy. Please. Let me in and we can just sit and talk." Gillian paused and listened through the door. After a few moments the door cracked open.

The room was an explosion of various shades of pink and a startling reminder of her own daughter's room from so many years ago. Gillian's heart jumped into her throat as a familiar pain stabbed at her chest and long-suppressed memories flooded her mind. Her psychologist friend would have called it a breakthrough moment; Gillian just felt like she was breaking—again. She took in a long deep breath and released it slow and deliberate.

Stacy saw the Detective's reaction to her room. "I know, it's really a lot of pink. Sometimes I think I may have out grown all this."

"Don't be in such a hurry. This just reminded me of my daughter's room a long time ago," Gillian said, and took another steadying breath.

"How old is your daughter?" Stacy asked as she sat on the edge of her bed.

Gillian continued to look around the room, taking in how clean and neat everything was. Meticulous was the word that came to mind, and not common for someone this age. "My daughter would have been 22 years old. She was killed by a drunk driver in a car crash a long time ago," Gillian answered softly as she sat next to Stacy on the bed.

Stacy could not contain her shock, and tears welled up in her eyes as she reached out for Gillian's hand, "I'm so sorry, I didn't mean to—"

"It's all right, I'm all right." Gillian consoled Stacy. She noticed some bruising on the young girl's left wrist just under the sleeve of her sweatshirt. Stacy pulled her sleeve down. Gillian had seen these kinds of things many times before within her job in Maryland. Domestic violence had no stereotypical family type. Rich, poor, middle-class and ultra-rich; abuse happened everywhere. "Did your mother or father do that?"

Stacy immediately shook her head. "NO. They would never, they, I—I knew you wouldn't believe me." Stacy pulled away and buried her face into her pillow on the bed.

Gillian was in full detective mode, and the girl's denial was not uncommon, but much more sincere. The look in her eyes was absolute shock at the suggestion. The hint of a bruise on the girl's lower back where her sweatshirt had pulled up was yet another indication of something not right. "I'm sorry, Stacy. You have to understand, I have to ask these kinds of questions."

"It's not what you think. You won't believe me," Stacy argued face down into her pillow.

"Okay, okay. It's all right. I understand. Something happened in that building. Something that scared you very much, and something you can't explain. I totally get it. That place is really creepy. Even in broad daylight, I can tell you. And to think you were in there when it was dark. I can't imagine."

Stacy turned her head from her pillow. "You've been inside?"

"Yes. Just this morning, we were looking for you. The report was that you had gone in and not come out. The Chief and Deputy Burelli and I all went in looking for you."

"Did you hear them?"

"Them?" Gillian asked. She could feel she was making headway

15

in gaining trust. They had a common experience, of sorts.

"The voices. I heard voices inside the building."

"As a matter of fact, I think I did. I may have seen something too, but I'm not sure," Gillian said and offered her hand to sit back up. "Please. I want to know what happened to you, and I promise I will not think you're crazy."

Stacy wiped more tears from her eyes. "You promise?"

"I promise. Tell me what happened."

Stacy sat for a moment fidgeting with her sweatshirt. "I went inside with my flashlight, and they closed the door behind me. I was really scared, so I went to the end of the hall as quick as I could. When I got there, I was about to start shouting the rhyme when I started hearing—"

"What? What did you hear?" Gillian asked.

"It sounded like children way down the other end of the hall."

"Was it possible you heard your friends outside?"

"No the other direction, deeper into the building. Then I heard a voice say, 'Get out,' right in my ear. I screamed and turned to look, and I felt a push on my back that burned. I dropped my flashlight and it broke. I couldn't see anything, but there was an awful smell. I thought I was going to gag."

"The voice, what did it sound like?"

"Like something demonic."

"Man, woman?" Gillian typed notes into her phone.

"Man or boy, I'm not sure, definitely evil. He just kept growling at me to get out, and that I didn't belong."

"So you couldn't see anything at all?"

"No, not even my hand in front of my face, so I reached for my cellphone to get a light, but the phone battery was dead."

"You normally keep it charged don't you?" Gillian asked, knowing teenage girls.

"Yes. It had a full charge, but I couldn't get it to come on."

"Then what did you do?"

Stacy stared down at her lap for a few moments. "Something grabbed my ankle. I started screaming and kicking but it dragged me."

"And you still couldn't see?"

"NO. I just kept screaming and I kept hearing a demon growling sound, and that awful smell. I thought I was going to die." Stacy cried.

"It's all right, you're all right now," Gillian consoled. "Why do you think it was a demon?"

"What else could it be? At one point it stopped dragging me and I stood up and tried to escape, but the demon took my wrist. It hurt so bad and was ice cold, and started pulling me down some stairs. I just kept screaming. Then I was pushed to the floor and I started crawling to try to get away."

"To where?"

"I couldn't see anything, but after being pushed into something like dirt and gravel, I was certain the demon planned to bury me alive. I was so scared. Finally I was able to stand up to try to escape again when I saw stars and a street light."

"You were out of the building? Where?"

"I don't know, I just know I was able to escape the demon's grip and started running for the light through the trees. Eventually I got to the street and ran to the next street light. I just kept running. I finally got back to the theater. There was a bus at the bus stop and I got on. It was the 'Cross County' bus to Belfare. So I went to my friend's house."

"Okay, so that's how you got all the way to Belfare…what's your friend's name?"

"Trish. Trish Harrison."

"How do you know Trish? She lives in a different town."

"Her dad and my dad work together at the shipyard. We've been friends since we were little."

"Okay. Wow. That was a scary thing," Gillian said, still typing notes into her phone.

"You believe me, don't you? You don't think I'm crazy do you?"

Gillian shook her head. "I don't think you're crazy. I think you're pretty brave."

"Brave?"

"Your girlfriends said in their statements that they all ran as soon as they heard someone scream. They left you behind to fend for yourself. And you got through it all on your own. That seems pretty brave to me."

Stacy nodded and wiped at her cheeks again.

"Can you show me that bruise now?" Gillian asked.

Stacy hesitated, then nodded and pulled her sleeve up. The bruise encompassed the girl's arm just above her wrist. She then pulled up her right leg and lifted her pant leg to expose a bruise around the bottom of her right leg, just above her ankle. "That's where it pulled me by my leg."

Gillian took a couple pictures from her phone. "May I take a picture of the bruise on your back?"

"I have a bruise there too? It burned for a couple hours but I didn't think I bruised."

Gillian took a picture with her phone then showed Stacy. There were three long red scratch marks over the top of a light discoloration that was the remains of a bruise.

"Oh my God. I had no idea," Stacy said and burst into tears again.

Again Gillian consoled Stacy. "You're going to be fine. I just have to ask, why didn't you wear a jacket, wasn't it a bit chilly to be wandering around at night?"

"I had my jacket on," Stacy answered.

"You did? Can I see it?"

Stacy nodded, "Sure." She pulled the dirty jacket out from her clothes hamper in her closet. Gillian held it up and inspected the back. There were no marks. "Are you going to arrest me now?"

Gillian shook her head. "No. We're not going to arrest you. We just wanted to make sure you're all right, and to possibly impress upon you the importance of staying out of dangerous buildings like the Stilles Asylum," Gillian answered attempting to give her best lecturing, non-lecture.

Stacy leaned over and gave Gillian a hug. "Thank you. Thank you for believing me."

***

"So you don't think her parents are the source of those bruises?" Trent asked as he turned from the Meyers' driveway to head back to the station.

"That was my initial thought, but her reaction was too genuine. I've seen denial a thousand different ways, and she is definitely convincing. But if it's not her parents, then we're looking at possibly someone inside the Stilles," Gillian said.

"I think we would have seen more signs of squatters while we were looking," Trent said. "The activities we experienced were just too weird."

"I know, none of that really makes any sense."

"And she didn't exit the building through the back door?"

"No. She said she came out a different way." Gillian's answer hung between them for a few moments. "Can we stop by the Stilles Asylum for one more look?"

Trent nodded, deep in thought, "Yeah, sure." He took the main roads this time, and drove up the main paved drive leading to the back of the Stilles' Asylum compound. They got out to examine the temporary fencing. There was a significant opening between fence segments on the south-east corner. Gillian squeezed through and headed to the back of the building. Trent needed to make the opening a little bigger but eventually fit through.

Gillian turned and looked back away from the building in the direction of the hole in the fencing. "Is that a light pole there?"

"Where?"

"There. Down through those trees, I see a power pole. Does that have a light on it?"

"Oh, there. Yes, probably a street light."

Gillian turned and faced the building, and was right at the coal-chute at the back. "Something has been bothering me all day about this," she said approaching for a closer look.

"What do you mean?"

The structure had a slight angle up toward the building, starting at about three feet high, with a cast iron cover fitted over the sides and a metal latch and lock. Gillian knelt down to investigate. "This." She pointed to a black smudge on the side of the structure.

"That looks a little like a black hand print," Trent said.

"Yes, but this lid is covering over the top of the smudge," Gillian pointed out. She took her finger and wiped at a part of the smudge and it came off onto her finger. "This is fresh."

"But that lid is locked, has been for years."

Gillian reached over to the lock and lifted it with ease. The lock and latch that should have been attached to the structure was broken off, only hanging on by the weight of the large lock.

"I'll be damned," Trent strained to lift the heavy lid to hold it.

"Look, the smudge continues over the top of the edge under the where the lid was. I'll bet this is where she came out."

Trent grunted his disagreement. "This lid is way too heavy for that little girl to lift."

"Adrenaline? She was nearly scared out of her mind," Gillian offered.

Trent continued to grunt holding the lid up at the odd angle over the opening, and shook his head. "I don't think so."

"Can you hold it a little longer so I can see in there?"

Trent nodded, "Make it quick."

Gillian shined her light inside, but everything was covered in black residue from years of coal storage. There may have been an opening but she could not be certain.

"Watch out, coming down," Trent warned, and let the lid back down as soon as Gillian stepped back.

"How much do you think that weighs?" Gillian asked.

"A hundred-fifty plus? See that welded ring, that used to connect to a block and tackle rig to open that when in use back in the day."

"I'm telling you, this is the only place that makes sense. In her account, she did not come out the back door, and this lines up with the hole in the fence, and what looks like a street light out there down through the trees." Gillian pointed just as a car pulled up the drive and parked next the PLPD SUV.

"Oh crap," Trent said under his breath.

"What?"

"Marty Feltzer, Kitsap *Tribune* reporter." Trent smiled and waved to the young man as he approached the fence. He was short and thin, with red hair and round-rimmed glasses, jeans and sport coat.

"Is that a bad thing?" Gillian asked. She had always maintained a good relationship with the local reporters in Frederick.

"Can be," Trent whispered back to Gillian. "Hey, Marty, what brings you out here?"

"Chief Johnson. Sources tell me you had an incident out here this morning, and seeing you're still here, seems their story is corroborated? What can you tell me? Anything official being put out?" Marty held up a small digital recorder.

"Nothing to see here, Marty. Just some kids getting themselves into trouble trespassing and getting a good scare."

"So, you're saying the urban legend of 'Jack-in-the-Box' has claimed another victim?" Marty asked, then pointed the recorder back to the Chief.

"No Marty, I'm not saying anything like that at all."

20

"My sources tell me a young girl was lost inside? Were you able to find her? Has she been identified? Anybody hurt?"

"Marty…yes some kids did something stupid here over the weekend, no one was hurt, and they're all under age, so I can't divulge any names," Trent responded.

Marty turned his attention to Gillian, "You must be the new detective for Port Latch Police, Detective McClary? Because of this incident, will you be re-opening the investigation into the mysterious 'Jack-in-the-Box' axe murder of Jeffrie Trace?"

Gillian shook her head, "I—"

"Boy, Marty, you don't miss a thing. Detective McClary is here with me to assist in wrapping up my report on this minor incident that happened over the weekend. The Jeffrie Trace case was never actually closed, so the detective will, of course, pursue any new leads as they make themselves available, and there was nothing new here to add to that case today. That's all we have to say. Okay? Marty, give me a break here. This is a nothing story."

Marty clicked his recorder off. "Hey, a guy has to make a living, and get all the facts I can before my deadline."

"Yeah, well tell Pete to stop trying stir up something out of nothing," Trent said.

Marty shook his head with a smirk and headed back to his car. "You know I can't divulge my sources."

Gillian and Trent watched as Marty drove off. "That was interesting," Gillian said.

"Yeah. Welcome to Port Latch. Now you know why some urban legends never die."

***

Chapter 2
Curiosity Killed the Internet Star

Tuesday, May 14th, 2019

Gillian searched Jeffrie Trace's murder on her laptop as she sipped from her first cup of coffee at the office. There were pages of search results from the top news agencies to the news wanna-be bloggers. The popularity of the murder became a story as well.

"Knock-knock," Darla said, giving the door-frame a light tap. Gillian nodded and waved her in. "I've got the case file you asked for." Darla placed the over-stuffed folder on Gillian's desk. On top of the folder was a cupcake with a single unlit candle.

Gillian cocked her head, noticing the cupcake, then glanced at her laptop to check the calendar. "It's that time of year again, isn't it?"

"The guys like to make big deals out of birthdays, but if you'd rather, I can keep it just between us."

"That might be best." Gillian pulled out the candle and licked off the frosting before dropping it into her desk drawer. "Us ol' gals gotta stick together, right?"

"Dear, forty-eight ain't old. Been there done that—a couple times now, going up and coming back down. I decided a few years back to just start counting backwards. I get younger every year," Darla scoffed with a wink. She turned to leave then turned around again at the door. "Are you sure you want to open that hornet's nest so soon though?"

"It would seem a few people believe I already have," Gillian answered, pulling a copy of the local *Kitsap Tribune* morning addition from her laptop bag. "I picked this up at the corner coffee shop."

Darla grimaced. "I had hoped you wouldn't see that this morning. I even hid the office copy in the foyer."

"Front page," Gillian replied with gusto. "*Jeffrie Trace Murder*

Case Reopened."

"Knock-knock. Gillian I realize this is just your second day, but are you certain you want to take on the Trace murder case so soon?" Bud squeezed into Gillian's office past Darla, holding a copy of the morning newspaper. "I lost a Chief of Police and a detective last time on this case."

"Mayor, um, Bud. I—"

"That would be the work of Marty," Trent interrupted as he stepped up to Gillian's crowded office door.

"Marty! I should have known," Bud scowled.

"He stopped by while we were checking on something at the Stilles Asylum," Trent continued.

"Checking on something?" Bud asked.

"Just looking for more details to finish Trent's final report regarding the Meyers' girl," Gillian explained.

"So you're not going to start messing around with the Trace murder case? Right away, I mean?" Bud asked with a look of relief. "The media had a field day with the City and Police Department last time."

"As Trent told Marty yesterday, I will only be investigating any new pertinent information or leads as they are discovered," Gillian answered. Bud looked as though a huge weight had been lifted off his shoulders. "But it would seem wise to at least get myself up to speed on the details as they stand now, so I would be able to identify any new pertinent information, if any should become available. Don't you think?" Gillian added, directing her question more to everyone than just Bud.

All three waited, looking to Bud for approval. He gave everyone a stern glance, then nodded. "Okay. Okay, I've got a council meeting to attend. Let's just hope the media doesn't go crazy on this like they did last time." Bud squeezed his way out past Darla and Trent, shaking his head. Darla followed Bud.

"Nice, I think you put Bud at ease," Trent said. "But really, are you going to start on that case?"

"I wasn't kidding. I believe I should at least be familiar with the case, especially if it's going to be such a hot-bed for the city every time something happens at the Stilles Asylum."

"Sure, I guess that makes sense. I'm going to finish up that report this morning so I'll—"

"I just emailed you my notes from yesterday," Gillian said.

"Okay, thanks." Trent gave the cupcake a curious glance that didn't go unnoticed by Gillian.

"Want it? I'm not hungry." Gillian held the cupcake out to Trent.

"You sure?"

"Yep."

"Okay, your loss. I'll see ya later." Trent snatched the cupcake and headed for the door.

"Later," Gillian said as she pulled off the file's large rubber band chuckled under her breath. *Men.*

***

Reading an autopsy report may seem like a macabre, nauseating or even gut-wrenching way to start a day, but their content was always so technical and dry that Gillian found the gross factor to be lost in the translation. This one was no different, and she jotted down the more pertinent points; Jeffrey Anderson, aka, Jeffrie Trace, Caucasian male, age 24, of good general health. Toxicology showed no signs of illicit drugs although levels for caffeine, taurine, glucuronolactone, B vitamins, guarana, ginseng, ginkgo biloba, l-carnitine, sugars, antioxidants, were off the charts, which matched up with his reported over-use of energy drinks.

Cause of death was not as obvious as one might think, despite the catastrophic injury to his forehead by blunt force trauma as described in great detail. The cause was consistent with an axe type sharp-edged instrument, but his death was not immediate. Likely knocked unconscious, the official cause of death was listed as exsanguination. *Poor kid bled to death,* she thought.

Gillian flipped through the report for more details on the actual instrument of the blunt force trauma, but there were none listed. Gillian thumbed through the whole folder once again, nothing. The murder weapon was not listed in custody.

Darla stopped by Gillian's office door. "Just made a fresh pot; thought I'd check on you. It's been quiet."

"I'll get some in a sec. Thanks, Darla. Are you very familiar with the Jeffrie Trace case details?"

"Dear, you would be hard pressed to find anyone in this county that isn't familiar."

"Okay, but I can't find anywhere in this report for information on the murder weapon. Where is the murder weapon?"

"Never found," Darla said.

"But…hold on, there's a picture here from a video clip, the caption says 'axe handle.' Where is that?"

Darla shook her head. "Never found. That video clip is from Jeffrie's video camera, the footage is at the time of death. The raw footage has been put onto a DVD, should be inside the file sleeve pocket. I think the original SSD card is in there too. But let me tell you, that's some scary footage. Don't watch that at night by yourself. Gives me chills just thinking about it."

Gillian slid the disk into her laptop and pulled up the AVCHD raw file and MP4. She clicked on the MP4 and the video file started with static, then a close shot of Jeffrie's face. *"All right, camera on. Test one, two, three. Audio on. Let's get this shit-show started. Dylan, make sure to get those standalone digital cameras tested and ready to set up on all four floors. I'm going to bust this fucking place wide open tonight."*

"I've got two per floor. I'm heading up now to put one at each end of the main halls," Dylan's disembodied voice answered.

"Jason, I want this main floor covered with laser grids, motion sensors and trap cameras. Nobody's going to get through any of this without any of us fucking knowing about it," Jeffrie directed.

"On it," Jason's off-camera view voice answered.

"I'm going to take an opening shot outside before it gets too dark, I'll be right back."

Jeffrie's camera view bounced as he walked out the back door of the large building. "I can't believe the city fucking made me pay a hundred and fifty fucking bucks for a permit to fucking bust this place. When I get done tonight, I just may fucking sue them for that and a few thousand dollars more to cover my cost of wasting my time here. I won't let those motherfuckers scam me."

The camera view steadied up on a wide angle of the back of the Stilles Asylum. "I'm Jeffrie Trace and welcome to another episode of 'Jeffrie Exposed.' Tonight I'm going to be taking apart one of most fake haunted buildings in America, the Stilles Asylum For Disabled Children here in Port Latch, Washington. Or should I call it Port fucking lame. When we got here after paying a hundred and fifty fucking bucks for a permit to have exclusive access, we all spotted movement in the upper windows."

The camera view zoomed in to the upper windows of the back of the building. A dark mass seemed to move past one of the windows on the third floor.

"What the FUCK! AGAIN? Did you fucking see that? They assured us the place is empty, but I can fucking tell you, they've already got someone planted inside to try to fucking scare us. Well, as you know, I don't fucking scare. My team and I are going to fucking blow this shit-hole wide open in this episode of 'Jeffrie Exposed.'" The camera angle changed to a close up of Jeffrie Trace's face and he held still for a few seconds.

"And, cut point." The camera view again bounced around as Jeffrie walked back inside. "You're not going to fucking believe this, Jason, I just fucking caught video of someone on the third fucking floor back windows. They are SO FUCKING going down tonight."

"Man, I'm telling you, I know what you mean. I've already been hearing a lot strange shit going on just while I've been setting up the equipment," Jason answered just off camera view.

"Dude, you're not going to believe this," Dylan's voice crackled over a walkie-talkie. "Someone just threw something at me up here."

Jason grabbed his radio, "Did it hit you? What was it? Where are you at? Did you see who it was?"

"I'm on the second floor landing. I didn't see anyone. I think it was a piece of a fucking ceiling tile or something, just missed me, but knocked over the camera I just fucking set up."

"Okay, that's fucking IT. I'm not fucking around, I'm already rolling...let's go after that motherfucker," Jeffrie ordered, and refocused the camera view on his face. "I'm at the Stilles Asylum for Disabled Children here in fucking Port Latch, Washington, and we're already getting evidence of someone trying to scare us with this fucking, fake-ass shit."

The camera view changed from Jeffrie's face to pointing ahead as he walked up to the end of the darkened main rear entry hall. Small bright green dots from the laser grid light covered every surface down the main cross hall.

"This place is SO fucking lame, they already have someone fucking upstairs making noise. Listen," Jeffrie paused. The audio hissed and the sound of some shuffling noises could be heard in the distance.

"Whoa," Jason called out.

Jeffrie's camera view spun around to see Jason looking back from where they had just rounded the corner. "What?"

"I just heard someone walking up behind us," Jason answered in a hushed tone trying to listen. "I fucking thought I just heard someone there."

Jeffrie's camera view turned back around down the main cross hall. The laser grid dots could be seen clear to the far end of the hall. "Shh, listen." Jeffrie and Jason froze to listen for several seconds.

"Guys, there's some fucking freaky shit going on up here on the fourth floor," Dylan's voice crackled from Jason's walkie-talkie.

"Jeffrie, look did you see that?" Jason called out. "I just saw some movement down there about half-way down."

Jeffrie's camera view adjusted to the spot. "I think I fucking saw something too."

"Dylan, we're getting some sounds and movement down here. Are you still up on the fourth floor?" Jason asked over the radio.

"Yeah. You guys need to fucking get here and hear this," Dylan replied back, his voice distorted in static.

Jeffrie picked up his pace, and the camera view bounced as he passed by a couple of closed wooden doors and reached the corner at the main entry hall. The camera's infrared light made the darkness seem to glow an eerie green. The large main entry double-door at the far end was framed with two large windows on either side. A slight glow of lights from the inlet, across the street and the shipyard on the other side of the bay, filtered through the dirty glass. A lone antique-style metal and wood bench sat against the wall across from an office door. There was graffiti on the dirty, deteriorating walls. The wallpaper was coming off in various locations all along the way. Jeffrie pointed the camera at a message scrawled on the wall between the old bench and a set of open double doors.

"How fucking quaint. The fucking urban legend says that if you fucking say this fucking nursery rhyme something bad is going to fucking happen." Jeffrie pointed the camera at his face with a smirk. "Let's fucking see." He turned the camera view back at the rhyme and read it out deliberate and loud. "Jack-in-the-box, shut up tight. Down in the dark, without any light. Jack-in-the-box, oh so still, won't you come out—"

"WHOA. Did you hear that?" Jason could be heard reacting off-camera. "I just fucking heard something."

Jeffrie pointed his camera back to his face and rolled his eyes. "Fucking, yeah right."

"I'm fucking serious. Back toward the other hall."

"Hey! Where the fuck are you guys?" Dylan called out from the radio. "You guys really need to fucking get up here. There's some fucking serious shit happening up here."

"Down here too," Jason could be heard off-camera replying on the radio.

"There's someone fucking with us, let's get up there and catch this fucker and be done with this fucking place," Jeffrie said as he pointed his camera around the hall then headed through the open double doors to the central stairwell that could take them to the fourth floor. Jeffrie and Jason's every step could be heard echoing up and down the stairwell as they hurried up to the top floor. Jeffrie's camera view bounced the whole way. Occasionally Jeffrie changed the camera angle to his face, then back again.

Every landing appeared the same as the one before, although each was covered with various levels of trash and loose debris. Jeffrie pointed his video camera toward the floor to show the digital camera Dylan had set up, and stepped over it. The camera did a shaky sweep of the main hall that was much like a mirror of the main first floor, without the double doors of the entry. Another set of windows filled that space. Jeffrie panned the camera around to show Jason stepping through from the stairwell landing, then back to his face. "The fourth fucking floor, where they fucking claim evil fucking ghost kids move and throw shit at you," Jeffrie said with disgust.

"Hey my fucking camera battery just died," Jason announced.

"Didn't you put fucking fresh charged batteries in?" Jeffrie said, pointing his camera at Jason.

"Yeah, I put fucking fresh charged batteries in everything," Jason protested. "It just fucking died." Jason pulled another battery pack from his fanny pack and loaded it into the camera.

Jeffrie pointed his camera back at his face and rolled his eyes again, before pointing the camera down toward the crossing hallway, were the glow of an infrared light source could be seen from around the corner to the left.

"Is that you, guys?" Dylan called out, before coming around the *corner.*

"Who do you fucking think?" Jeffrie scoffed.

"Fuck. This battery is dead too," Jason said.

"You fuckers need to see this. I'm telling you there is some shit going on," Dylan said.

Jeffrie's camera bounced in the direction of Dylan as he walked over. "There's nothing fucking going on except a serious fucking hoax. This is just too fucked up to be believable," Jeffrie argued.

"I don't know, man. You gotta see this," Dylan said, turning through an open door into a large room.

Jeffrie's camera followed directly behind Dylan, sweeping through the room. Old, dirty, worn-out toys were scattered about, and a small child-sized chair sat in their path. "This is just fucking sad. Fucking sad, man. They're really playing on the sad-spooky factor in here," Jeffrie said.

"Dude, I moved that fucking chair out of the way when I came in here so I wouldn't fucking trip over it on my way out."

"So fucking what?" Jeffrie asked.

"So. SO I moved that fucking thing over there next to the wall, walked down to the end of the room to set up a fucking digital camera and when I turned around I nearly tripped over that same fucking chair back in the middle of the fucking way," Dylan explained.

Jeffrie swept the room with his camera, looking for anyone hiding in the shadows. "There's someone here fucking with us. Stop fucking with us, I will fuck you up!" Jeffrie called out.

"Did you catch anything on the digital?" Jason asked.

"I haven't checked yet, I've been chasing down some strange noises. Lemme go check," Dylan said and walked over to the camera mounted on a short stand. Jason moved the small chair off near the wall before joining Jeffrie and Dylan to check the recording.

"Fuck," Dylan announced.

"What?" Jeffrie asked, pointing his camera back and forth between Dylan's face and the digital camera in his hand.

"The fucking battery is dead," Dylan said.

Jeffrie aimed the camera to Jason's face.

"Don't give me that look. I put fresh batteries in all the cameras."

Jeffrie panned down at the floor, "Look, man, this kind of shit just makes us look fucking incompetent. Do we have any more fucking batteries?"

"Yeah I got a whole fucking bag full downstairs, but I'm telling you, these batteries had a full fucking charge," Jason argued.

"Well go back downstairs and bring some more fucking charged batteries," Jeffrie ordered.

"Yeah, yeah." Jason switched his flashlight on and turned to leave, but stopped short, "FUCK!"

"What?" Jeffrie and Dylan both asked.

"That fucking chair," Jason said.

Both Dylan and Jeffrie turned to look. "What about it?" Jeffrie asked.

"I moved that fucking thing over next to the fucking wall just before I walked over after you guys." Jason's voice cracked. Jeffrie pointed his camera at Jason's face then down to the chair that was sitting right in the middle of the floor again.

"Fuck. Did you hear that?" Dylan asked. Everyone hushed to listen.

"Voices. Sounds like voices," Jason whispered.

"Sounded like laughing or giggling?" Dylan suggested.

"Do you have your digital audio recorder going?" Jason asked.

"Yeah, it's still working. Hopefully something is fucking coming through," Dylan said, holding the recording device more out front with his video camera.

"Fuck, do you smell that? What died?" Dylan asked.

"Smells like a hoax to me," Jeffrie smirked.

"Uck! Smells like road-kill!" Dylan winced.

Jeffrie grabbed a small flashlight from his back pocket and shined it around the room along with the camera to catch any evidence of someone in the room, not wanting to rely on just the infrared lighting from the onboard camera light.

"I'm telling you, someone is fucking with us. Somebody check that fucking chair for fucking wires or fucking something," Jeffrie ordered as he continued to scan the room. As the camera moved past the doorway into the room, a dark mass was captured. Jeffrie aimed the camera back. "I just fucking saw someone." He ran for the door, the camera view shaking and bouncing with every fast step. "When I catch you I will fuck you up," Jeffrie threatened, and continued in the direction the dark mass appeared to move, out toward the main hall and stairwell.

30

Jason and Dylan could be heard following Jeffrie through the camera audio, and Jason's flashlight created odd dancing shadows on the walls that showed up on Jeffrie's camera view. The camera continued showing Jeffrie pursuing something back toward the stairwell. With a quick sweep to show the rest of the guys following, Jeffrie flew down the stairs as fast as he could, trying to keep the camera focused down the stairs. A dark mass could on occasion be seen slipping just out of view further down the stairs.

"You motherfucker. I'm going to enjoy exposing you and this fucking hoax operation you've fucking got going on here," Jeffrie taunted, and continued the chase past the main floor and down to the basement level. At the bottom, Jeffrie paused at a set of open double doors and pointed the camera at his face. "I've followed this fucker down to the basement level, and if any of the fucking information they gave us is fucking correct, this is the only way in or out of the fucking basement." Jeffrie lifted the camera at an angle to catch all three of them in the shot as they caught up with him. "Now we catch this fucker red-handed in this hoax haunting."

"Hey, my flashlight just died now," Jason complained off-camera.

"Mine too," Dylan answered.

"Good thing one of us put fucking good batteries into his fucking own flashlight," Jeffrie huffed, then shined his flashlight to the right first through the double doors into the dark hallway. The camera showed the floor was covered with paper, trash and debris. Then a metallic clang echoed through the hallway from the other direction, and Jeffrie swung the light to the left and the camera to his face again. "Got you now, you motherfucker."

As he moved the camera view back in the direction of his flashlight, the light flickered, dimmed then went out. "Goddamn it, Jason. What's with these fucking batteries?" Jeffrie asked as he put his dead flashlight back into his pocket and readjusted the camera viewfinder, using its light in an attempt to illuminate the very dark hall, then took some cautious steps further toward the metallic noise.

"I keep hearing something," Jason whispered. "Like someone talking."

"Just keep talkin' motherfucker," Jeffrie directed down the hall.

"Me too," Dylan added. "I can't quite tell what it's saying though. Sounds demonic and smells like hell too."

"Is that it, motherfucker? Am I chasing some fake fucking

31

demonic Jack-in-the-box?" Jeffrie taunted. He turned the camera in toward another open door, lighting up a room filled with piping. Further in the camera caught the features of an old furnace. The light from the viewfinder was not adequate to show much more than a few feet in front of the camera and created odd shadowing with the infrared lighting.

Something could be seen flickering past the camera view, then a clanging noise off into the distance. "The FUCK? You're throwing shit at me? You piece of shit," Jeffrie shouted.

"I think that was a tin can," Dylan answered off camera.

Jeffrie panned the camera over to the top of a large metallic box with debris scattered on top, grabbed a piece of flooring and flung it back into the darkness in the direction that the can had come from. "I can throw shit too. Are you getting pissed off? Are you Jack-in-the-box? Shut up tight? Down in the dark, without any light?"

The camera view was shaky and the battery light started flashing. Jeffrie turned the camera back toward his face for a close up, and noticed the blinking red battery light on the view screen. "Goddamn it, Jason. This battery is dying too."

"I'm telling you, I put—"

"Yeah, fucking yeah, you keep telling me. I gotta get this motherfucker exposed before my camera dies completely," Jeffrie complained.

"My camera battery is getting low, but I've got you covered from behind," Dylan called out from off-camera view.

The camera pointed back to a cluttered corner of the room, when another object glinted in the infrared light and flew past. The sound of something sounding like wood dropping to the floor could be heard in the distance.

"You motherfucker. Jack in the fucking box, shut up tight? I've got you cornered now, motherfucker. Down in the dark, without any light," Jeffrie taunted as he moved closer.

"Be careful, man, this guy might fucking freak out or something," Jason said well off camera.

"Jack-in-the-box, oh so still. Won't you fucking come out?" Jeffrie paused as though expecting an answer. A low mumbling sound seemed to emanate from the dark corner.

"Was that growling? Did you fucking hear that? Demonic growling?" Dylan asked from off camera.

Another flash flickered through the camera view, just missing Jeffrie. The object landed with a loud thud, and there was a scattering sound on the floor close by.

"The FUCK?" Jeffrie expressed his growing anger.

"That looked like a fucking piece of brick or something from my camera view," Dylan announced.

"You're fucking pissing me off, Jack. Jack-in-the-box. Jack-in-the-BOX. Like the rhyme says motherfucker, won't you come out, Jack! COME OUT JACK," Jeffrie demanded as he moved closer and closer.

The camera captured a dark mass tucked into a dark corner of the room and an unrecognizable sound like a groan or growl emanated from that direction. Without warning the mass darted forward and a bright flash of something flickered in the infrared lighting coming straight at the camera. The sound of metal chopping into wood rang out, and the camera view was distorted with a violent shaking before dropping to the floor.

"FUCK ME! RUN!" Dylan shouted. Jason's screams accompanied their sounds of scrambling through debris to leave the room, into the distance off camera.

The video showed the camera was now laying on its side, the auto-focus continuing to adjust, then readjust in and out of focus on a wooden handle object across Jeffrie's outstretched arm on the floor. Both his arm and the wooden handle seemed to be twitching, as another low mumbling, growling sound emanated from off camera along with a closer gurgling noise. A dark unfocused mass moved past the camera's view in the background.

For a few seconds the low battery light blinked in the video, as dark fluid flowed onto the floor between the camera view and Jeffrie's twitching arm. There was one more unintelligible off-camera sound just as the gurgling noise ended and Jeffrie's arm stopped twitching. The video turned black and then to static.

The hairs on Gillian's neck were standing straight up. Everything happened so fast, she wasn't at all sure what she had seen.

Darla brought in a fresh pot of coffee. "Just hearing that video gives me the creeps."

Gillian held up her cup while Darla poured. "That's some crazy evidence of a murder. And no suspects?"

"Oh there were a few thoughts on that, but nothing that could be charged," Darla scoffed.

"You mean 'no one,'" Gillian corrected.

Darla shook her head. "Jeffrie Trace had plenty of enemies, and Joe tried, but couldn't find a single suspect within miles of the place. Plenty of people blamed this on some demonic force, but that's kind of hard to bring up on charges," Darla half chuckled.

"Joe?"

"Detective Joseph Tulford. You're sitting in his old office," Darla said giving the small room a long look around.

"Ah," Gillian glanced back down at the case file. "Is there more? Any other physical evidence from the case?"

"That's all stored at the county seat, down in the basement. I'll have them send everything over, might take a day or two."

"Thanks, this certainly is a head-scratcher," Gillian answered then took a sip of her coffee.

***

The drive up to the main entry of the Stilles Asylum seemed far less inviting than just twenty-four hours earlier, with a misty fog covering the grounds instead of the bright spring sun. Gillian thought about how much those changes in weather conditions at a moment's notice were just like back in Fredrick. *If you didn't like the weather, wait five minutes,* she recalled.

She parked the car on the large concrete pad facing the building. There were a couple of guys from the city maintenance crew finishing up the fence repairs but they gave her little notice. The misty fog blanketed the grounds and surrounding trees, giving the whole area an eerie feel of quiet solitude and shrouding the large building enough to obscure the top two floors.

Gillian spread out several depositions from the Jeffrie Trace case, along with a few of the crime scene photos, and read through them as she picked at a deli salad. The grounds had an old-world charm and classic beauty accentuated by the dense fog. Still, she had an odd overwhelming sense of being watched but tried to chalk it up to being somewhere new, a long way from what had been home for most of her life.

Jeffrie's companions, Dylan Roe and Jason Dunlap, were cleared of any wrongdoings, and the depositions read nearly identically, up to and including the point of the attack in the basement. They had chased a dark figure from the fourth floor down to the basement and then Jeffrie approached. Everything happened fast; they were scared out of their collective wits and left the scene. Through his camera, Dylan said he saw the axe strike Jeffrie's face in the glow of his IR light and the glow from his flashlight. Jeffrie then fell to the floor. He claimed, "I just knew there was no way someone could survive that. I knew he was dead."

Gillian again reviewed the autopsy; the official cause of death was exsanguination. Even if they had stuck around, there was likely nothing either one could have done to stop the massive hemorrhaging from such an attack and they would have likely come under attack as well. Their instinct to run saved their lives.

Gillian paused on that stark thought a moment, no longer sure if she could finish her salad. She couldn't shake the feeling of being watched as if there were eyes piercing through the fog from every window in the building as well from the surrounding grounds. The hairs on the back of her neck raised, and she could feel her heart starting to pound. The fog felt darker and thicker with each passing minute, as though swallowing up the whole grounds in a dark shroud of despair.

She was startled by a tapping on her window that made her gasp and jump in her seat to discover one of the maintenance guys just outside the car door.

"Are you Detective McClary?" he leaned down and asked through the glass.

Gillian rolled down her window just enough to answer, "Yes."

"We're finished and we need to leave for another job. I called Chief Johnson, and he's on his way, but he's going to be awhile. Can we give you the keys to the new locks to give to the Chief?"

"Uh. How did you—"

"Small town," the man interrupted. "Besides, I can see you're opening up the Jeffrie Trace Case again." The man shook his head. "Are you sure you want to jump right into that mess? You seem like a nice lady, and you just got here."

"I'm actually not—" Gillian paused. She realized the man could see all the files and crime scene photos spread out on her lap and passenger seat. "I mean to say, I'm just reviewing the case, that's all."

"Uh-huh," the man nodded. "Can I leave you the keys? We really need to leave now."

Gillian nodded and rolled the window down the rest of the way, "S-sure, I guess. I can wait for him here."

The man handed her a small key ring with some new keys hanging from it. "You take care now," he said and climbed into the maintenance truck that headed the back way out down the wooded drive.

Gillian rolled her window back up, feeling a fleeting moment of relief. The maintenance man seemed nice and not menacing at all. She even felt a little silly for getting worked up until she glanced around and could see the area taking on an even more unfriendly feel. The fog was getting thicker and darker, obscuring the Stilles Asylum down to the ground. She could barely see the fence across the backside of the building. A quick check on her cellphone indicated a quarter to one in the afternoon, but the grounds seemed much darker as if it was after sunset, so she turned on her headlights. Gillian felt acutely aware she was sitting there alone, and the sensation of being watched grew ever stronger and menacing. She tried to not allow her imagination to run away, but she couldn't help thinking of all the horror flicks she had seen with a scene like this. She felt like she was surrounded by something, but she wasn't sure what, even paused before glancing in her rear-view mirror, expecting to see someone sitting in her backseat staring back at her. Her heart was pounding in her ears, and she pulled her purse closer, feeling for her service revolver holster inside, when headlights shone up the main drive with a faint glow in the darkened distance. A vehicle paused at the fenced area then turned towards her.

Trent pulled up in the PLPD SUV and rolled his window down. Gillian rolled hers down as well. "Hey," he said.

"Hey," Gillian sighed in relief.

"What on earth are you doing out here?"

"Oh, just having some lunch, and waiting to give you the keys for the new locks."

Trent noticed the files and crime scene photos on her passenger seat. "Can't get enough of that case?"

"Just some lunch reading. I'm still trying to get a feel for what happened and put the pieces together. There just seems so much is missing. Detective Tulford's notes are vague in places."

"You should talk with Joe."

"Really? I thought—"

"He retired. He's not dead," Trent chuckled. "Although, he may not want to actually talk too much about this case. It is the reason he left."

"Is he still in the area?"

"Yeah. He's a manager over at Handy's Hardware, off Mile Hill Road. Probably there right now."

Gillian started to tap the name into her cellphone to look up directions.

"Just go back down the main entrance here, turn right at the bottom of the drive, take the very next right, go all the way to Mile Hill Road, turn right again, and Handy's will be in the strip mall on the left about a half mile," Trent directed.

"Okay thanks. You think he won't mind?"

"I don't know. I've never brought the subject up with him, and he's never volunteered anything. It has been a couple years, so maybe he'll open up for you, and maybe he can fill in some of the gaps."

"Okay," Gillian started her car.

"Hey?" Trent asked.

"What?"

"Keys?" Trent reached out.

"Oh, right." Gillian handed over the set of keys. "Almost forgot."

***

Trent's directions were spot on, and Gillian was amazed at how just a few short miles could make such a difference in the weather as she turned into the parking lot for Handy's Hardware. The fog was breaking up and the sun was shining through, lifting that feeling of dread and heaviness she felt at the Stilles Asylum.

The small strip mall had seen better days as there were mostly shells of businesses boarded up. Handy's Hardware and a pawn shop were all that was left.

"Hello, thank you for shopping at Handy's, can I help you with anything?" the young girl behind the cashier counter said.

"I'm looking for Mr. Joseph Tulford."

"Oh. I believe he's back in plumbing. Straight back and to the right, last aisle over."

"Thank you." Gillian found a gentleman with gray hair and glasses, wearing a shop's apron. He was pricing and restocking a shelf. "Mr. Tulford?"

"Yes, may I help you?" His smile dimmed when he turned. "Detective McClary."

"How—"

"It's a small town."

"So I've been told," Gillian sighed.

"Your photo in this morning's paper didn't do you justice."

Gillian chuckled. "I think they got that from an old driver's license photo."

"I've been expecting you and at the same time, half hoping you wouldn't come."

"Mr. Tulford I—"

"Joe," he interrupted. "Just Joe, please."

Gillian nodded. "Joe. I'm Gillian."

"Gillian. Nice to meet you."

"Is now a good time?" Gillian looked around and saw there were no other customers.

"Sure, just a second." Joe walked to the end of the main aisle. "Susan, I'm going to take a smoke break."

"Sure thing, Joe."

"This way," Joe gestured toward the back of the store. Gillian followed him through an 'employee's only' swinging door, past boxes of hardware, and out a back loading dock door. He continued out toward an old picnic bench by the back fence, and pulled out a pack of smokes. "Is it all right?"

"By all means, this is your smoke break."

"You've got questions?" Joe asked, lighting up his cigarette.

"A few." Joe cocked his eyebrow with a look of skepticism. "Okay several," Gillian confessed. Joe took another puff and sat down at the bench, knocking some ash into an old coffee can. "The murder weapon—"

"Never found," Joe answered. He took another puff. "Myself and over sixty other men scoured the inside of that facility top to bottom, every nook and cranny. Nothing. And before you ask, I had over a hundred men scour the grounds and adjacent grounds. We found antique ammunition; we found horseshoes, boot buttons, uniform buttons, coins—TONS of coins, and other tools dating back to the late 1800s. No axe."

"Okay, I'm not being critical but your report on all this is so, so—"

"Edited."

"Vague," Gillian offered.

Joe took another drag, and stared off past the back fence into a field. "What I found was not allowed into my report."

"What? What did you find?"

"Pure evil."

Gillian didn't flinch or show any emotion. After the many years working with domestic violence, she had learned never to react to what might sound far-fetched or unreasonable. She chose her next words with care, "How do you mean that? Literally or figuratively?"

"I mean absolutely pure unadulterated evil. That building, and whatever is in there is pure evil. You can feel it the moment you step onto the grounds. And inside is worse. Have you been inside?"

Gillian nodded. "Yesterday. Trent, Deputy Burelli and I went in to search for the girl that was lost."

"Did you hear them? Feel the electricity? Did you see it?" Joe asked.

"Yes, I believe I did see and hear some things that didn't make much sense while we were inside."

Joe shoved the lit end of his cigarette into the side of the coffee can and tossed the butt inside. "That thing, whatever that thing is, owns that place, and it is straight from hell. Did you see the video?"

"Jeffrie Trace's video, yes. Just this morning."

"Did you see the other video?"

"The other video?"

"Dylan's video. Dylan Roe had a camera going at the same time from behind. He caught that evil on his camera too. Pure blackness from the depths of hell. It's not human!"

"There is nothing in your report about—"

"I was forced to remove that, edit, revise my reports, my findings," Joe said clinching his fist. "The Kitsap County Sheriffs Office and Washington State Police were brought in to review my findings. Suggestions were made. Suggestions that were made clear to me, required my cooperation to save my career. My career—" Joe scoffed at his own comment. "I had no career after Jeffrie Trace's murder."

"I'm so sorry. I didn't mean to upset you," Gillian reached out but Joe pulled away.

"I'm sorry, I'm not upset. That was a long time ago, and I'm past that. I've made my peace, come to terms, as they say. I'd just hate to see someone else throw their career away on this though. Are you sure you want to get into this mess so soon?"

"Honestly, I'm not reopening the case. It's just such a 'hot-spot' in this community and I'm just trying to understand what happened and get a handle on the facts. Trying to figure out where this all stands."

Joe perked up as though a second thought came to mind. "I can tell you, this case goes clear back to 1966 and the murder of Ruphord Stilles, and possibly earlier than that. They wouldn't let me put that in my report either, but I'm sure of it. You should see all that I uncovered. It would make a believer out of you too, I know it."

"You think the Jeffrie Trace murder is related to the murder that closed the place over fifty years ago?" Gillian asked just to make sure she had heard right.

"Absolutely! That place has been riddled with evil ever since that murder."

"You mean the Urban Legend?"

"Yes! Behind every legend is a sliver of truth. There is an evil there that is the root of that legend and those murders!"

"Joe!" Susan called out from the loading dock. "I need a manager key on the register."

"Okay, right there." Joe turned to Gillian. "I've got to go. Don't throw your career away on this. But if you insist, go back to the source. They're linked, I'm sure of it. It was all there in my original report. That evil has been there a long time!" Joe walked Gillian back up to store entry without another word, then went straight to the register to help a customer. Gillian waved as she left. She had so many more questions, but felt this was a good start. No need to rock the boat on this first visit.

Just one thought came to mind. When digging for the truth, you have to remember to dig a way out before it gets too deep. If Jeffrie's murder was related to the one in 1966, this case just got a whole lot deeper, and Gillian knew she needed to always know the way out.

***

Chapter 3
The Root of Evil

A pink glow enveloped the highest clouds to the west, painting the final pigments of a day made up of a palette of colors found at Gambrill State Park in November. The bright red, orange and yellow leaves of the Chestnut Oaks, Red Maples and Black Gum trees contrasted against the brilliant blue sky and the unseasonably warm day made for a perfect Saturday to meander the many trails and vistas. The sunset from the Tea Room patio, overlooking the city of Fredrick to the southeast, was the highlight of the day, the city lights sparkling in the distance as the sun sank below the horizon.

Gillian rested her head against the passenger window. She watched the passing trees on the narrow and winding Gambrill Park drive, highlighted by the headlights of their car as well as the diminishing pink sky. She listened to Kristin and Daniel sing along with the song on the radio, laughing at the new and funny words they both made up as they played their game for the short drive home. The end of a perfect day.

Gillian was glad she had insisted they all go and enjoy a beautiful and rare day when everyone was available to be together. Their work schedules had become more and more conflicting, and finding any time to be together was a treat in an otherwise new normal of separately together under one roof. Spending one day together as a family would not make up for the time lost, but was a nice start. Gillian promised herself she would make this happen more often.

The heaviness that enveloped her when she turned to look at Daniel and Kristin was stark, overpowering and pressed her hard into the seat. "No! No, no, no NO! NOT AGAIN!" The glare of the oncoming car headlights filled the interior from the driver's side with a sudden, overwhelming and blinding brilliance. Gillian sat up in a cold sweat with the sound of crunching metal and breaking glass still ringing in her ears.

The excruciating pain was far deeper than simple flesh and bone, reaching down to a core she never believed possible before, and she held her breath for a moment, afraid to move. She soon took notice of a dark mass taking shape just in her peripheral vision along the wall of her bedroom. Refusing to take the chance to turn and look, she could see from the corner of her eye, the dark shape moving slowly along the wall as the room turned frigid. Her breath became visible from the glow of a streetlight shining through her bedroom window. When she dared to turn and look, the shape coalesced and rushed at her. She felt it pass straight through her body, screaming, "YOUR FAULT!"

Gillian flinched and opened her eyes. From her pillow she could see in the darkness the red glow from the digital clock next to her bed; 05:23. She was certain her psychologist friend would remind her that it had been months since the last time she had experienced similar dreams, and this was only a minor setback in what could be considered years, if not a lifetime of recovery.

Since the morning alarm was only twenty minutes away, Gillian decided to get up and start the day a little early. She had a report to finish up and send off to the prosecutor's office regarding a recent burglary at a local barista shop. A busy first week on the job for a town that was supposed to be a "quiet" change of pace.

***

Darla was hanging her jacket on the hook behind her desk when Gillian arrived. "Morning. You know the first person in the office in the morning is responsible for making the coffee. Are you trying to take my job, or you just hate my coffee that much?" Darla asked.

"Morning, Darla. Just couldn't sleep," Gillian said on the way to her office.

"Oh. You okay?"

Gillian paused, "Sure, just new surroundings, and I promised to get my final case report to the prosecutor's office this morning."

"Well don't be losing any sleep over that," Darla scolded.

"I won't, I promise."

After a few minutes Darla stopped by Gillian's office with a fresh pot of coffee and a package. "This came in the late express mail run after you left yesterday."

43

Gillian was proofing her report and held her cup out without taking notice of the package. "Thanks."

After a couple more hours and another cup of coffee, Gillian sent out a digital copy of the report, sat back and finally took notice of the simple brown paper package addressed to her on the corner of the desk. The return address was only a P.O. box number from the local post office at Port Latch.

"Hmm. Curious," she mused aloud. Gillian took the wrapping off, taking care to not damage the return address. Inside was a bulging folder with Port Latch newspaper clippings and police reports. As she thumbed through the reports, they seemed to date as far back as the early 50s up to 2014. She then sorted through the clippings and found many were photo copies dating back to the 1940s and 50s, up to 2014, appearing at first glance to be related to the Stilles Asylum for Disabled Children facility, and the latest ones related to the Jeffrie Trace murder.

Clearing the folder of any remaining papers, a tattered and worn business card dropped out. "William Hartfield, Lead Researcher, Puget Sound Paranormal Research, PSPR," Gillian read aloud, then scoffed as she shook her head and set the card aside.

Looking back over the photocopies of the paper articles, she noticed hand written notes along the margins. One stood out in particular, "root of the evil," with a question mark on an article regarding the disappearance of the Stilles Asylum for Disabled Children facility maintenance man, Frank Mills, on June 24th, 1952. Gillian sifted through the police reports and found one for the corresponding date. The case was closed, no evidence of foul play. Frank was assumed to have just left his live-in job at the facility. Gillian noted that further down in the report, a curious point was made that none of Mr. Mill's personal belongings were listed as missing from the facility.

Paper-clipped to the article was another photocopy of what appeared to be an employee record from the Stilles Asylum for Disabled Children facility for a Ruphord Stilles, with a change of employment status note from apprentice to full-time position of facilities maintenance, starting August 1st, 1952. A single hand-written word on the margin, 'suspicious?' Gillian noted Ruphord's last name was the same last name as the asylum namesake. *Relation*, she wondered?

Gillian spent the rest of the morning matching up news clipping dates with any corresponding police reports, or other documentation found in the pile of papers, including several police documents regarding the Jeffrie Trace Case that appeared to be original pieces removed from the formal case file. She read through a few of those pages. The report described evil spirits at the facility, and forces beyond normal understanding. The words 'evil' and 'paranormal' were used quite often. This was Detective Tulford's deleted report. The anonymous sender of the package was obvious.

"Knock-knock," Trent stood at Gillian's office door. "Fridays I usually head on down to the Harbor Deli for lunch. Interested?"

Gillian looked up with distraction. "Hmm, sure. I didn't pack a lunch today."

"Great. I'll meet you at the cruiser."

"Yeah, sure. I'll be right there. Thanks." Gillian scooped up a few of the documents into the folder and stuffed it into her shoulder bag before following Trent.

The drive to the deli was quiet and did not go unnoticed by Trent. He showed Gillian to his favorite corner seat inside the small deli, overlooking the marina. "Everything all right?"

"Sure, why?"

"I know I've only known you a few days, but you seem kind of quiet today." Trent pulled a couple of small menus out of a condiment holder at the end of the table, handing one to Gillian.

"I didn't sleep well, it's a rental bed...I woke up early."

"That barista heist get to you? We caught the guy red-handed, I saw the investigation report you sent to the prosecutor's office this morning. It's a slam-dunk."

"No. Nothing to do with that. Just getting used to the new surroundings, I think."

"Oh, sure that's probably all," Trent said.

A young girl brought over a couple of water glasses and took their orders then returned to the kitchen.

"She's the owner's youngest daughter, just graduated from high school last year," Trent offered up some small talk.

"Nice. I had a similar first job when I was her age." Gillian stared out at the marina. The morning had started out foggy but was starting to look like it might lighten up.

"I love coming here; I love the view. My grandfather kept his 25-

footer here at this marina for years."

"You've been here all your life haven't you," Gillian said.

"Yes. My grandfather was a respected elder of the Suquamish tribe. He helped raise me after my father died."

"I'm sorry for your loss. May I ask?"

"Sure, although there are few details. He was Navy Seals, killed in action October 3rd, 1982...I was only four. The operation was and still is classified," Trent said gazing out at the water.

"So your father and grandfather are—"

"My grandfather was my mother's father. I never met my father's parents. They're some well-to-do folks from the East coast. They never understood how their son would give up a prestigious university opportunity for a career in the Navy Seals, or could get involved with someone like my mother."

"Because she was Native American?"

"No, although I'm pretty sure there was some of that too, but my mother did not come from 'money,' as it was explained to me before my mother passed away from cancer a few years back."

"I'm so sorry. I didn't mean to bring up—"

"No, no. It's fine. It's all a part of life."

"Then dare I ask about your grandfather?"

"Sure. He was my hero growing up. Taught me so much about my heritage, traditions, family."

"Was?"

"He passed away not long after my nineteenth birthday."

Gillian shook her head. "I'm so sorry I really didn't mean to pry into so much personal tragedies."

"It really is okay. I'm at peace with it all, and I'm not completely alone. I have cousins and childhood friends all over the place here," Trent explained as they both made room for their food.

"Will there be anything else?" the waitress asked.

"I think we're good for now," Trent answered looking to Gillian who nodded. The young girl smiled and placed the bill on the table.

After a few bites of his sandwich, Trent wiped his mouth, "Okay, I guess it's my turn."

"Seems only fair," Gillian answered through a napkin, attempting to be polite.

"I see a very nice wedding band on your left hand, but you're here alone," Trent observed. Gillian glanced down to her left hand, and kept her mouth covered to finish her bite. "Oh, that was too personal. Now I'm sorry. Forget I asked—"

Gillian shook her head, "No, no. It's okay." Gillian waited to finish chewing then put the napkin down after drawing a deep breath. "A psychologist friend of mine would be very happy to see me talking about it."

Trent's eyes got wide. He realized he completely overstepped the boundary, "No, really. I'm sorry, I shouldn't have asked."

"My husband and daughter were both killed in an automobile accident in November 2005," Gillian answered with zero emotion. She had developed that answer for years, practicing over and over, but she never worked on a delivery that ever came out with any more feeling then that of an autopsy report. Sterile. Dry. Removed. Cold.

Trent put his chin to his chest. "I am so sorry. I should know better than to ask personal—"

"I'm okay," Gillian interrupted. "Really. I—I met Daniel while I was in college getting my B.S. in Criminal Psychology. He had just passed the bar and was working with the Fredrick County DA. We got married right after I graduated, and I was still trying to figure out where I wanted to take my career when Kristin was born a couple years later. I stayed home and took care of Kristin while Daniel continued up the ladder in the DA's office. Once Kristin started school, I realized I needed to do more with my degree, and Daniel told me about an opening with the Fredrick Police Department that worked with people in crisis and that really interested me. So I applied, graduated from the police academy and started working in the Domestic Crimes Investigative Division, dealing with domestic violence and abuse, children in crisis and the like. My father had died while I was in college from long-standing complications with diabetes, after which my mother had become very withdrawn and moved in with her sister, my Aunt Katie, in Boston. My mother continued to decline both physically and mentally and passed away a couple years after Kristin was born from pneumonia brought on from a real bad lung infection. After Daniel and Kristin—" Gillian paused taking in a long breath as she turned her gaze toward the marina. She could see patches of blue sky as the fog was lifting, which all felt metaphoric as she told her story. "After the accident, I just buried myself in my work, got my masters degree along with a few other degrees, and just concentrated on work. With everyone that was truly

47

important in my life gone, I was just going through the motions, day after day." Gillian turned back toward Trent with a forced smile. "After fourteen years, I decided I needed a change of scenery, and a few months ago, I found the opening here at Port Latch. I applied and—well, here I am." An awkward silence fell between them for several long minutes so they both concentrated on eating. "Changing the subject," Gillian said again through her napkin.

"Yes, please," Trent agreed, desperate for relief from his embarrassment.

"I got a package today."

"I saw it come in late yesterday and was wondering."

"I'm pretty sure it's from Mr. Tulford." Gillian turned and pulled the folder from her shoulder bag.

"Joe?"

"When I talked with him a few days ago, he told me a lot was removed from his official reports on the Jeffie Trace murder by some state authorities, and said it was very important that I see the material. I didn't think he would send it right away, but—"

"That sounds like Joe."

"There's a lot of clippings and police reports dating back to the early 40s." Gillian pulled some of the clippings from the folder.

"Joe really believed there was more to the whole urban legend thing."

"When I asked about the Jeffrie Trace Case and the missing murder weapon, he said the building and the grounds both were searched thoroughly."

"Oh yeah—"

"I just kind of did the math, and realize you were working here then. So you were part of the search?"

"Certainly. That's why I hate being in that place so much. Same with my two deputies. We were all involved, metal detectors and everything." Trent handed back the clippings.

"Joe truly believes something unnatural and evil is responsible."

"Joe was completely convinced," Trent agreed.

"What about you? What do you believe?" Gillian asked. She was not trying to be facetious; she really wanted to know, without judgment.

Trent raised his brows, but soon realized Gillian did not appear to be joking or judgmental. He wiped his mouth with his napkin and glanced out at the marina for a moment. "My grandfather taught me that there are many strange beings in this universe, unexplained, and inexplicable. And, many are not very nice. Some could be well defined as 'evil.'"

"And do you think there is something in that old building that is evil?"

Trent sat back in his chair, took in a deep breath and scowled. "I think that what I believe isn't relevant. What I believe is possibly beyond any proof as necessary and required for a court of law, or beyond even possibly simple rational thought. What I believe are stories taught to me from my grandfather, based on traditions and legends passed down over generations. So when you ask me if there is something 'evil' in that building, I can't honestly say with any modern rationality. I believe there is something—something not right, but what that is, again I don't know. I do know I watched a good man obsess over that building and whatever is inside there, and walked away from a career over his beliefs. I sure hope you're not going to do the same thing."

Gillian smiled and shook her head. "That sounds like that would be a crazy thing to do. A psychologist friend of mine tells me she believes I'm not crazy, so I think I'll hold on to that belief."

Trent chuckled under his breath. "But, you are going to dig into it further, aren't you."

"Well. Two people I've recently met, and highly respect, believe something isn't right about that place, and now the detective part of me really wants to know what 'that' something is."

"You know Bud is not going to like this."

"We don't have to tell Bud do we?"

Trent leaned into the table, "No. We certainly do not."

"What about Darla?"

"Darla? She knows what you're thinking before you do. But if you let her know the plan, she knows how to keep a secret."

"Really? By the way, did you like that cupcake the other day?"

Trent looked confused. "Sure? Why?"

"Just wondering," Gillian said.

***

Sunday, June 2nd , 2019

49

The weekend was spent juggling the movers bringing boxes and furnishings in, and the rental furniture store moving their furnishings out. By Sunday the stack of flattened cardboard boxes in the corner of the small living room attested to the long hours of careful placement of belongings that make a new residence a home.

All that remained were two boxes, one labeled *Kristin*, the other *Daniel*. Two 2x2 foot square boxes that were now the sum total of all that remained of her family that Gillian could not bring herself to look at, sell or give away. Now both sat stacked in the far corner, out of the way but never out of sight, unopened since the day they were packed fourteen years ago. Gillian knew her psychologist friend would tell her that this was still an improvement. At least the boxes were no longer being hidden in the darkest reaches of a closet, but instead out in the open and acknowledged. Gillian gave them a glance and sighed. "Not yet. Soon, just—not yet."

Stepping through the small dining area she noticed a familiar fragrance; one that seemed to always permeate her last house, Daniel's favorite cologne. Throughout the years she figured it was just part of the woodwork of that old house. But in this new rental house, there should be no cause for that familiar fragrance unless—

Trying not to panic, Gillian sniffed at the air and headed straight for the two boxes in the corner of her living room. She knew that packed inside Daniel's box was a decorative decanter of his cologne. She continued to sniff around the box, afraid something had happened during the move and possibly the decanter had spilled or worse had broken. The fragrance was gone, just the musty smell of old cardboard from the two boxes. Gillian stepped back to the dining room, all she could imagine was some of his cologne was clinging to the table in some way, even though she could no longer smell the cologne anywhere. In a strange way the familiar fragrance made her feel more at home and for a moment she felt as though fourteen years ago had never happened, and she could see Kristin sitting at the table eating a snack with Daniel. A bittersweet moment that felt more like scratching a persistent itch with a razor-blade. Gillian let go a heavy sigh as her family faded away to reality. *When will missing them stop hurting so much?*

With a nice hot cup of tea to relax and sitting at her more familiar dining table and chairs, she pulled the folder of clippings and police reports closer and sorted through the thick pile for a few moments of mental distraction. She had managed a few days earlier to get everything organized and in chronological order but still had not gone through each piece with any detail. The mysterious disappearance of the Stilles Asylum maintenance man was the oldest piece. Gillian set that aside, and moved onto the next article, dated May 26th, 1966, regarding the horrific axe murder of Ruphord Stilles, at the Stilles Asylum on May 25th, 1966. Paper clipped to the article were photocopies of the police report and a few grainy photocopies of crime scene pictures. She was just glad the photos were in black and white, as the gruesomeness of the scene was bad enough without full color.

She read through the report. The victim had been chopped into pieces, many of which were never recovered, including the head, all of the left leg, most of the right leg and all of the left arm. Also missing was the weapon, assumed to be an axe. Gillian flipped through several more photocopies of pictures and articles. One was of a picture taken at the time of the installation of a new furnace for the facility, donated by a local charity. In the picture were several people involved including Frank Mills, head maintenance man, Winston Farwether, facility administrator, and the charity representative, Mr. Robert Moore. Their names were all hand written on the photo over each of their heads in red ink. Just behind Frank nearly out of the photo was another young man with 'Ruphord' written over his head. On the wall next to Mr. Moore, a fire axe was hanging on the wall circled in red ink.

Gillian searched through the police report once more to be sure. The murder weapon and assumed tool of Ruphord's demise was listed as never found. One of the crime scene photos had an angle that included that portion of the wall, and the area was again circled in red ink, indicating where the fire axe should have been found but was, indeed, missing.

Gillian dug down to the bottom of the pile into the Jeffrie Trace murder articles, and pulled out a picture taken from the video that showed the handle of the axe laying over Jeffrie's arm, and took a careful examination. The sway of the handle appeared the same, but she would need to be sure if that was a simple manufacturing coincidence. Were all fire axe handles made that way?

She could see where Joe was going with this, there were certainly

51

several circumstantial pieces of possible evidence, but it was all just that so far—circumstantial. As much as Joe was ready to believe this was all the actions of some evil force, Gillian continued to search for something more down to earth. Believing in evil was easy. There was enough evidence of evil all over the world, enough truly wicked people doing truly wicked things to other human beings, but she was not quite ready to give this mystery away to that theory just yet.

The tea was doing what she had hoped, and Gillian retired to the comforts of her own bed for the first time in weeks, since packing out of her place in Fredrick a month earlier. In the familiarity of her own sheets, pillows and blankets she drifted off to an easy sleep, with only the thoughts of another day in a sleepy little town. The whole reason for moving away.

The sound of crunching metal and shattering glass echoed in her mind once again and forced her to sit up wide awake. "Not again," she whispered choking back tears.

***

Tuesday, June 11th 2019

"I really appreciate you coming along with me on calls like this," Deputy Pierce said to Gillian, as they pulled away from the small apartment complex. "I sure hope we did the right thing. I would normally be hauling someone in for booking."

"If they do what I suggested, everything should work out. That boy doesn't need to be locked up for a mental crisis. With the appropriate diagnosis and care, he could be helped. I've been in contact with the mental health agencies and they all seem very capable," Gillian said. "It's just a matter of will they do what needs to be done."

"Domestic issues, and calls like this can be some of the most dangerous. More officers end up shot, stabbed and killed on domestic dispute calls. We all train to keep our service weapon real handy; you can't be too careful. You just never know what mess you're walking into," Pierce said.

"Oh, I know. I've been in some pretty tight situations over the years."

"If you don't mind me asking, I heard you have several degrees in this sort of stuff."

"I don't mind. I have a Masters in Criminal Psychology, and varying degrees in Psychology, Sociology, Domestic Violence Intervention and Counseling, Child Psychology, Child Abuse Intervention and Counseling, with a few minors and certifications in other mental health conditions related to both adult and child ADD, ADHD and PTSD counseling."

Deputy Pierce sat back in his seat in awe, "Wow. How did you have time to go through all that schooling?"

"Well, let's just say it just helped me focus on my job in Fredrick." Gillian didn't feel the need to admit out loud that all the training and certifications were also her desperate attempt to self-medicate her own trauma. That years of helping others was in some way a selfish experiment to help herself.

"Certainly doesn't sound like you had much time for anything else."

"Nope. But that's all right. I'll write up a report of this incident for you to file. It shouldn't take too long…you should have it by the end of the day. I'll follow up with his mother in a couple days, to see if they need any further encouragement to seek appropriate treatments."

The deputy pulled the cruiser into the back lot of the station. "Here you go, thanks again for the assist."

"You're welcome, give me a call if you need help on something like this again."

Back in her office, Gillian attached her report to the electronic file and hit send. Taking a sip of her cup of tea, she sat back in her chair and glanced at Joe's over-stuffed folder. She was determined not to dig into the folder on a regular basis, not wanting be accused of obsessing over the material. Bud was out of town for a few days, and Trent had made sure everyone else was aware of her intentions on the case materials from Joe, so Gillian took a moment to indulge.

She slid the folder closer and moved down another layer into the pile of articles and reports. After the stack of Ruphord Stilles' papers, there were several cases of transients that moved into the emptied building after the closure in 1966.

First was an Army Vietnam disabled veteran who had occupied the empty building along with some teenage female associates in 1967. Sergeant Jonathan Billings had been suspected of drug and sex trafficking from the facility. There had been some reports of abuse among the girls, but never any arrests on his warrants because Mr. Billings went missing without a trace. The girls' statement to the police was that the facility was haunted by some dark and evil force.

Another similar story followed with another suspected drug dealer and transient in 1969. James Conway had a long rap sheet, dating back to the mid-fifties. The Stilles facility was popular with homeless transients and James became a leader of the next group. There were several complaints of assault and battery, and eventually a bench warrant was issued, but no arrest. James disappeared again without a rational trace. Those at the facility claimed a dark evil entity took him away. Although there was no mention of an axe, or any listed evidence of any foul play, the report was filled with descriptions of evil spirits throughout the facility. Joe wrote out several notes regarding the haunting reports along the borders of the reports.

The stories continued, seventeen cases of missing people up until 1992, when the county finally terminated utility services from the entire property. All with a very similar MO—people missing without a trace, no evidence of foul play, only reports of dark evil spirits. Without running water and power that could be illegally turned back on in the electrical room, transients staying in the facility discontinued breaking in for an extended stay. By that time the urban legend had a solid foundation of past events and local high school crowds were breaking into the facility to taunt the evil spirits. Those that were initially reported to have gone missing inside, were typically found to have turned up later somewhere else as a 'run-away,' all still continuing the legend with tales of a dark evil entity and the threat of attack by axe.

After 1992, the reports and stories in the folder changed more to tales told by ghost enthusiasts coming to the facility from across the country for a thrill. A familiar name started to pop up rather regularly; Bill Hartfield, a local paranormal investigator. Gillian remembered seeing that name and rummaged through some of the loose paper clippings to find the business card. She could tell by the wear, the card had been kept in a wallet for a long time. There was a faded phone number scribbled on the back that was different from the number on the front of the card. Gillian compared the writing style to the notes written on the borders of the many reports and news clippings; it was not Joe's writing style.

Gillian propped the card up next to her laptop screen and typed the name into the browser. Several links popped up for a site; Puget Sound Paranormal Research, PSPR. She clicked on the first one and the link was dead. Continuing down the list, she found that all of the links referencing Puget Sound Paranormal Research, PSPR were dead, so she checked for history on the URL and the site. There was an article explaining that the URL had gone inactive just two years earlier in 2017. One final link was a blog site that mentioned the Puget Sound Paranormal Research group had disbanded. However, there were several links to posted video clips of the group at locations around the state, with many listed to be at the Stilles Asylum. Gillian clicked on a couple, but the files were so grainy and the sound distorted that the video files were difficult to view.

"Knock knock. I'm out. The cleaners are going to be here in just a few minutes. Are you planning on moonlighting with them tonight?" Darla asked from the hall.

Gillian was perplexed by the question, and took a quick glance out of her office window. What she thought was still daylight was actually a street light. She had completely forgotten she had turned on her desk lamp some time ago. "Oh my. I guess it would be a good time to leave."

"Just checking," Darla chuckled. "You seem pretty wrapped up in your research project."

"Yeah, maybe a little too much for today."

***

One advantage of being a detective is being good at acquiring information. For example, Gillian was able to find out that Mr. and Mrs. Joe and Mary Tulford lived at 2719 Cedar Rd W just outside of Port Latch, and that today was normally his day off. Also that he had purchased several gallons of paint, and brushes, and mentioned to his co-workers that he had planned to do some painting on his backyard fence since the weather was expected to be sunny and clear.

Gillian had some questions regarding many of Joe's notes, various articles, and how well he knew Bill Hartfield, so she decided to take a chance and stop by his residence. When she pulled up along the side of the road in front of the address, there was an older woman in long pants and plaid shirt with a broad-brimmed gardening hat and apron. She was pruning some of the plants along the front yard white picket fence.

"Mrs. Mary Tulford?" Gillian asked, as she stepped up to the fence across from the woman.

"Yes?"

"I'm Detective—"

"Detective McClary," she interrupted. Although the woman had a smile on her face, Gillian noted a bit of a chill in her voice.

"Have we met?"

"In a way. My husband described you to a 'T.'"

"I hope that's a good thing?" Gillian held her hand out.

Mary put her garden clippers in a pocket of her apron, took off a garden glove and reached across the short fence to shake Gillian's hand. "I suppose that depends." Mary's answer was dry.

"I've just come to ask Joe a couple questions—"

"You got the package?" Mary interrupted.

"Uh, yes and—"

"Everything there is to know is in that package."

"Well, yes, Mrs. Tulford, Joe's notes are very extensive, but—"

"Detective McClary—"

"Gillian, please."

"Gillian. You don't understand."

"No, I guess maybe I don't."

"My husband has obsessed over that case for years. Pulling together pieces, information and evidence, that in the end no one would believe. He was obsessively meticulous with every detail."

"I understand, I—"

"I watched my husband walk away from the job and life he loved for that obsession, only to sink into a depression so deep, I was nearly unable to reach him on his worst days."

"I really believe I can understand what—"

"Please, listen. When he sent you that package, he did so because he believes in you and that you will do right by him. A weight has been lifted from him." Mary paused to clear her throat, and her emotions. "Gillian, I have my husband back. Can you understand what I'm saying? What that really means? He's been lost in the details of that evil place, that darkness for the last five years. Since he sent you that package and all his work on that case, he has finally let go. He has been set free. Please don't drag him back down into that abyss again. I may not be able to pull him back out next time."

Gillian let Mary's words sink in. She knew the power of obsessions. She knew the darkness that can envelop a person's soul over a single pointed vision.

"Mary, did someone drive up?" Joe asked as he stepped from around the side of their home. He was wiping paint from his hands on a rag. He paused a moment when he saw Gillian, but regained his smile and joined them at the fence. "Gillian, this is my wife Mary."

"We've met," Mary said.

"Yes, lovely woman. I stopped by to," Gillian paused and glanced at Mary to see her pleading with her eyes. "To thank you for entrusting in me with your work and sending me that package."

Joe pressed his lips together and nodded. "I just hope it's helpful."

"Oh my, yes. Extremely." Gillian's words hung in the air. "Your work was extremely thorough," she added for good measure.

"Okay then, well nice seeing you again. I've got paint brushes I need to finish cleaning before the paint dries up. You understand," Joe said and turned to go back around the side of the house, he turned one last time and waved before disappearing around the corner.

"Thank you," Mary said wiping the corner of her eye with back of her hand.

Gillian managed a polite smile and nodded. She took a long gaze at the house and the meticulous landscaping Mary was maintaining. "You have a beautiful home."

Mary nodded. "Again, thank you."

***

The worn business card was propped on the front of Gillian's laptop screen for a couple weeks or so. She had spent that time going over the files in the folder Joe had left, and found so many had notes referencing Mr. Hartfield and his paranormal organization. Since Mrs. Tulford had requested Joe be left out of any further investigation, that left only Mr. Hartfield to talk with, if he was still willing.

Still, Gillian could not shake her feeling that the whole phenomenon of paranormal research and ghost hunting was a hoax.

There were plenty of videos online that exposed the fakes, including Jeffrie Trace videos. Then again, an explosion of television programming continued to sell the idea of paranormal activities around the world as facts. Her Christian upbringing and Sunday school teachings of the bible were very strict regarding life after death, demons and angels, excluding the idea of ghosts in general. As she had grown, and not continued so faithfully down the path of Christianity, her own beliefs in life after death seemed to reside somewhere in between the Christian ideology and the theories that Joe was subscribing to, that a ghost or non-living evil entity could commit murder.

On a whim she picked up her desk phone, dialed the number on the business card and received a disconnected-number automated message. The results were expected, but the detective in her said she needed to try that number first. She then dialed the hand-written number on the back of the card.

"Hi, you've reached William Hartfield, Paranormal Researcher. Please leave a message after the tone—(beep)."

In that moment Gillian realized she had not decided how she wanted to approach the idea of talking with Mr. Hartfield. After all, this really wasn't any formal questioning, and officially not even police business—yet. While trying to decide on the tone of her message, she had hesitated too long, and the messaging service hung up. "Crap."

Gillian hung up to clear the line and try again, but the phone started ringing before she could pick up, and when she did answer, she heard a man on the other end.

"Joe?" he asked.

"This is Detective McClary of the Port Latch Police," Gillian replied.

"Oh. I'm sorry I just missed a call from this number that used to be—"

"Yes, this is Detective Tulford's old desk number. Are you Mr. William Hartfield?"

"Yes, but you can just call me Bill. Joe always did. So you're the new Port Latch Detective, the papers say you're opening up the Jeffrie Trace Case again?"

"Mr. Hartfield, that case was never officially closed, but I have been reviewing some of the files and details and I was wondering if you would discuss some of the details that Joe had that referenced you and your organization."

"Uh, yeah. Yes, sure, absolutely." Gillian could hear his answer grow with genuine excitement. "I live on Bainbridge Island, I can meet you there in Port Latch in about an hour?"

"Well, I don't really need you to drive all the way here. Can I meet you somewhere in between?"

"Oh, right. Sure. Do you know where the Silverdale Marina is?"

"Hold on," Gillian typed in and located the marina on her laptop's browser. "Okay, got it."

"There's a gazebo at the park there, on the end of the cul-de-sac just past the marina, rarely used this time of day, meet me there say, in about a half hour?"

"I'll meet you there."

***

The drive didn't take long at all, and the directions were easy enough. The gazebo was as Bill said it would be, empty, and Gillian sat at the picnic table and realized this was going to be another one of her favorite places with a well-maintained park and the Dyes Inlet. The view was spectacular, with sailing boats, and paddle-boarders enjoying the water.

There was very little traffic coming to the end of the cul-de-sac, and Gillian noticed an older model sedan pull up right next to her car in front of the gazebo. The driver was wearing a brown split-tail riding coat, a brown fedora that nearly covered his thin rat-tail, and carried a large, over-stuffed, aged-leather satchel briefcase. When he looked up, she could see his broad smile behind a grey-stubbled beard and piercing grey-blue eyes behind his glasses. He looked very different from any of his videos.

"You must be Detective McClary? They certainly didn't use a very flattering picture of you in the paper," he said stepping up next to the bench table.

"They did not. And you must be Mr. Hartfield."

"Please, just Bill. Mr. Hartfield was my Dad." He set the satchel on the table with a thud.

Gillian gave the case a long glance. "I didn't realize you were going to bring all your notes."

Bill chuckled, "Naw, this is just a few items I had handy. All the rest are in my barn in several storage bins."

"Uh—all regarding the Stilles Asylum? Or Jeffrie Trace?" Gillian was amazed there might be that much material.

"Well, yes actually both." Bill's blunt answer hung in the air a moment while Gillian processed his reply.

"I have to be honest with you, Bill. I really don't subscribe to all this weird paranormal investigation stuff you see all over the TV." She didn't mean for her statement to come out as blunt as it sounded, and tried to soften the harshness with a light chuckle and an awkward nod.

Bill gave her a moment for her comment to settle, then put both hands on the table and leaned in. "Well. Thank goodness for that. All that paranormal TV junk investigation…is just that; junk. Most of that is fake, and what isn't fake is edited to seem like more than it is."

"I'm sorry I really didn't mean to come off attacking your profession," Gillian said.

"Don't be sorry. There are a lot of people trying to make a quick buck off the latest rage, and lately paranormal investigations, into ghosts and the like, have been all the rage. But you know that."

Gillian nodded.

"So, now you've got questions?"

"Yes, I do," Gillian agreed.

"I want to help answer those questions as best I can, and maybe along the way, show you the difference between what I do, and what you see on TV."

"Okay," Gillian paused in thought. She wasn't sure where to go next.

"Where to start?" Bill asked, as though he was reading her mind. Gillian pulled out the folder from her shoulder bag. "Ah, Joe's notes."

"You recognize these?"

"Of course. We worked on these reports for many months."

Gillian tried to decide what to ask about first.

Bill gestured towards the folder. "Before we get into it, just ask me some general questions. You must have some."

"I appreciate that." Gillian paused. "First, I have to ask, do you really, truly believe in ghosts?"

Bill sat back. "Great first question. If you mean the Hollywood, sheet-covered, chain-dragging, wailing version of a ghost? No. However, I've witnessed energies, sounds, lights, and apparitions that in many cases I couldn't explain, and after careful, and thorough debunking, would be identified as a ghost, or after-life energy. Keep in mind there are several variations of spirit paranormal activity."

Gillian sat back and crossed her arms in thought, trying to process his answer.

"I know that is a lot to take in, without providing any supporting evidence."

"And you have non-controvertible supporting evidence?"

"For individuals with an honest, open mind; yes," Bill said and put his hand on his satchel.

"All right. Are ghosts evil?"

"By most accounts those that I've personally encountered, no. That idea that all ghosts are evil mostly comes from religious concepts. Now, that's not to say none are evil. I've also seen and been in the presence of entities that I'd say are non-human, and very much an evil energy."

"Non-human?"

"Absolutely. There are some entities, many would call 'elemental' or 'cosmic' energies, often the source of many folklore and ancient myth."

"Evil?"

"Mostly you might say they come from a different concept of morality, and thus can come off as evil. Again, much of that would be derived from the religious concepts of demons and devils."

"Stilles Asylum?"

"Joe very much subscribed to that notion. I was not completely convinced."

"Okay, next question. Could a ghost, by your definition, kill?"

"There are stories that say so. Joe certainly believed so. I have personally witnessed attacks by spirit energies that have injured people, causing severe cuts, scratches and bruising. There is a corroborated event where a young man had provoked a spirit while carrying a knife, taunting the spirit of an individual that had stabbed someone in that house with an identical kitchen knife. The man set the knife down on a table and the knife flew up and stabbed him in the back after he turned from it. There's video evidence showing the knife lifting and flying and striking the man, aided by only an unseen force. Luckily he was not killed, but was rushed to the hospital with a serious knife wound."

"Wouldn't that be considered an evil spirit?" Gillian asked.

"Many would say so, but I also believe there are some spirits that are simply very angry, and if they're able to gain enough strength, could move objects and on occasion possibly cause injury."

"Now you're starting to sound like a lawyer."

Bill chuckled. "Sometimes I do feel spirit energies often get a bad rap. Most spirits I come across just want to be left alone. Others want someone to talk to so they're not forgotten. There are also paranormal encounters that are called a 'residual haunt.'"

"What does that mean?"

"A haunting that is simply like a recording of an event in the past playing over and over. Some call it a non-intelligent haunting."

"Non-intelligent—"

"Yes, the energy is not aware of anyone's presence."

"As opposed to an 'intelligent haunt?'"

"Exactly. That's when the spirit energy interacts with us. Sometimes they're happy to have visitors, sometimes not so happy."

"You make ghosts sound like regular people," Gillian said, shaking her head.

"Well, if you think about it, most spirit energies were real people who lived in this world, and when they died, they just stayed behind."

"Why?" Gillian asked.

"Why are they staying behind?"

"Yeah. Why have they not gone, you know, into the light. Gone off to heaven?"

"Wow, you really are asking some great questions," Bill answered, as he pulled his fedora off, scratched at the back of his head, and then placed it back on.

"I'm a detective, remember?" Gillian chuckled.

Bill chuckled too. "From much of my research, as well as many other respected investigators, some spirit energies appear to gravitate back to a place of familiarity, like a home they lived in for years, a business they worked at, or a place that is comforting. Some are angry, and in that anger, don't want to leave or possibly because of the anger, are not able to leave. Some energies don't realize or refuse to believe they have crossed over, are no longer alive and so again, they remain in a place of familiarity. Others seem to attach themselves to a site, or even a person, again either not knowing where to go, sometimes wanting to watch over loved ones, or too scared or confused to leave that location."

"Like murder victims or crash victims?"

"Yes, exactly."

Gillian shook her head, "I just can't. I don't like that idea. I hate to think someone might be stuck at some lone crash site or murder site alone. I just can't."

Bill could see from the look on Gillian's face, there was a raw nerve being struck, and hard. "That is hard to take sometimes, especially when there are children's energies involved."

"Oh my God, I really can't go there. That just breaks my heart to think of children or loved-ones being stuck in some awful place or on the side of a road somewhere," Gillian said, turning away. She let the soft breeze from the inlet soothe her thoughts a moment. Bill let her take her time. After a few moments Gillian pulled herself together. Her psychologist friend would have been proud that she only needed a few minutes this time. Something Bill had said earlier drifted back into her thoughts. "You said you've seen evidence of spirit energies causing injuries, like scratches and bruising?"

"Yes. Often scratches come in threes, and in places that scratches should not have been possible, like under clothing with no evidence of any abrasion from above or through the clothing."

Gillian turned and gave Bill a stern look while pulling her cellphone from her shoulder bag. "Like this?" She asked and accessed the photos on her phone she had taken of the young girl, Stacy. There were no images of the young girl's face, only the injuries, including the three long parallel scratches on her back, and the bruising around her wrist and ankle.

Bill lifted his glasses and took a closer look. "Yes, these images are exactly consistent with injuries acquired by spirit energies. Although this bruising around the wrist and ankle is much more intense, still overall very consistent. Where did you get these photos, may I ask?"

"Actually I really can't. Let's just say, she is underage, and had an encounter at the Stilles Asylum, a few weeks back."

"I read that article. I was curious if there had been more to that story." Bill returned Gillian's phone. He opened his satchel and rummaged through, pulling out several photos and handing them to Gillian. "These are several photos of encountered injuries while on investigations."

Gillian sifted through the large prints. So many were of scratch marks on people's backs, legs, arms, one poor woman's cheek. Some of the scratches were deep enough to create welts and draw blood. Other images were of bruising, and in one particular case, it was shaped like a hand print. "Are these all from the Stilles Asylum?"

"Several, but not all. I do investigations all over the state."

"You have more evidence?"

"Far more than I brought here today, but let me pull out some more photos." Bill rummaged again through his satchel and pulled out more large photos.

"Are these from all over or only Stilles Asylum?"

Bill took another glance at the photos before handing them to Gillian. "These are from the Stilles."

Gillian sifted through. She wasn't exactly sure what she was looking at until one in particular.

Bill noticed a change in Gillian's demeanor. He studied the photo. There was a dark shadow in a doorway, that was shaped like a person, as though peeking out from around the door frame. The black mass resembled features of a head and shoulders. "Oh, that's Jack," Bill said, as though he were about to make a formal introduction. Gillian's gaze at the photo grew more intense. "You've seen Jack?"

"I don't know what I saw, really. Whatever it was, this is very close," Gillian finally admitted.

"Well I'm sorry for the overused cliché, but you look like you've seen a ghost."

Gillian gave Bill her best skeptic scowl, "This doesn't look like a ghost. This looks like a person."

"Yes, they are often called 'shadow people,' and are another representation of spirit energies. Although some paranormal investigative professionals believe 'shadow people' are more of an elemental being like I mentioned before, and not so much a 'human entity.'"

"No really this has to be a person," Gillian insisted.

Bill shook his head. "Look closer. See the graffiti on the wall

64

behind? You can see the graffiti continue on through the shadow form there. See?" Bill took a pen from his shirt pocket and used it as a pointer.

"Camera trick?"

"No camera tricks. And this particular photo was taken during a daytime investigation, that light on the walls' graffiti is daylight from the window just on the other side of the door. That shadow form should not exist there on that side of the door frame, with the light coming from the window like it was."

Gillian continued to stare at the photo and shake her head in disbelief. They both felt the shift in the breeze bring a chill to the air with the setting sun.

"You know the deli just up the street from here has a great bisque and probably the best coffee this side of the Sound. We can continue there. Interested?" Bill asked.

"You know that actually sounds good. I have so many more questions."

"No problem. I'll do my best to answer them one at a time."

***

The bisque was everything Bill had said it was and more. Even his praise of the coffee was not an exaggeration. The silence may have been due to hunger and getting down to the business of eating, or simply that Gillian had so much to process. Whether or not she'd remain a skeptic was still undetermined.

Gillian looked around the small deli. There was a small group of diners in a corner booth across the room, so she leaned in a little. "Do you believe that shadow person in the photo to be Jack from the legend?"

Bill took one last swipe of his spoon across the bottom of his empty bowl of bisque and set it aside. "Yes."

"What makes you so sure? Do you have some conclusive evidence?" Gillian also set her empty bowl aside, and cradled her coffee.

"Contrary to what you may have seen on TV's paranormal investigations, and I purposely avoid the term 'Ghost Hunting,' there's a lot more research and investigation into the history of the site, or the people involved. I've been investigating the Stilles

Asylum since 1997, both onsite to verify that activity has been duly challenged and debunked, and researching the records, and people or witnesses with direct knowledge."

"So did you reach out to Joe or did he reach out to you?"

"He reached out to me. I'd been on a couple of those TV shows in the early 2000s. I was a bit of a local celebrity back then, and was still naive to TV editing and a production agenda, as opposed to attempting to prove the science and study of the paranormal and spirit energies. Joe wanted to know pretty much the same thing as you. Do I truly believe, and what proof do I have? When he found out about how much research I actually do, he wanted to tap into that resource."

"So all the notes and questions he wrote down, you found or researched?"

"Exactly. But he wanted to keep it quiet. Jeffrie was quite a celebrity online and was said to be signing a lucrative TV deal soon."

"So I guess everything in this folder is all there is," Gillian said a little disappointed.

Bill gave the folder a once-over glance and scoffed. "If that's all you have, that's nothing. I wasn't kidding when I said earlier that I have bins filled with research on the Stilles Asylum."

"But what evidence do you have that the shadow in the photo or the shadow I saw is the legendary 'Jack?'"

"My research," Bill said as though there could be no other answer. He glanced at his cellphone and saw the time. "It's getting late. This place will be closing soon, and I certainly don't want to keep you from Mr. McClary any longer tonight."

"Mr. McClary," Gillian paused. "Daniel and my daughter, Kristin, were killed in an automobile accident many years ago." Her psychologist friend would be proud she had spoken their names without hesitation—a real breakthrough.

Bill sat back, feeling embarrassed. "I'm so sorry, I saw your ring, and assumed—"

"That's all right. I'm getting used to explaining. Everyone knew back in Frederick, I rarely had to explain."

"Again, I apologize, I should not have assumed. Look it is getting late. I have a couple of investigations over the next couple of days I've been asked to attend out of state, but I'll be back on Saturday.

Can we continue at my office? I have so much more I can show you including what evidence I've collected over the years at the Stilles Asylum. I believe I have the answers you're looking for."

"I would like that. I'll let you know. I'm still very much on the fence with all this. Call Joe's old number when you get back, it's forwarded to my cell," Gillian said, as she scooped up the folder and her shoulder bag.

Gillian wondered on her drive home if she was heading down a rabbit hole. Bill was very good at answering her questions, but she had so many more—there seemed to be no end.

***

Chapter 4
Proving Jack

L iving in a small town apparently included a few perks that Gillian was fast learning about. Somewhere along the way, word got out that she enjoyed having lunch parked in her car on the grounds behind the Stilles Asylum. So when she pulled up on this very nice sunny Friday, she found the city crew unloading a metal picnic table where she normally parked—a nice sunny spot with a full view of the whole complex. Recently mowed, the grounds had a park-like appearance.

When she got out of her car and walked up to the table, she nodded a thanks.

The older gentleman approached from the truck. "Weather seemed too nice to be sitting in your car eating lunch. This table was just refurbished with no particular place to go. So we thought here would be just as good as any."

"Well I thank you for thinking of me," Gillian replied and sat down at the bench with her lunch. She watched as they drove off down the main paved road. Even sitting a few hundred feet away in the clearing, the buildings' immense size was foreboding. Many people had told her how 'creeped-out' they'd feel sitting this close to the Stilles Asylum. To Gillian the Stilles Asylum, despite all the bad publicity, was truly a grand structure, and reminded her of the architecture and heritage of many of the buildings in Fredrick and the East Coast, particularly on such beautiful days like today. Gillian allowed a fond memory of the times when she and Daniel would take Kristin to some of those city parks overlooking the grand historic buildings. Kristin loved those visits and picnics so very much. Now Gillian found herself staring, and in that moment also realizing, she felt once again, as though someone, or possibly many sets of eyes were gazing back. She wasn't sure if she was feeling uneasy from the creepy factor, or because there was a loneliness about the place. She was so mesmerized that she hadn't noticed the

PLPD SUV cruiser coming up the main driveway.

Trent pulled the cruiser up next to her car, got out with a small plastic bag, and stood next to the table. "All right if I join you? Or is this a private party?"

Gillian looked up and smiled as she gestured to the other side, "Please. They just set this up for me only moments ago."

"I heard," Trent said as he sat down and pulled a to-go container out and opened it up.

"You heard?"

"Small town, remember?" Trent pulled out a thick cold-cut sandwich.

"So I've been told," Gillian said shaking her head with a chuckle. "I thought you always went to your favorite deli on Fridays?"

"I did. They serve take-out too. So I decided to go there, get a to-go and then see if I could join you here."

"I don't remember telling anyone I was coming here today," Gillian said with a forced sarcastic scowl.

Trent pulled his sunglasses down enough to look over the top and gave her a raised eyebrow glance.

"Right. Small town," Gillian chuckled again.

"Haven't heard much news lately, you've been playing your cards pretty close to the vest. How's the project?" Trent asked between bites.

"Researching mainly. Do you know William Hartfield?" Gillian asked.

"Bill? Sure, why?"

"Trustworthy?"

Trent put his sandwich down, sat back and wiped his face with a napkin, "Joe trusted him implicitly. I don't know that I know him well enough to make that much of an informed opinion. Why?"

"He's invited me to his office to go over some of his research on the Stilles Asylum."

"Has he acted inappropriate or something? Are you having concerns? Feeling threatened?"

"No, no, no. I just wanted to get your take on him. He seems legit. What I've found online has some people praising his ethics in the paranormal arena, and many in the more mainstream scientific community calling him a crackpot. Of course, many in the mainstream scientific community call anyone not toeing the line in scientific discovery crackpots, so it can be hard to take that opinion completely serious. Know what I mean?"

"I know what you mean. My grandfather often talked about how blind the mainstream scientific community was toward native lore, myth and legend, not taking in consideration that the lore and myths were often based in very tangible facts, even if they didn't make scientific sense, often dismissing everything to fantasy…or worse—hallucinations."

Gillian found her gaze fixed on the windows at the back of the Stilles Asylum, convinced she was seeing movement. Not just the reflection of passing clouds, but actual dark shapes, and often in several windows at a time. "How often do you feel like someone is watching you here?"

Trent took another bite, and shook his head, "I try not to think about it."

"Fair enough, but every time I've come here, I get the feeling I'm being watched, and just as often I feel like I'm seeing movement in the windows. How certain are you that there's no one living in that building?"

Trent turned enough to almost glance at the building, but stopped and turned back. "I don't think anyone can be completely one-hundred percent, but we've got the entries locked pretty well this time, and the old coal bin hatch has been re-welded with a new lock. If there's someone living in there, I can't image where that would be. We've searched every square inch of that place. Plus there's no water or electricity."

"So you think there are only ghosts living there?" Gillian asked.

Trent could see by the look on her face that she, once again, was not being sarcastic. "Let's just say I hope there's no living person in there. I think that would be a fate worse than death."

"Chief. This is dispatch," Darla's voice crackled over Trent's radio.

Trent reached over to his shoulder radio mic, "Trent, go dispatch."

"Got a disturbance call at the tire shop, Sarah says she's got a disgruntled customer making threats. She requested you, but I can dispatch Case or Robert if you're not done with lunch."

"Dispatch, I'm done. Let Sarah know I'm on my way, Trent out."

Gillian sat back and raised her brows with surprise, "Small town."

Trent scooped up his lunch leftovers and tossed them into the bag.

"Very small town."

***

Saturday, June 29th 2019

Bill sent the address and Gillian's cellphone GPS provided the directions. She felt a sense of familiarity as she crossed over the Agate Pass Bridge onto Bainbridge Island, driving on the two-lane road, all so reminiscent of Frederick's narrow, back roads, lined with a forest of cedars and maples along with a heavy undergrowth.

She drove down a narrow single-lane gravel driveway through dense forest that eventually opened to a large pasture surrounded by well-kept white fencing. There was a horse-training arena just beyond, as the driveway wound further along. With a couple of turns the drive angled toward a modest older white two-story home, with a partial wrap-around porch and an overly large parking area in front. A well-maintained bright red barn sat just beyond the house and first parking area. Trucks and horse trailers were parked on the side of the barn. Gillian was becoming concerned that she may have been taken to the wrong address until she noticed Bill's older sedan.

Feeling that was a safe place to park, she pulled in and got out just in time to see Bill exiting the house and heading in her direction with a wave. "Hey, there you are," he greeted.

"Hey, here I am," Gillian waved back. "This looks like a horse-training facility."

"And that would be correct," Bill said, gesturing back toward the barn. "This was my folks' place. I got it after they passed away a few years back."

"Nice place...so you train horses?" Gillian followed Bill to a white painted fence attached to the side of the barn where they could see the pastures and training arena. There were a few horses in the pasture and a woman working with a horse in the training arena.

"Actually no. I just rent out the training arena to several local trainers along with a few stalls on one side of the barn. It helps to pay for the upkeep, some food and keeps the lights on."

"Were your folks horse trainers?"

"Naw, they did the same thing, renting out the space. The original owner that built this place back in the twenties trained horses though.

71

When my folks bought the place when I was a kid, they didn't want to lose the charm of what the original owner had. Now this place is practically a historical landmark."

Gillian nodded. "This is beautiful."

"Thanks. Let me show you to my office." Bill gestured to a door on the opposite side of the barn away from the arena. "This is my side." Bill opened the door for Gillian.

The interior was a combination of rustic barn, and modern architecture, with exposed wood beams, a few pieces of well-aged horse-riding tackle and equipment as decoration set against professional finished painted drywall, and reclaimed wood wall boards. The floor was varnished floor planks and the office furniture was a combination of rustic and new modern—nothing like what she expected to see. Along the back wall were several large TV screens, computers and various pieces of electronic equipment. There was an open hallway that continued on to another similarly finished space with open storage shelving and bins.

"Very nice," Gillian expressed looking around.

"My ex was a professional interior decorator," Bill answered Gillian's unasked question.

"Well this all certainly explains the hat and long riding coat the other night."

"Oh that. Well, yeah. I grew up around horses, and one of the perks is I get to ride some of them once in a while. I get all the best parts of being around horses; riding without owning and upkeep," Bill chuckled. "AND, all the manure I can handle for my garden."

"You garden too?"

"Well, that might be a bit of a stretch. But I do have all the manure I could ever need for a garden."

Gillian grinned. "Fair enough. So how was your trip? Catch any ghosts?"

"Ha-ha," Bill scoffed, then noticed Gillian's expression was serious and not joking. "Really?"

"Yes, remember I'm not convinced, but I am curious. Or is there some kind of privacy agreement you have to keep so you can't discuss the cases?"

"No, no. I can discuss the cases. My first stop was in Portland, at a private residence. I was able to calm their fears through some simple debunking."

"Really? No ghost?"

"Nope. And seriously that happens more often than you'll hear about on TV too."

"So what was the cause of their distress?"

"First they have some serious issues with their wiring, causing huge EMF spikes throughout the house."

"EMF? Are you talking about Electromagnetic Fields?" Gillian asked.

"Yes, exactly. High concentrations of EMF can cause very real physical effects, like headaches, fatigue, nausea, paranoia, feeling like you're being watched and hallucinations. That particular client has an older home with very poor wiring and grounding, causing severe EMF signals."

"That was all it was?"

"Well, that and some very drafty doors and windows, causing things to move unexpectedly whenever a door or window was opened in another part of the house."

"Isn't EMF used by paranormal investigators to confirm when spirits or ghosts are present?"

"EMF meters are often used, but you have to know their limitation and be mindful of false positives."

"But mainstream scientists insist there is no connection with EMF to ghosts or spirits," Gillian argued.

"Yes. Mainstream science discounts many things. They also fail to come up with explanations for having EMF hits where there is no electricity or any other scientifically known cause for the detector's reactions at some locations. I don't use it as proof of a spirit energy but to let me know when I'm finding unexplained environmental conditions at an investigation."

"Don't paranormal investigators claim that spirit energies or ghosts draw energy from excessive EMF to manifest or move objects?"

"You've been studying up," Bill said impressed with her line of questions.

"I'm trying to understand all this."

"You and me both. The field of paranormal investigation is in constant flux—new theories, new technologies. And, yes, there are several theories regarding EMF strengthening spiritual energies."

"So how was the other place?"

"The what?" Bill asked.

"The other investigation. One was a bust, what about the other?"

"Oh, the second site. That was the old Mansfield Poorhouse in Oregon, now a Brewery, Inn and restaurant. It's believed the poorhouse has been haunted from back when it was used for the destitute and disabled at the turn of the last century. The owners have often allowed investigations on the property to validate or debunk some of the claims by guests and staff. I was asked to come down and help with a team that's training new investigators. The activity is quite prolific and you can get experiences on nearly every investigation. I used to do training at the Stilles for the same reason."

"So did you?"

"Did I—Train?"

"No, I mean, did you have any particular experiences you can't explain?"

"Hold on just a second, I loaded this up on my computer after I got home this morning." Bill logged onto his computer and all the large screen TVs lit up. Bill pointed to a seat next to his desk. "Here have a seat, this is an EVP from one of the rooms that is especially active."

"Electronic voice phenomenon?"

"Exactly," Bill clicked on the file and it played:

"Is there anyone here tonight?" A young woman's voice asked on the recording. She paused and left some space for a reply. *"Can you tell us if you're here? Can you tell us your name?"* she repeated, and again paused for a reply.

In the hiss of background noise a scratchy male voice whispered as though right into the microphone of the small recorder. *"Just leave me alone."*

"Wow," Gillian exclaimed. "That was clear. You're sure no one in the room was playing a trick?"

"Good. Debunk the data. That's what I teach. So for some background info on that EVP. We had the whole wing of the building to ourselves, all three floors, no staff or guests. This was on the third floor at the end of the building. There were two gentlemen in the group of seven—not including me. The room in question is known for activity and we had each of the new investigators go into the room one at a time, to practice the process for EVP recording and camera setup. Sharon was the last one in the room that night;

everyone else except me was waiting in a sitting area at the far end of the hall some fifty feet away. I was outside the closed door the whole time, listening for her technique. She didn't hear the voice at the time of the recording, and felt as though she had no responses just like everyone else that night. It was only after she left the room and we all listened back on her session that we heard this EVP response."

"I'm just not convinced it's not something more than a fluke; a one-off. Could have been anybody's voice really," Gillian said, trying not to sound condescending.

"Good, still debunking. Remember I've been there a many times before too, helping to train different groups. I recognized that voice from previous visits." Bill pulled up another file and played it:

"Why are you here? Do you just like being here? Is something making you stay?" The male voice asked, leaving pauses between the questions for a response. Gillian recognized the voice, it was Bill, and she pointed at him. Bill nodded and pointed at a blip coming up on the audio file as the cursor was moving long the file.

"Leave me. Go away." the scratchy male voice said, again as though whispering straight into the microphone.

"That sounds like the same voice," Gillian said, as she leaned forward with interest. She could feel a chill across her arms and neck.

"Yes, and I have a dozen more EVPs from that same room over the years…similar responses and all the same voice. We call him the 'angry old man.' I have done some extensive research, and unfortunately, there are too many people that have passed through that facility over the years to narrow it down to just one person. But I have three good candidates, including—"

"Okay so how can you be so sure about Jack at the Stilles," Gillian interrupted. "There were hundreds of people who came and went through that facility over the years."

Bill stopped and stared at Gillian for a second, needing to catch up on the conversation. "Boy you switch gears in a hurry, don't you?"

"Detective here. I have a goal to not only try to understand all this, but to come to a real tangible conclusion."

"Okay, back to the Stilles," Bill answered, turned back to his computer screen and opened up another folder filled with audio and video files. "Let me find some audio files that—"

"Is there just the one shadow figure at the Stilles? Or several?" Gillian interrupted.

Bill turned again and gave Gillian a hard glance. "How many times have you been in the Stilles?"

"Just the once, but I often go and sit behind the building during lunch. I'm not sure, but I think I keep seeing movement in the windows, and not just one; sometimes several at once."

Bill took in a deep breath, and let it out slow and deliberate. "I've seen that too."

"Do you have any explanations? Mainstream science tells me that it must be my mind and eyes playing tricks. I'm seeing movement from reflections of clouds and wind moving the windows. It's a phenomenon known as 'Paredolia,'" Gillian said.

"If what you and I have seen are tricks of the mind, I would think that recording that phenomenon would end the discussion." Bill turned to select a file. The video started showing the back of the Stilles Asylum at night. The camera was set to night vision mode, with static IR lights shining up at the back of the building. Bill stood up, reached out and pointed to a window on the upper floor, just as a dark, undefined figure appeared to walk past several windows. At that same moment another figure appeared to stand up at another window and look out. Bill pointed out the second one as well in the static video shot.

"I see people in the building," Gillian stated.

"I was there by myself, the place was locked up tight. There was no one inside the building," Bill explained.

Gillian shook her head. "I just can't believe that's true. This is all circumstantial. I certainly can see why Joe was working with you on this, you seem to have a wealth of data collected here, but I'm not convinced. How do you know there is a Jack involved here? Going back to what appears to be the beginning of the urban legend of Jack in 1966, where Ruphord Stilles was brutally murdered, there was no suspect found or listed and no murder weapon found. So, I have a hard time believing that dark mass I saw was some legendary figure named Jack."

"Okay, I apologize, I made a very presumptuous comment. That shadow form you saw may not actually be Jack that time. I've seen several shadow-figures there over the years, but I know he's there, and was there—"

"How many?" Gillian interrupted.

"I don't have an exact count, but I've documented a few regulars."

"Regulars?"

"Yeah, like there are some that are short and really fast moving. They like to climb walls, so we call them the 'Wall-Hangers.' They can be really creepy at times, and seen day and night. Then there's one that we lovingly call 'Stinky,'" Bill chuckled.

"Why?"

"Whenever we saw that one, we got a whiff of a god-awful sickening smell, like seriously putrid."

"That sounds awful."

"I'm telling you the smell is worse, but at least that one seems to be pretty shy, and generally stays well away."

"What about the one you think is Jack?"

"That one seems more curious, and you will see him peeking around corners, like he's trying to see what you're doing," Bill explained.

"But how can you be sure that one is Jack, or that Jack even existed?" Gillian argued.

"Oh I know Jack existed, I have first-hand witness accounts." Bill got up and headed back to the storage area. "I'll be right back, hold on." He rummaged through some bins. "Back in 2003 I was doing more research and got a lead on a gentleman, Martin Kulp, that lived in Spokane; he'd been a resident at the Stilles from 1958 to 1965," Bill's voice resonated from the long hall. "His father had dropped him off after his mother died, when he was 8 years old."

"That sounds horrible."

"Oh it gets worse. Martin had witnessed his father beat his mother to death in a drunken rage, and then proceed to tell the police she simply fell down the stairs. Before dropping his son off at the Stilles, the father swore he would kill his son if he ever told anyone." Bill walked out from the storage room with a Hi-8 digital video tape and player. He plugged it into some cables on his desk and turned it on. The video displayed on a smaller screen on the side of the larger main computer displays. The video jiggled and zoomed in and out, then finally settled into a static shot of a very old-looking Caucasian man, thin white hair, deep wrinkles and when he started to speak, was missing several teeth.

Gillian did the math and couldn't help comment, "If he was

dropped off at the Stilles at age 8 in 1958, and this was shot in 2003, he should be only 53 years old. This man looks like he's in his seventies or eighties."

"Martin had lived a very difficult life," Bill said as he fast-forwarded the video. "I'm looking for the parts about the legendary Jack." Bill saw what he was looking for and hit play mode:

"...so after hitching a ride to Montana at, what 15 years old?" Bill asked.

"Yeah, 15," Martin answered, almost in a daze of the memory. "Never looked back. Took me years to realize there was nothing wrong with me, that I wasn't mentally disabled like they all made me out to be." He took another sip from a bottled water.

"Now, while you were there, did you ever meet anyone named Jack, you know from the urban legend of the Stilles?"

"Oh yes. There was a boy that everyone called 'The Jack,'" Martin said.

"The Jack?"

"He was about my age I guess. Everyone said he had been a favorite of Ruphord's attention for many years."

"Ruphord's attention?"

"We were all at some point tortured and abused by Ruphord in one way or another, but Jack was a particular favorite. Ruphord's abuses were mostly toward younger kids and putting them into a metal box in the basement after he was done—" Martin cleared his voice and closed his eyes for a moment, then continued, "Jack ended up in the box more than most. Ruphord was often heard reciting that stupid nursery rhyme."

"Didn't anyone ever report Ruphord's activities and abuses to the authorities?" Bill asked.

"There was no one to report it to. Some of the older kids tried to protect the younger ones, but many of the older kids seemed to be almost as bad with the abuses as Ruphord. The nurses, and every other adult there just looked the other way."

"That's a familiar story I've been hearing," Bill commented.

"There was an older boy when I first arrived, named Tommy that tried to protect the younger boys and girls from Ruphord. But after a few years he eventually disappeared. Ruphord made sure to let everyone know the furnace was Tommy's final resting place."

"Oh my God," Bill exclaimed.

"There were a lot of children that went missing that way. There were no records for many like me," Martin added.

"Like you how?"

"If a child showed up on a weekend, there was no paperwork of their arrival, there was no official record of their existence. They were just dropped off. Ruphord could do what he wanted, and no one cared, there was no one ever intending to come back for them or keeping tabs on them."

"So what happened when Tommy disappeared? Who protected any of the little ones?"

"Funny thing that. Jack often acted like a small boy, even as he got older, like he was always six years old. But after Tommy disappeared, Jack just started acting like Tommy, very defiant, protective, a complete personality change. Completely different from how Jack normally acted. Even calling himself Tommy. Of course Ruphord would just take him down to the basement and Jack would be locked in the box again. Sometimes for weeks at a time."

"That's just awful. How could he survive like that?"

"Ruphord would often drop rats, sometimes alive, sometimes dead into the box for the current occupant to eat. I never did eat any when I was in the box, but I was never in as long as Jack."

"Oh my God, that is disgusting treatment."

"I tried to get him to come with me the day I left, but he just insisted he needed to stay and protect the others," Martin said. "But I know I was talking with Tommy that day. Jack was always talking about his mother coming back to take him to school."

"Did he ever mention his mother's first name? Or a last name?"

"No, just that even after several years, his mother would be coming back to pick up him and his sister Jillie."

"Jillie?" Gillian sat up in her chair. Bill paused the tape.

"Yeah, I've never found anyone that could corroborate any more on that detail, so I—"

"I heard that name spoken that day in the Stilles." Gillian's heart was pounding as though she had taken a shot of pure adrenaline. "I thought one of the guys was calling me."

"I've got recordings of that name being said at the Stilles, and usually by what sounds like a small boy calling out."

"No this was no boy that called my name," Gillian assured.

"Are you certain?"

"Very."

"Again, I haven't been able to verify that detail of Jack having a sister. Like Martin, I have had other interviews where people said Jack would often call out for Jillie, but no one had ever seen her, and with no records it's hard to take any of that seriously. I keep looking for more witnesses."

Gillian shook her head, deep in thought, and let out a heavy breath.

"Maybe we should take a break. Can I offer you a coffee or tea?" Bill offered.

"Maybe just some water," Gillian nodded. Bill headed down the hall to a small kitchenette and bathroom. She could hear Bill getting a glass and running some water.

"I've got the best well on the island, no need for bottled water here," Bill bragged.

"So all of your recordings, I'm guessing are similar voices talking about Jack?"

"Absolutely not. The bulk of the recordings, EVP sessions and spirit box sessions are of children, but there are also voices from the days of the garrison—soldiers and doctors. The Stilles has a very rich history, and there's a lot of energy stored there from over the last hundred plus years."

"Children," Gillian sighed and shook her head. "That's just so sad."

Bill set a glass of water on a small side table next to Gillian's chair. "Even after all the years I've been doing investigations, hearing voices of children from the other side is never easy. Although some groups, mostly religious, will argue that the children are actually demons, attempting to manipulate you."

"Joe seems to be rather religious from what I've noticed in his notes." Gillian pulled the folder from her shoulder bag. "He often talked about demons and evil spirits. Was that because of the children's voices in your recordings?"

"He's certain that there is evil in the Stilles Asylum. I do think a good portion of that was because of the children's voices."

"That just breaks my heart, to think there are spirits of children being tortured there," Gillian said taking a sip of water.

"Well, I do have several recordings on EVP and even just sounds we've heard in person, that sometimes sounds like children crying.

But honestly, on the fourth floor where many of the youngest ones lived, there are many recordings of children playing and laughing."

"Why do you think?"

"Well, some I believe to be residual haunting as we talked about before. But not all are, let me show you." Bill turned to his computer and opened up another digital video file:

The video showed a static night-vision shot of Bill sitting on the floor. A few feet away a toy ball was resting near a small device. Child-sized chairs could be seen arranged around behind him in the darkness.

"Is there anyone here that would like to play with me?" Bill asked, then waited for a response. *"I brought a nice new ball for you to play with. It's all right, work hours are over. You can play."* Bill paused the video.

"The children all worked on the first floor shoe and clothing production areas, and from witness accounts, anywhere from fifteen to eighteen hours a day, except Sundays," Bill explained.

"Clothing production?"

"The facility had a contract with several prison systems across the country, producing shoes and some clothes for state and federal prisoners."

"That's horrible," Gillian replied. "That should have been illegal."

"Actually it was, but again, there was no oversight on the facility. The only ones that were 'supposed' to be working were only those 16 years and above, but in actuality it was anyone that could, disabled or not."

Gillian leaned toward the large screen, "What's that next to the ball?"

"That's a device called 'THE-POD' that detects changes in temperature and surrounding energy fields. If you put your hand next to THE-POD it will sound an alarm, or if the temperature changes by any preset amount. I use it next to objects a spirit energy may try to interact with. Watch—" Bill started the video file again:

"I'm going to sit here and wait. If someone would like to roll the ball toward me, I will roll it back." Bill said. After a few seconds THE-POD lights turned on and an alarm sounded. *"Don't worry about the sounds and lights. It's all a part of the game; it won't hurt you. You can play with the ball."*

After a few moments more the ball began to move ever so slightly at first, the whole time THE-POD reacted. Then all of the sudden the ball lifted a few inches from the floor, hovered a moment, then dropped, bouncing a couple times before stopping and rolling a few inches from its starting point.

"Hold on," Gillian exclaimed. "That just lifted up—on its' own." She could feel every hair on her body standing straight up.

"Yes." Bill grinned from her honest reaction.

"Was there anyone else there?"

"Just me that night. But wait until you hear this." Bill pulled up a secondary audio file. "This is what I picked up on my digital recorder." He clicked on the file.

"Is there anyone here that would like to play with me?" Gillian recognized Bill's voice from earlier.

"I will," the voice of a small child answered.

"You didn't hear that?" Gillian asked. "That's as plain as day."

"No, I didn't until later when I went over all my recordings. Check this out." Bill continued with another file.

"I'm going to sit here and wait. If someone would like to roll the ball toward me, I will roll it back." Gillian heard Bill's voice again. Then THE-POD alarmed, followed by what sounded like several children laughing.

Gillian felt the hairs on her neck go straight up again, along with every hair on her arms. At the same time she felt a deep sickening churn of her stomach at the thought.

"You've got to see this," Bill continued and started the video file again. While Bill was watching the ball bounce and roll slightly, several of the small chairs could be seen moving closer, scooting an inch or two at a time.

"Oh my God, did you notice that when it was happening?"

"I thought I heard something, but again, it wasn't until later when I reviewed my footage that I saw that, and picked this up—" Bill started another secondary audio file and there was the sound of chair legs dragging across the floor, then more young voices. The clearest child voice said in a very excited tone, *"My turn next."*

Bill could see Gillian shaking. "Are you all right?"

"You didn't react to anything. Doesn't any of this faze you? That, in itself, is very suspicious."

"I've been doing this for a very long time. I've trained hard over the years to not react and 'freak-out' like you see on TV so often, because I'm asking for something to happen. I'm expecting it, and grateful to be able to experience, and document the event. Sometimes it still gets to me; I can be startled at times, but I was in good form that night, keeping my cool while witnessing some real fantastic things."

Gillian stared at the last frozen video image of Bill with the chairs behind him, the voice of a child saying, 'my turn next' echoing in her mind. She finally turned to Bill, "This is absolutely my worst nightmare."

"My point here, Gillian; they are not always sad. They just want someone to play with."

"You're not helping," Gillian's voice was shaking, and she cleared her throat. "This is incredibly sad. If any of this can be believed; you're telling me innocent children are stuck there, in some awful place in some awful after-life." Gillian got up, paced a few steps then rushed out the door.

"Oh crap," Bill said under his breath. He had thought she would be all right with all this. That this was what she was looking for. He followed her out the door. "Gillian?"

A late June evening, the sun was just starting to sink in the west, and Bill found Gillian standing by the fence looking out over the pastures and training arena. He stepped up next to her without saying a word. He wasn't actually sure what he should say anyway.

Gillian picked at a sliver on the fence, then squared her shoulders and took a deep breath. "When I awoke three days after the accident, I already knew the worst had happened. I don't know how, I just knew. The first responders on scene later told me the car that struck the driver-side was traveling at least 70 mph, and there were no skid marks to indicate the use of any brakes. The doctors assured me neither Daniel nor Kristin would have felt anything. They died instantly," Gillian said softly and somewhat disconnected.

"I'm so sorry for your loss."

"The driver was a young woman on drugs. Her two young children died at the scene as well. She survived and spent ten years in prison for vehicular homicide." Bill listened and nodded as Gillian spoke. "The day she was released, she got a gun and shot and killed herself at that very intersection."

"Jeez," Bill said shaking his head.

"On some nights people have reported hearing the crash, metal crunching and glass breaking, and a gun shot on other occasions."

"I could understand—"

"I cannot allow myself to believe that my family might be trapped there on the side of that road, in some 'after-life' hell—"

"And there is nothing to say they are," Bill interjected. "All that is being reported could easily be explained as just a residual haunt. Remember, sometimes they are just a recording of an extremely devastating or catastrophic event."

"Yet, nearly every day I can't escape the feeling. That somehow it is all my fault, and my family's paying that awful price."

"How long ago was all this?"

Gillian took another long deep breath. "Fourteen years."

"You can't blame yourself because you survived," Bill said with care.

"I know, I know. A psychologist friend of mine is constantly telling me to get over my 'survivor's guilt' and move past this. So what do I do? After fourteen years of dragging myself through all this emotional turmoil, I move to a different coast, start a new job, and immediately begin investigating a murder in a facility filled with the ghosts of children."

"Well you're starting to sound a little less skeptical." Bill said. Gillian continued to stare out into the pasture with no reaction. Bill tried a different approach. "Look, I've been a lousy host, let me cook you up some dinner."

Gillian finally turned and scowled. "No, I'm fine. I should be going."

"No, really. I must insist. Please. We've gone over quite a bit of material today. It's a lot to think about, the least I can do is feed you, and we can maybe let some of it sink in while we share a meal. Do you like salmon? I've got some fresh salmon in the fridge, just waiting for the grille—there's plenty for both of us."

Gillian continued to scowl, but realized it had no effect on Bill. Maybe she was losing her touch. She shook her head in defeat, "Okay, but I'm helping."

Bill raised his brows in surprise, "Deal."

***

The sun was down behind the Olympic Mountains but there was

plenty of light left in the sky. Gillian and Bill had finished up the dishes and stepped outside on the front porch to let the dinner settle.

"You certainly know your way around a grilled salmon," Gillian complimented as she found a spot on a bench on the porch.

"Thank you. It's one of my specialties. But I must admit, your touches on that salad made the meal."

"You had all the ingredients, I just put it together."

They both sat for a while enjoying the evening.

"I—"

"Something—" Bill interrupted by accident.

"I'm sorry," Gillian chuckled, "Go on."

"No, no. You were saying?"

Gillian waited a second, not sure she wanted to bring the conversation back up. "I just can't help wonder. Everything you've shown me is, on one hand, quite compelling—"

"But?" Bill added.

"But. My gut reaction is still that there is someone physically there. I just can't believe a ghost can kill."

"One of the common threads from everyone I've interviewed, is that they are certain Jack or Tommy, whichever personality you want to call him, killed Ruphord."

"But he was very much alive then and was never caught," Gillian argued. "The report doesn't even list him as a suspect."

"Yes, and the other common thread from those I interviewed is that Jack never left the building. Many believe he died there and his body has never been found."

"Thus, lending to the legend of Jack-in-the-Box," Gillian continued. "But what do you think?"

Bill stretched his neck and grimaced in thought. "I've been on the fence for a long time, but lately, I just can't believe he's alive. I'm really thinking, like so many others, that he died somewhere in the building likely years ago. Let's be serious, if he were still alive, he'd be nearly 70 years old. Not impossible, just not likely, especially living in those conditions."

Gillian shook her head, "And so you're willing to believe his ghost has been roaming around the building, then suddenly able to kill Jeffrie Trace nearly 50 years later? Talk about, 'not likely.'"

"Yet, I'd say also, not impossible, and what about the other missing people in Joe's folder?"

"Missing. No evidence of any foul play, no bodies. Circumstantial at best."

"Yet still missing, right?"

"Okay, I guess we have some valid points on either side, just nothing conclusive," Gillian suggested.

"I can agree with that," Bill relented.

"By the way, can you do your audio analysis on any recording, or does it require something special?"

"Nothing special. I just get the best results from first generation recordings."

"Have you ever done any analysis of the Jeffrie Trace recordings?" Gillian asked.

"By the time the crime labs got the originals back to the case files, the state had closed their investigation and Joe had left the department. I did some analysis on bootleg copies found online, but they were too degraded."

"There's nothing in your process that can damage the originals is there?"

"Absolutely no chance of damage. I simply upload the files to my computer and run my audio programs on that," Bill attested.

"Would you be interested in doing some analysis on the originals?"

"Do you have them with you?" Bill asked with excitement.

"No, I wasn't sure what I was coming out to see. But I can bring them out and allow you to upload the files. I can't give you the originals to keep though."

"No problem at all. Absolutely I would love to run an analysis on anything you can get me. Just let me know when."

Gillian picked up her shoulder bag and made sure Joe's notes were tucked inside, "I really enjoyed dinner. I want to see more of what you've found at the Stilles, but I really need to be going now."

"I understand, and you are more than welcome anytime to go through more of my evidence from the Stilles," Bill said, as he walked Gillian back to her car.

"I'll be in touch regarding those original files."

"I'll be waiting!"

***

Gillian looked up from her lunch and realized the fog had rolled in once again, thick and dark. So much so, she was barely able to see the back of the Stilles Asylum, and completely lost sight of where she parked her car. She had a sudden feeling of being exposed and vulnerable, and more troubling, not alone. The feeling of a thousand staring pairs of eyes was a constant at the Stilles Asylum, but there was something more this time. Gillian strained to see through the thickening fog, a shadowy figure-form walking toward her from the direction of the Stilles Asylum, and the hairs on her arms and neck stood straight on end. Her heart was beginning to pound with adrenaline, her purse and service revolver were nowhere in sight.

The figure continued closer and Gillian started to see more features that appeared familiar in some strange way. The figure was a young woman, wearing jeans and a light blue blouse with dark shoulder length hair and stopped just a few feet away and turning to face back to the Stilles Asylum as though addressing an audience.

Gillian gasped when she saw that the back of the woman's head was missing, and the realization of who she was sank in. This was the woman that caused the wreck fourteen years ago, and Gillian started to shake, and feel disorientated, "This can't be!"

The woman turned back, blood running from her mouth, holding out a small hand-gun as an offering, "Your turn," she demanded.

"NO!" Gillian tried to scream out, but all that she could muster was a guttural rush of air from her lungs. "NOOOO!" She tried again, as the woman stepped closer, still forcing the gun toward Gillian. Still there was only a rush of air from her lungs that now seemed to hurt from the force.

"I paid my debt. It's your turn!" The woman stepped closer.

Gillian sat up from her bed, "NOOOOO!" The word rushed from her lungs and reverberated in the small dark room. After a few moments she was able to realize she was in her bed, and tried to stop shaking while not completely breaking down into tears. "That's a new one," she whispered, afraid to admit her thoughts out loud. She knew her psychologist friend would call this a major setback.

**

Chapter 5
Well-house

Tuesday July 2nd, 2019

Gillian waved to the city workers as they left the Stilles Asylum. She was meeting Bill to transfer data files to his laptop, and the Stilles Asylum had become a regular lunch spot for her over the last few weeks. Gillian felt the location was a perfect place to meet and Bill agreed. Gillian couldn't help notice a new large shade umbrella had been added to the picnic table and shook her head. The temps had been rising over the last few days, and she guessed the guys were concerned she might be too hot in the direct sun. She wondered why people said it always rained in Washington. She set her lunch out and cranked open the umbrella. The thermometer in her car read mid-seventies already at noon, so maybe the guys knew their stuff, because the shade felt nice.

Bill's sedan rumbled up the drive just as Gillian began eating her salad. He parked next to her car and got out with a laptop and a wicker hand basket. "I don't remember a picnic table out here."

"The city maintenance guys set it up…isn't that nice?"

Bill sat down across from Gillian. "I think someone has an admirer."

"No, really? You think?" She shook her head in mock disbelief. She rummaged inside her bag for the camera SSD card with the original capture files and handed it to Bill.

"Well, this place really cleans up nice. Almost like a city park, if not for the feeling of a thousand eyes staring at your back from the large ominous building a couple hundred feet away." Bill put the SSD into a slot in his laptop. After a couple clicks from the touch pad, he set the laptop aside and opened the wicker basket.

"You feel them too?" Gillian asked. "It's like having an audience; a real creepy audience just staring at you." She stared at the back of the building. With only the rare cloud in the clear blue sky, and hardly a breath of a breeze, there could be no reason for movement in the windows. But there it was. She shook her head, hoping to clear her mind.

Bill pulled out a small tripod and aimed a digital camera at the building. He reversed the viewfinder, setting the camera off to the side to record. "It's been a long time since I've been out here, so I'm going to try to capture whatever I can." He pulled a sandwich from the basket along with a small digital audio recorder that he flipped on.

"I didn't know we'd be officially on the record today."

"Oh no. That's not for us. That's to capture any EVPs. I've had a few in the past when I wasn't expecting any activity." Bill took a bite of his sandwich.

"I enjoy having lunch here," Gillian said between bites. "How many years again have you been researching this site?"

"Since 1997." Bill answered.

"You must know just about all there is to know about this place. Like how is it that Ruphord had the same last name as the facility here? I haven't found anything on that, and that's such an odd coincidence."

"Actually not at all. Children brought to the Stilles Asylum without paperwork, or as infants with no names, were often given names, but instead of John Doe or Jane Doe, the name of the facility was used like John Stilles or Jane Stilles."

Gillian scowled at the thought. "Why?"

"From my research this wasn't done only at the Stilles but across the state and country. As the disabled children grew older in the system, they were eventually moved to adult facilities, or sometimes released, and their last names gave them a form of legal identity. Those that were released often changed their names though, which complicates searching for survivors. Tips come mostly from word of mouth between the few who've kept in touch," Bill explained.

"Like having their own secret emotional support group?"

"Exactly. From what little I've been able to find, Ruphord was brought to the Stilles as an infant sometime around 1934. Some stories say his mother's name was Ruth Ford, and that became the root of his first name. But I haven't been able to find any trace of a Ruth Ford in this area at that time to authenticate that story. But everyone seemed to agree that Frank Mills took a particular interest in Ruphord from the start, and not in a good way."

"The articles reported that Ruphord worked with Frank as custodian and eventually took over when Frank left," Gillian recalled.

"It's clear that Frank groomed Ruphord his entire life…kept him very close. Some people have claimed Frank made Ruphord what he was later in life, ruthless and deviant. The hard part though is trying to separate truth from legend," Bill explained.

"Well, I can certainly see why Joe came to you for answers. You seem to have them or at least can find them."

"One would think. But I still find myself asking a lot of questions. This place is just so rich in history. The original garrison history is nearly as fascinating as all that has happened since."

Gillian nodded, "Like what?"

Bill looked around and gestured, "The garrison grounds used to be so much larger and included the veterans' cemetery all the way back to Mile Hill Road to the south, and where the Veterans Home is now. The woods right back here had an orchard with cherry, apple, plum, and pear trees. I've been back in there a few times and you can still find some of them, although they're all overgrown and they've all gone mostly wild."

"I'm surprised I don't see more wildlife around here. On my street, there are squirrels everywhere."

"Animals are particularly sensitive to paranormal activity. They generally don't stick around, and with this place feeling so active all the time, it doesn't surprise me in the least."

"I've never heard that," Gillian said.

Bill pointed toward the two outbuildings nearly hidden in the tree line along the back gravel drive. "Over there, that larger building was the ammo house, 'The Powder Block' they called it—used to store their ammo and black powder supplies. Story goes when the Army left they buried the underground storage bunker, so all that's left is that little building above ground."

"Any activity there?" Gillian asked.

"I've been inside a few times, never got any hits for anything. It was used for storage for years, so there's a ton of junk piled up last time I looked inside."

"What about the other little building?"

"That's the old well house."

"Chief Johnson said something about the city cutting the water; did they just shut off the well?"

"Actually that well is tapping a year-round natural spring—you can't shut that off, there's an overflow drain pipe that goes straight under the Stilles basement level and down to a drain pipe under the road into the bay."

"Okay so I guess I misunderstood about the city water."

"No, no. Back in, I believe it was 1952, the well water went bad making everyone sick. At that time there was a new water main going in across the ravine to support growth at the Veterans' Home. So in an emergency repair, they brought a water mainline to the Stilles and re-plumbed into the main waterline in the building. In the basement you can still see the original brick and mortar cistern that the well filled for the building water supply back when it was the garrison."

"1952?"

"I believe so, why?"

"Did they ever figure out why the well went bad?" Gillian asked as she turned to give the small outbuilding her new-found attention.

"The rumor was a raccoon crawled in and drowned."

"You'd think they'd fish a raccoon body out to clear that up."

"That spring well is deep...easily a hundred-fifty to two-hundred feet deep, so if it sank, probably not." Bill could see Gillian was working something out in her mind as she continued to stare at the well house. "What are you thinking?"

"Frank Mills disappeared in 1952."

"Yeah, he just walked away from his job and disappeared."

"But in the police report none of his personal belongings were listed as missing. Who leaves and takes nothing?"

"How did I miss that? I'm sure I've seen that police report."

"It was buried in a side note." Gillian got up and walked toward the well house.

"Well if you're thinking someone murdered him and dumped his body down the well, the pipe is only eighteen inches across at best...too small for a grown man's body."

"Whole," Gillian answered sounding a little distracted by the conversation and continued to approach the well house.

"Right, that's what I'm saying, the hole is too small."

Gillian tried the door. The hinges were stiff, but with additional effort, the door opened. There wasn't much inside; an old broken wheel chair and some chair padding on the ground. There was a large pipe sticking straight out about twenty-four inches from a concrete pad, with two smaller pipes coming out at different heights leading back into the ground toward the Stilles Asylum. The larger pipe had a hinged cap lid and Gillian reached to lift it up. The hinges were tight, but she was able to peer inside the dark opening.

"That top pipe is the overflow line, that lower one was the building mainline that fed the cistern in the basement. If you notice, the original engineers took advantage of the topography, this well house is slightly higher on the grounds than the main floor and basement of the Stilles Asylum. They didn't need a pump here, they just let nature and gravity do their jobs to fill the cistern in the basement. The water was pumped from there inside, at least until the city water main was hooked up to replace it," Bill explained.

"Do you know if this pipe was ever searched?" Gillian asked, still trying to see down into the pipe. The water line stopped right at the top pipe leading out, and there was the sound of water rushing into the pipe.

"I've never come across any articles or anything about this pipe being searched for a raccoon body."

"So no searches?"

"None that I'm aware of," Bill said with some frustration.

Gillian took her cellphone from her back pocket and dialed. "Darla, hi it's—of course you do. Do the city maintenance guys have a long pipe inspection cable with cameras? What? Yes Mr. Hartfield is here. Yes, I'll let him know. We're having lunch and—yes they put up a nice shade umbrella. Darla I need to know if—right, pipe inspection cable with a camera. Are you sure? Great. Can you put in a request to have the well house main well pipe inspected to the bottom here at the Stilles Asylum? No formal requests needed? How soon—no need for right this second—okay, I'll hold."

"Tell Darla, 'hey.'"

"Well of course they will. Fifteen minutes? Okay we'll be here. All right. Bill says 'hey.' All right, thanks." Gillian put her phone back into her pocket. "They have one on their truck and will be here in fifteen minutes."

They walked back to the bench and finished their lunches waiting on the city guys. They showed up in ten minutes, drove right up to the well house, and pulled equipment from the side panels of the truck.

The older gentleman asked, "Detective McClary. Did you lose something down that old pipe?"

"Actually no, and I just realized, I don't know your names."

The man grinned. "My name's Bob, and that's my assistant Daryl. Is there something in particular we're looking for?" Bob unpacked the portable monitor and got it connected to the inspection cable on the spool.

"The bottom," Bill replied.

"I would expect that to be pretty mucked up and filled with silt." Daryl smirked.

"Actually the flow of water going into that overflow drain pipe, would tell me that spring has a pretty hefty flow-rate and probably keeping the bottom fairly clear of silt and dirt," Gillian said, giving all of the gentlemen around her something to think about for a moment.

"That makes sense. Can I ask what this is about then?" Bob asked.

"A hunch," Gillian said.

"Anything you're thinking you want to see?" Bob asked as Daryl sent the end of the cable down into the pipe.

"Gravel and rocks, maybe a clay bed," Bill said.

"And what is it you don't want to see?" Bob asked as he adjusted the camera angle down and got the light turned on for visibility.

"Bones," Gillian answered.

"Animal or human?" Bob asked.

"Neither." Bill responded, feeling his lunch turn in his stomach at the thought.

They all gathered around Bob to view the monitor as he guided the camera angle while Daryl kept the cable going down the pipe slowly and carefully. There were several places on the way down where the casing of the pipe could be seen to be worn with scaled and flaking material.

"We'll likely see a lot of that at the bottom," Bob said, making note of the wear on the aged pipe. "I believe this is the original pipe."

"How far down now?" Bill asked.

"One hundred seventy-eight feet," Daryl noted from the spool counter.

"The clarity is remarkable," Bob said. "Okay, Daryl, slow down I think I'm seeing the bottom now." The light at the end of the cable caused a glimmer on something and Bob angled the camera for a better view. "Down a little more, Daryl, real slow."

The coloring was remarkable on the large flakes of pipe casing that littered the bottom. Bob used the cable's articulated end to move some pieces around for a better view when a large piece slid out of the way.

"Stop," Bob ordered. Daryl paused as everyone gathered around the monitor. "That's one hell of a hunch Detective."

"HOLY SHIT!" Daryl exclaimed, shaking and stepping back from the monitor.

"That's a skull," Bill proclaimed.

"That's no raccoon," Bob clarified.

"And that looks like a large, long bone and possible vertebrae to the side." Gillian traced on the monitor screen with her finger.

***

The evening sun was well into setting as Gillian, Bill, Bob and Daryl sat at the picnic table watching the WSP officers tape up the crime scene, taking pictures and jotting down plenty of notes. They had already gotten statements but didn't want anyone to leave just yet.

Trent walked away from the taped-off area. "The Captain says we can get the city truck out of the way in a few minutes, but they want to keep the pipe inspection cable down there for now, as not to disturb any possible evidence. They're about to set up the light generators and bring in some forensic equipment to retrieve the larger bone fragments. Then they plan to use a vacuum pump to suck out any smaller pieces of evidence and bone fragments." Trent sat down on the bench next to Daryl and Bob. Gillian and Bill were on the other side also facing the scene while he reviewed his camera footage.

"I sure hope they know how to take care of that cable. That thing's expensive," Bob huffed. "Those State people sometimes think we're all made of money."

"They know, Bob. It'll be fine," Trent assured.

"Was that Marty I saw you with earlier—looking for another scoop?" Gillian asked.

"Yeah. I told him everything I was allowed for now and promised him an exclusive, if we get the case back. The Captain says if the body is determined to be related to a case older than ten years, they'll notify the FBI to check their missing persons' cases. If they come up empty they'll hand over jurisdiction back to us. If it's something newer, and still not on the FBI's list, the State will keep it."

"I think they're going to find this case dating back to 1952," Gillian suggested.

Trent pushed back his Chief ball cap and leaned back. "Well they'll let us know, as soon as they find out."

"Do we have any genealogy information about Frank Mills to pass on, so they can try a DNA match?" Gillian asked.

"Doubtful," Trent answered. "You know there was someone we all know was missing a skull; Ruphord."

"Can't be," Bill spoke up. "Ruphord was missing a significant number of upper teeth. From what we briefly saw on the monitor of that skull, there were too many teeth in the maxilla to be Ruphord's head." Bill continued to examine his digital camera footage and shake his head.

Gillian asked him, "What's the matter?"

"At the exact moment we spotted the skull Daryl shouted...just watch the windows," Bill explained as he handed an earbud to Gillian and played back the video.

Just as Daryl shouted, nearly every window in the Stilles Asylum showed signs of movement, and as though a thousand pairs of eyes were suddenly watching with great interest. Gillian felt that creepy feeling again, and the hairs on her arms and neck stood straight out.

"You tell me, are my eyes playing tricks or is something moving in those windows?" Gillian asked, trying to shake off the chills.

Bill shook his head. "That's going to have to be your call. You're the skeptic."

Gillian turned to Trent. "What permissions do I need to request for Bill and me to do a thorough search and investigation inside the Stilles Asylum?"

Trent was slow to turn, "You'll need to know someone in the Port Latch Police Department to sweet talk the mayor into not having a fit when he finds out that's what you plan to do."

Gillian sat back and grinned. "That's all?"

Trent let out a heavy sigh, and bobble-headed a tired nod yes. "But can it wait until these State guys are out of here? We don't need them giving us crap over all that too."

"Agreed," Gillian answered, then turned to Bill. "So. Did you get any EVPs from that little digital recorder too?"

Bill looked a bit sheepish. "Uh, oh the digital recorder? Uh, yeah well, I'll have to run it through my audio program to clean it up, probably just nothing though." Bill squirmed.

"Are you all right?" Gillian asked.

"Me? Oh sure. Just excited to get back inside the ol' Stilles Asylum, you know. Need to get the team together and ready," Bill stammered.

"Now I don't want some large crowd of people in there. There are health issues to be concerned with, kicking up too much asbestos dust and all."

"Lately, my team generally consists of me, and one other to help carry and set up gear. Since I will assume you are planning on coming along, the team will likely be you, me and Charles."

"Charles? Who is Charles?" Gillian asked.

"Let's just say, Charles is my new guide to the other side."

***

The State Police took forty-eight straight hours to go through the well house pipe and small building with a fine-toothed comb, before giving the all clear. The FBI said to let the case go back to the LEOs and would take back jurisdiction only if their research came back with anything of interest. No sooner had Trent given Gillian the news than she was on her way to Bill's office. He had something important to share, and now, so did she.

She knocked on the barn office door when she arrived, not exactly sure of the protocol.

"Come on in, Gillian," she heard Bill's voice through the door.

"How did you know that was me?" she asked.

Bill was sitting at his desk, and pointed to another monitor up above the main computer screens. There were several security camera views shown, including one of the door outside his office. "I'm so glad you could get here so soon, I've got some stuff you've got to see and hear," Bill said.

"Me too, I just got word from Trent—the State Police are done and cleared out of the area at the Stilles, the FBI will contact us if they find something in their case files and need to take back jurisdiction, but for now, we're good to go for our investigation inside."

"Great news, I'll let Charles know we're on. When?" Bill asked.

"How long do you need to get things together?"

"I've got my bags packed and ready for a moment's notice, and Charles is pretty much available at a moment's notice as well."

"Tomorrow's Friday—let me check with Trent—he had mentioned that he would rather we do this on a weekend, so he can be available for emergency support if needed. So maybe this Saturday?"

"Okay, and you're still certain you want to do this during the day and not a standard night investigation?"

"Let's be sure we get this straight. I'm looking for a person or persons of the living variety. You and your friend are coming along to help with that search because you're more familiar with the building. I'm willing to help with your investigation as long as it doesn't hinder mine," Gillian was candid, hoping it wouldn't be a deal breaker.

"Fair enough. I've done plenty of daytime investigations, and at the Stilles as well. So I'm good," Bill assured.

"Okay, so what have you found?"

"I thought you'd never ask." Bill grinned from ear to ear, then turned toward his large computer screens. "Have a seat."

Gillian made herself comfortable and scooted the chair a little closer to the desk. "Ready."

"Okay first, this is Jeffrie's video as you can see right after he started the file. Let me speed forward, and, there…look in the windows. Seem familiar?" A shadowed figure appeared in one of the windows on the third floor on the back of the Stilles Asylum. Bill ran the file at half speed and the shape simply slid out of the window frame.

"Jeffrie was pissed there. He saw that with his naked eyes and was certain at that point that someone was in the building and going to mess with their investigation. He was primed and ready to attack."

"Yeah that video is filled with cursing," Gillian added.

"Yep, a Jeffrie Trace trademark as it were. So okay fast

forwarding to inside. Here he is talking with Jason. Dylan has already gone upstairs to place some digital cameras. Dylan calls down and claims someone has thrown something at him and Jeffrie goes off again to start his investigation. Now listen here as he's walking down the hall, right here. Listen."

Bill turned the volume up on his speakers, and a hissing noise got even louder when there was suddenly an unknown voice, *"You don't belong here—"* followed by a deep growling sound and something else.

Gillian turned to Bill, her eyes wide. "That was clear. What about the growling noise he heard? That almost sounded like someone wheezing in the background."

"I heard it too, and that makes sense. The Stilles garrison was turned into a military hospital during World War I, and there was the Spanish Flu outbreak in 1918 along with bouts of Tuberculosis, and I have caught audio of 'wheezing' and 'coughing' residual haunting sounds in the past. Now listen as they are going down this hall there are some wooden doors there on the side. I'm familiar with those doors; one room was used as a staff sleeping quarters, and the other a secondary office space. If you look here, I'll slow down the video, the doors are closed and neither Jason or Jeffrie are touching them. As they pass you can hear the doorknobs rattling, and as Jeffrie changes the video angle back to his face you can briefly see both doors are opening slightly. They apparently didn't notice that at the time."

"This is amazing. I'm getting goose bumps just watching this," Gillian admitted.

"This video is absolutely full of background noises, and voices everywhere, but let me get to some of the most incredible ones." Bill fast-forwarded the video to a point where Jeffrie stood in a wider hall pointing his camera the nursery rhyme scrawled in paint. Bill played the video from there, "Listen here."

The hissing in the background got louder and Jeffrie's voice could be heard: *"Jack-in-the-box, shut up tight. Down in the dark, without any light. Jack-in-the-box, oh so still, won't you come out,"* followed immediately with another voice, *"Yes I will"* and another voice said, *"Stop scaring him."* Immediately after Jason said, *"WHOA. Did you hear that? I just fucking heard something."*

"Those voices sound so creepy, and they were actually hearing them at the time. These aren't EVP only, they actually heard them," Gillian stated.

"Yeah, they were hearing all this. This is some of the most incredible audio and video I've seen in a long time. I've tried to analyze this before but all I could get my hands on were bootleg copies of copies online that were too degraded to get any of the clarity I'm getting here with this first generation version."

"You sound pretty stoked," Gillian said.

"Let me get to the end, that's where this whole thing will blow your mind." Bill fast-forwarded further. "Here they are down in the basement, after chasing a shadow figure down into the furnace room. Jeffrie is really pissed off here and completely provoking and taunting; listen."

Bill started the video: *"You're fucking pissing me off, Jack. Jack-in-the-box. Jack-in-the-BOX. Like the rhyme says motherfucker, won't you come out, Jack! COME OUT JACK,"* Jeffrie's voice shouted, followed by another growling voice that was decidedly not Jeffrie's voice, *"Leave. NOW. Stop. Scaring. HIM."*

Bill paused the video, "That was just before Jeffrie was hit by the axe."

Gillian sat back in her chair rubbing the hairs on her arm, "Unbelievable."

Bill nodded and fast-forwarded the video to near the end where the 'low battery' light continued to blink in the bottom right corner of the video, as a dark fluid flowed onto the floor between the camera view and Jeffrie's twitching arm. Bill turned up the volume again, and the same voice could be heard in a low grumble, *"Leave. Us. Alone."*

"And you still don't think this thing is alive? A real person?" Gillian asked.

"Throughout this video there are shots of shadow figures moving inhumanly fast, darting through spaces like no living being I've ever seen. A lot of this I recognize from the regulars we've documented in the past. If we're suddenly talking about actual living beings, we're getting into the realm of Cryptids like a Rake or some other shape-shifting creatures."

"Whoa, wait a minute. What are you talking about now?" Gillian asked.

"I'm talking about things outside my wheelhouse," Bill turned and gave Gillian a serious look of concern. "So I have to try to believe I'm dealing with a very powerful spirit energy, because that's what I know how to deal with."

"Are you saying I shouldn't go there looking for a living person?" Gillian scowled.

"I'm saying the living thing you are trying to find, may not be what you think you're looking for, and something way beyond our control. Whatever it was that killed Jeffrie that night, did so without remorse. If that is a spirit energy, it's strong enough to wield a large axe with deadly accuracy, along with an abundance of other objects of various weight and size. IF that thing is alive—again—it showed no remorse, no moral compassion, and I have no idea what it is truly capable of in the long run. Murder for certain."

"I don't understand, are you saying we shouldn't go and search inside the Stilles Asylum at all now?" Gillian asked, shaking her head.

"Not at all. I've investigated that facility hundreds of times and never once felt threatened. BUT, I've never gone in threatening like Jeffrie did. So what I'm suggesting is we need to be guarded about any and all of our actions the whole time we're in there. We need to be sure we are being respectful, and as the voices seemed to be warning; do not scare him."

***

Gillian hung her car and house keys on the hook just inside her door relieved to finally be home after such a long day. The drive back from Bill's office felt long tonight. There was so much to process, so many audio and video files they reviewed, and with each one that might answer a question, so many others posed even more. Was it real? Was all this paranormal activity just a hoax?

Stepping into the living room where her house was now filled with all her familiar furnishings that had felt like home, tonight suddenly felt different. The air felt thick, difficult to breathe with a hint of tobacco, like from a gentleman's pipe. The lights also seemed dimmer than usual, as though the darkness of the evening was fighting back the light. She set her shoulder bag on the dinner table, when she felt, as much as heard, a strange noise coming from the direction of her bedroom. Did she hear someone call her name? She couldn't be sure. When she looked, there appeared to be a dark shadow-mass disappearing through the door into the darkness of her bedroom. Gillian immediately pulled her service revolver from her purse-holster, releasing the safety. "I am a police officer, and I am armed. Come out with your hands up." She had been in situations before where she had to defend herself in police operations, and was always able to do so with full confidence, but this time she felt different. She couldn't shake the feeling of electricity dancing over her entire body. Her nerves were lit up, and she felt the hairs on her entire body standing straight out. Why was this different?

She moved closer to the bedroom door, her revolver in a standard tactical two-handed ready safe position pointed toward the dark room. "I repeat, I am a police officer, and I am armed. Come out with your hands up," she announced again.

Per her training she visually cleared the opening and was able to reach for the light switch just inside the door, still at the ready with her service weapon. The single overhead light came on, but again appeared to be fighting the darkness to fill the room. With a quick sweep of the room she spotted a dark shadow-mass up in the far wall corner at the ceiling, where no shadow should be even possible.

As she stepped in to get a better view, the dark mass faded and the light in the room appeared brighter. The feeling of electricity all over her body stopped, and the hairs on her body calmed down and the air seemed far less heavy but very cold. Still trying to understand what she had just seen, Gillian's training kicked in once more and she continued to clear the room and closet, also checking that the window was still locked. After checking the bathroom, and all the windows in the entire house, including the front and back door, she finally put her service weapon back in to the purse-holster, not really sure what had happened.

Was this just her imagination? How could that even be real? Maybe she was just over-tired, thinking too much about all this paranormal stuff, but now she wasn't sure if she could go to sleep. She sat at her dining table trying to make sense of it all, feeling a little embarrassed at her actions, and fairly certain she would not want to mention any of this to Bill, let alone Trent. Sleep eventually found her on the living room couch with all the lights on in every room and her purse-holster tucked under her arm.

***

Chapter 6
Into the Darkness

Saturday, July 6th, 2019

Trent leaned up against a mid-90's jacked-up Ford 4x4, soaking up the Saturday morning sun in a ball cap, jeans, light denim, long-sleeved shirt with the sleeves rolled up and sunglasses, staring out above the trees surrounding the Stilles Asylum. Gillian parked behind his truck along the fence and walked up with two very large coffee-to-go cups. Trent didn't even turn to look, putting his left hand out as though holding something. Gillian filled his waiting hand with one of the cups of coffee, and leaned back against the truck as well. Trent nodded and took a sip without a word, then grinned his approval.

The silence of the peaceful morning behind the Stilles was broken only by the occasional screech of a distant eagle beyond the treeline, and finally by Bill's sedan as he parked closer to the gate of the fence surrounding the asylum.

Gillian greeted Bill and saw his passenger opening his door. He was a very large man, dressed like he was going to a resort lounge in tan slacks, matching dress shoes and sport coat. The car raised a couple inches as he stood and towered over the side of the sedan, and Gillian couldn't help feel he should be stepping right off the front line of a professional football team. She could see his shaved coffee-colored head and black tightly-trimmed beard, shaved under his nose, and oddly enough he was wearing a large blindfold over his eyes. As he stood he turned to face the grounds as though he was actually looking at something through the blindfold.

Bill came around to meet Gillian, holding a finger up to his lips. "Don't say anything yet. Charles likes to get a feel for a place he's never been to and people he's never met before actually seeing them and talking." Gillian just nodded as she watched Charles who appeared to be watching something near the well-house, before finally turning to them. She was having some difficulty envisioning this large man as a psychic medium. She was expecting something completely different. She wasn't exactly sure what, but not this.

Charles extended an immense hand directly towards Gillian as though he could actually see her, and she responded in kind. She was awestruck as her hand disappeared into his warm, pillow-soft palm. Wrapped in his large fingers, he inspired a long-forgotten memory of holding her own father's hand when she was a very young girl four or five years old. She remembered her father's hands so soft and warm and how she would often envision herself crawling into his protective grip and hiding away there from the world, safe and warm.

Charles took her hand with both of his and nodded, "Thank you. I'm Charles Beaumonte the Third, nice to finally meet you Detective McClary." His deep resonating voice seemed to penetrate the far reaches of her very soul, but she noticed his initial smile disappear into a look of concern behind his blindfold as he appeared to be scanning the area around her. "I'm so sorry for your losses. I can feel the heaviness and see the darkness that has been weighing down upon you for so long."

Gillian looked to Bill and he nodded. "Call me Gillian, and I'm fine, really."

"That is what your friend tells you," Charles said with soft assurance. Gillian felt an honest disappointment when he let go of her hand and turned to the asylum, again as though he could actually see the building through his blindfold. "Bill, I'm feeling a bit overdressed today."

"You never let me tell you about these places before we go, so that's all on you," Bill chuckled.

"The Stilles Asylum. I have seen this place from afar, but never this close," Charles said in awe. "So bright and busy. So full of activity. So many souls wanting attention."

"It always feels like a thousand eyes staring at me whenever I come here," Gillian said.

"At least," Charles answered as though distracted.

"Do you still want the blindfold on now that you know where you are?" Bill asked.

Charles held his hand out toward Bill, "Just a moment more." He turned once more toward the well house as though studying something there, then nodded and took off blindfold with a deep breath.

"Seeing something?" Bill asked.

"Yes. A very dark and scared spirit, hiding and afraid," Charles said. "Many secrets. Dark secrets," he continued staring out toward the small building.

"Any names coming out of that?" Bill asked.

"He's afraid I am revealing his presence by looking at him. He's really afraid of some entities here at the asylum, or more accurately the garrison," Charles said and turned to face Bill and Gillian.

Gillian was taken aback by Charles brilliant copper-colored eyes and tried not to stare. "Isn't that really the same place?"

"Physically yes, but there's a difference between space and time," Charles explained.

"Well my goal today is to do a thorough search inside this physical location for any living persons that could explain a few things going on around here," Gillian said.

Charles rolled off a deep chuckle with a broad grin. "To the point. I can appreciate that."

Bill popped the trunk and pulled out some gear bags, opened one up and passed around some professional-grade face masks. He handed the other gear bag to Charles who made the large bag appear tiny compared to his large frame. "I've got floor plans from notes and drawings I've made over the years investigating here, I'm thinking we should start at the top in the attic and work our way down to the basement last, a basic top-down approach. Gillian?" Bill asked. Gillian nodded in agreement. "Then Charles and I will place various recording devices and cameras at key locations throughout on our way up, and pick them all back up on our way out," he continued.

Gillian nodded. "How detailed are your floor plans?"

"Fairly detailed, I'm pretty sure I have most possible hiding places listed. I've ordered actual blueprints from the U.S. Army archives but they haven't arrived yet."

"How long have you been waiting?" Gillian asked.

Bill scowled, "Years."

"Okay then. Well, Trent has the fence and door already unlocked and he's standing by and I have a radio to call for help if needed," Gillian said, taking one last sip of coffee and starting for the door.

She pulled out the radio from a back pocket and gave it a click. "Radio check."

"Loud and clear," Trent answered, still standing by his truck, and raising his coffee cup as well.

Everyone masked up and stepped inside the door. "Charles, we'll do a standard coverage; I've got the mini-digital cameras already mounted on the little stands. I want to cover the main passages from end to end and on each of the floors, starting right here at the door," Bill explained.

"Roger," Charles said in a military snap, as he reached into the gear bag and pulled out a mini-digital camera on a stand, spread the legs, pointed the camera toward the other end of the first hall and turned it on after Bill and Gillian entered. He set a digital audio recorder down in camera view a few feet in front and turned it on.

"We were here about halfway down this hall when we started hearing strange sounds, "Gillian said, keeping her voice low.

"I think I've already heard some familiar low whispering," Bill added. "What about you Charles?"

Charles followed along from behind, "Oh they're here, all around. Like mosquitoes buzzing in my face, all testing me."

"What do you mean?" Gillian asked as she shined her LED down into a dark doorway just past the first opening to the side of the building with direct outdoor lighting from the windows.

"They know I can feel them and hear them. I've got one in particular that is very persistent. Like having someone shouting in my face," Charles explained.

Gillian turned to see Charles squinting and turning his head as though trying to avoid something or someone in his face. "I don't see anything."

"Shhh, listen," Bill hushed. "I'm hearing more whispers." Bill had reached the first crossing passage at the end of the hall and pointed out a spot for Charles to place another camera and digital audio recorder.

Gillian nodded, as she recognized the main crossing hall in the center of the building from Jeffrie Trace's recording. She walked past two doors on her left, making note that they were open, and shined her LED inside in a quick sweep, before continuing on. "That sounds like conversation between several people," she noted, and glanced back to Charles as he placed a camera and audio recorder where Bill had pointed.

Bill continued on ahead to the main entry hall, gesturing down another main hall for camera placement and back the other way to gain full coverage of the area before moving on toward the main stairwell. Charles nodded and made quick work of placing the cameras and audio recorders while Bill and Gillian searched in doorways and smaller rooms on the first floor.

Bill pulled out his floor plans and showed them to Charles. "Each of the next three floors all have this basic floor plan. I'll have you place cameras here, here, here and here on each of the floors to cover the main passages. We'll meet you at the top floor at the end of this end passage here, where the stairs up to the attic are located."

"Roger that," Charles answered with a military tone, and started up the stairwell.

Gillian walked over to the bench just outside the stairwell across from the office door of the old main entry. The rhyme was painted across the wall in bright red paint, exactly how she had seen it in Jeffrie Trace's video, and a cold chill ran across her neck and down her back. "This just gives me the creeps."

"As often as I've been in this building, both day and night investigations, that still gets to me too," Bill said as he opened the office door across the hall from the bench to take a quick look inside.

"Go. Now."

"Sure, I guess we need to keep going since this will likely be a long day," Gillian agreed.

"What?" Bill asked.

"You said we need to be going. I was just agreeing."

Bill stared and raised a brow. "I didn't say anything."

Gillian did a quick scan around the room with her LED, acting like a bright spotlight even though the room was lit from the windows by the main entry doors, and light came from the office's outside windows. The hairs on her arm stuck straight out and made her feel uncomfortable.

Bill held out his digital audio recorder. "We think we're hearing you, but we're not sure. Can you say that again? Don't be shy. Speak into this device, and we will be able to listen back later to hear you." He paused and held the recorder out hoping for an audible response.

"I know what I heard," Gillian said under her breath with some frustration.

"I believe you," Bill answered, then pointed out toward the stairwell. "I'm hearing voices that sound like they're coming from there."

"Charles?"

Bill shook his head. "His voice is too deep...it's not what I'm hearing."

"Should we—"

"Yeah, let's head on up."

With their LEDs to light the very dark steps, they both climbed the stairwell as quietly as possible listening for any anomalous noises or voices along the way. Although their steps echoed up and down the stairwell, there was also the distinct whispering sound of a conversation that seemed to be coming from above. As they passed the third floor, Bill indicated Charles was setting up recording equipment there.

Bill reached the top and guided Gillian to the attic stairwell. "This way," he pointed. They passed the main crossing hall, and continued toward the back of the building.

Gillian paused at a steel cage door. "This is an elevator?"

Bill turned back. "Yeah. The actual lift is permanently locked at the bottom on the first floor, and all of these old-style cage doors are welded shut. The bottom door is the one boarded over and probably why you didn't notice it."

Gillian pointed her LED into the darkness of the elevator shaft through the locked metal cage doorway. She could hear shuffling noises and other sounds that seemed to be echoing out from the darkness. Pointing up, she could see the mechanics of the elevator cable lift system just above at the attic level. "Do you feel that breeze?"

"I have no doubt there is some movement of air through the shaft. I have set up cameras and audio recorders in there over the years, but never had any particular evidence of activity. I think most noises there are carried through from other parts and amplified by the shaft," Bill explained.

Gillian held her hand up and gestured. "Did you hear that?"

Bill nodded. "Not sure what though."

"Sounded like giggling or children playing," Gillian whispered. "From the shaft?"

Gillian shook her head and pointed back up the hall to the main hall intersection. "That way?"

Bill nodded. "That would make sense. The room with most of the children's paranormal activities is just down that way at the end of the hall. That's where I got that video of the ball and chairs moving."

Charles came around the corner from the other side of the main hall. "I can see now why you've been wanting to come back here all this time. This place is astounding. I don't think I've ever been anywhere with this much activity." Although soft, his deep voice resonated throughout the space.

"But have you seen anyone alive? We're looking for someone actually here, in person," Gillian pressed.

"'Here,' is a relative term," Charles assured.

Gillian sighed in frustration, "I need to be certain there is no physical presence to buy into all the paranormal explanations. I need solid physical proof."

Everyone let Gillian's words hang in silence to reflect on her rational concerns for a few moments, but also to listen to what sounded like footsteps right above their heads in what should have been unoccupied attic spaces.

"Everyone take a digital camera and a secondary LED, just in case. It can get really dark up there and there is a lot of junk to get tangled up on and fall over," Bill suggested and took some cameras from the bag Charles was carrying. "We'll leave the bag here and head on up." Bill opened the door to a very dark narrow staircase.

Every step creaked as they ascended to the top, even more so under Charle's weight and size. Gillian looked back to see his frame taking up nearly every inch of the stairwell behind her. Even with the bright LED flashlights, the darkness of the attic seemed to fight back, absorbing every light particle after only a few feet of distance.

The air was hot and heavy, and smelled like mold and deteriorating wood and cloth. There were boxes of children's clothing, and more boxes of shoes in various stages of assembly. Stacks of rails for baby cribs, hospital beds and pieces of wheelchairs, crutches and boxes of artificial limbs that seemed to go on and on into the darkness. They all felt a chill at that sight.

Gillian couldn't help herself and asked, "Is there anybody up here?" They all paused their movements and waited for an answer.

Bill pointed off to the far side, and whispered, "Shuffling sound, like someone moving through the boxes."

Gillian pointed her LED in that direction but there was nothing to be seen as the light seemed to be swallowed up before reaching the far side.

"Charles, are you getting anything here?" Bill whispered.

"There are a few entities up here trying to hide, confused why we're here, but mostly I'm being pestered by an old man. He's been following me from the moment I arrived," Charles answered a bit annoyed.

"What has he been saying?" Bill asked.

"Doesn't make a whole lot of sense so far. Mostly yelling to 'stop,' and 'I got them,' however it may be a possible reference to the unconfirmed existence of Jack's sister, Jillie, because he has mentioned that name, Jillie a couple times in a frantic tone."

"Right, Jack's sister," Gillian exclaimed. "I wonder if that's the voice I heard that first time?"

"Maybe he was drawn to you because of your name similarity?" Bill wondered out loud.

They all pondered that thought and continued to search to the far corners of the large attic space, listening to unexplained sounds of footsteps. The heat eventually became too much and they retreated back down to the fourth floor. Bill pulled out some bottled waters and passed them around.

Using Bill's hand-drawn floor plans, they continued through all the spaces of the fourth floor. Gillian was struck hardest by what was being called the children's playroom, where there were several small chairs and toys strewn about the room. They all heard plenty of whispers and a few giggles, much to Gillian's continued heartbreak, but again did not see anything or anyone.

Charles gathered up equipment as they left each floor, per Bill's plan. The third, second and first floors were littered with more pieces of hospital bed parts and broken wheelchairs, and still no sign of any current squatters. Most of the trash left laying around appeared to be from the nineties or earlier.

"Okay, we've got the basement left, and I would suggest we take a break here, have some lunch and come back and tackle that. There are a lot more hiding places down there, and it will likely take nearly as long to search." Bill suggested.

"Can we leave the recording equipment up and running while we're on our break? I don't want to leave any gaps in our search that someone might be able to slip through," Gillian said.

"Absolutely. I often take breaks during an investigation and leave the space with recording gear to see what I can capture while we're not poking around."

"Okay, then I'm ready for a break and something to eat," Gillian agreed and looked to Charles to see if he agreed too, but he was staring down the stairwell toward the basement. "Charles? You all right?"

Charles nodded and placed a new camera from the bag on the stairs leading down to position it for the widest coverage.

"You getting a feeling?" Bill asked.

Charles set up an audio recorder a few steps further down. "Yes, but I could use a break."

"What are you picking up?" Gillian asked.

"Something different. Confusing and—different."

***

Bill pulled a cooler from the trunk. "Okay everyone, as promised I did bring some lunch for our break." He set the cooler on the table and pulled out several packages of cold cuts and bread, with condiments and a bowl of potato salad. "I've got some leftover meatloaf for making sandwiches too, plus all the utensils and plates, along with more bottled water and sodas. So dig in."

"So, nothing so far?" Trent asked as he built a sandwich.

"Nothing physical," Gillian said with some disappointment.

"We've had some interesting experiences, and I can't wait to go through all the digital camera footage and audio recorders to see what we find, but unfortunately for Gillian, no physical persons so far. We'll check through the basement next and see what we can find down there," Bill explained.

"Charles, you were seeing something?" Gillian asked.

"Not so much seeing as feeling. I was getting a feeling of some very different energies," Charles said, through bites of a meatloaf sandwich.

"But you do 'see' some things sometimes, right?" Gillian asked. "I'm not really familiar with how a psychic medium functions."

"Not all psychic mediums function the same way. Some are more empathetic, others are more clairvoyant, and still others, well—they

111

see dead people," Charles chuckled.

"So how long have you been a medium? Was this something you were born with?" Trent asked, and Gillian nodded wondering the same thing.

"I wasn't born with this gift. I was in the Army on my third tour in Afghanistan five years ago, part of a forward scout unit, Second Lieutenant," Charles started, then cleared his throat. "Our armored vehicle hit an IED. When I woke up out of a medically-induced coma two months later with severe brain trauma, I was still on a ventilator but was greeted by my squad at the hospital every day for a week. They would sit and talk to me, assuring me everything was going to be all right. When the day came that the nurses pulled the ventilator out, I asked them to be sure to let my squad know, so I could finally talk with them. The nurses didn't understand my request. Finally after a couple days the Major came in with a chaplain to let me know what had happened. I was the sole survivor of my squad from the IED explosion."

Gillian held her napkin up to her mouth and felt a tear starting down her cheek. "I'm so sorry."

"Don't be. I've come to an understanding of sorts. I've spent the last few years seeing the world in a completely new light. Life is not what we think it is. I don't have all the answers, but by doing investigations like this with people like Bill, I've been able to help myself and others to find their way."

"You said you 'see' things differently?" Trent asked.

"The best way I can describe that is like a photo negative when I close my eyes. In the darkness, life energy or spirit energy glows. The more energies gather together, the brighter the glow. And, like a moth to a flame, more energies are attracted to the brighter spots."

"So there is something to be said about the old saying when you die, 'go to the light,'" Trent said off-handed.

Charles nodded. "However, not everything attracted to large collections of light is nice. There are very dangerous dark energies, or spirits—some might say demons, that are also attracted to large gatherings of light, and prey off that energy, feeding off the fear they are able to generate."

"So that's what you meant when you said the Stilles Asylum was 'so bright,'" Gillian said.

"Exactly. In this region, the Stilles Asylum is almost like a beacon on the hill. Imagine a baseball field in the middle of nowhere, with all the field lights on in the middle of the night," Charles explained. "You can spot that from miles away. I've seen this beacon on the hill since I moved back three years ago—"

"And since 2014 and the death of Jeffrie Trace, this place has been closed off to the public," Bill interjected.

"So that's why you've never been here before," Gillian added.

Charles nodded as he finished the last bite from his sandwich.

"Are we ready to return? Gillian?" Bill asked. Gillian nodded while wiping her mouth with a paper towel. "Charles?"

"Ready."

"Trent?" Gillian asked.

"Standing by as requested," Trent said with a smirk.

* * *

All three stood at the staircase, with fresh batteries in their flashlights, digital recorders and camcorders, along with extra flashlights, staring into the darkness to the basement. The entire building seemed different—quiet as though waiting for something to happen, but no one was sure what. Charles even noticed the old man who had been in his face all morning was no longer there.

Bill pointed his flashlight at the digital camera Charles had set up earlier. It was knocked over and the digital audio recorder set two steps below was moved several steps down. "We've had some activity that will be interesting to see on the playback," he said in a whisper.

Gillian could also feel the difference in the building and asked Charles, "Are you seeing or feeling anything going on?"

"Everything has gone very quiet," Charles answered in as much of a hushed tone as his deep resonating voice could muster.

"Why?" Bill asked.

"There's a kind of reverence or respectful attention being paid that I don't understand yet. Will you let me take lead down the stairs, Bill?"

"Sure, if you think that best."

"I do," Charles answered and started down with slow careful steps. Gillian didn't realize it at first but Charles had his eyes closed as he stepped further into the darkness, his flashlight seemed only

113

able to penetrate a few feet ahead. Like the steps above, they curled back around and he stopped at the bottom where there was once a double door frame, but the doors had been removed. He briefly shined his light to the right and then turned left. Bill paused only long enough to set a digital camera down on the floor pointing down the hall, and Gillian followed close behind.

Charles came to an intersection of another hall, paused a moment to sense left, then turned right. Again Bill placed another camera down on a short stand and pointed to the left. The hall opened up into a much larger space filled with bed frames, shelving and various other old worn and broken furnishings. A narrow aisle continued through the middle and Charles took a few more steps before stopping, continuing to sense, with eyes closed, further down the path.

"Are you seeing anything on the SLS camera?" Bill asked Charles.

"Sorry I keep forgetting…using it now. There's something going on down there."

Gillian kept checking her pant legs with her flashlight and Bill turned back to see what she was doing. "What's wrong?"

"I keep getting caught on something," Gillian whispered.

Bill shined his flashlight around, but couldn't see anything near her legs. "What do you mean?"

"I keep feeling something tugging on my pants," Gillian said pointing her flashlight down. In that instant the material pulled away from her leg as though being pulled by some unseen force. Gillian gasped trying not to scream in shock. She could feel her skin crawling with goose bumps. Bill let out a gasp as well and pointed his digital camera down to attempt to document the incident.

Gillian felt a tap on her arm on the opposite side, and spun around startled, "Someone touched me."

"Someone or something?" Bill asked.

"I felt a hand," Gillian answered, trying to keep from overreacting, but she was already feeling out of control, and shined her flashlight all around, casting odd shadows in all directions.

"Shhh," Charles hushed them.

"What are you seeing?" Bill whispered.

Charles pointed his light down further ahead of the path, where the room narrowed back down to another hall. "Activity. Some kind of ceremony," he answered as quietly as he could. "We're disturbing something."

Bill stepped closer to Charles and tried to position his FLIR camera to get a view.

"I'm seeing military men. This looks like a changing of the guard, but really doesn't make too much sense. It's like there are two, possibly three, different eras in the process, the uniforms are all different."

Gillian was still trying to see what was pulling her pant leg, shining her flashlight at her leg, as Bill tried to reposition himself for a better camera angle to catch what Charles was seeing at the end of the hall.

Gillian stopped as Bill continued behind Charles, and shined her flashlight into the piles of junk on either side of the narrow aisle. She felt as though the air was getting thick and there was a distinct pungent smell of rot and decay drifting in around her.

"Leave. Now. You. Don't. Belong. Here," a voice said low with an edge of anger right in Gillian's ear. Startled, she turned and screeched out when a dark human-shaped mass with bloodshot eyes appeared behind her. She lost her balance and fell back, dropping her flashlight as she hit the floor. Instantly she felt something vice-like and ice cold grip her ankle and swiftly drag her several feet away from Bill and Charles.

"OH HELL NO YOU DON'T," she screamed out kicking at anything and everything with her other leg while grabbing at the floor to stop from being dragged further, but she had no grip on the slick concrete flooring. A moment of helpless panic set in, reaching straight to the depths of her mind and soul like she had never felt before. *How do you defend yourself from something you can only feel but cannot see?*

Bill was startled by Gillian's screams echoing throughout the basement. He turned to see, in the glow of her flashlight rolling across the floor, a dark mass over her legs as she was being pulled away. He went to help all the while attempting to capture on camera what he was seeing. "Gillian!"

Gillian was surprised that when Bill shouted her name the dark mass let go of her ankle and vanished into the darkness.

"Is everyone all right?" Charles' deep voice boomed through the spaces of the basement as he turned with his flashlight to give some

115

light on the situation.

Bill knelt down and helped Gillian sit up on the floor. "Are you all right?"

Gillian was shaking, feeling as though her heart was pounding in her throat and took a few deep breaths to calm herself before nodding. "I think so. Did you see that? And that smell! What was that?"

Bill sniffed at the air, but shook his head, "Can you walk? We should leave," Bill suggested.

Gillian retrieved her flashlight nearby, "No. I'm fine. Just startled. Someone grabbed me. I want to know who."

"I really think you have just experienced a shadow-figure up close and personal...we should leave," Bill attempted to be firm.

"No. We still have more of this basement to investigate. I need to know if this is a something or a someone down here."

"Okay, if you insist, but I think you need to stay between us from here on out," Charles suggested.

"I agree. I think you're being singled out," Bill added.

Gillian nodded and dusted herself off as she stood back up, determined to refocus on the task at hand, "Charles, what were you seeing down there?"

"I'm not sure yet, but stay here. I want to check something out. I'll be right back."

"Whoa, where are you going?" Bill asked.

"Just down here to get a closer look."

Bill and Gillian watched as Charles walked towards the beginning of the hall, pointing the SLS camera. Just a few feet beyond was the west wall of the basement. His frame nearly filled the entire space, but after several seconds he stood at attention, saluted, then turned around and walked back.

"What was that all about?" Bill asked.

"It's a bit hard to explain but they recognized my former rank in the Army," Charles answered.

"Are they still there?" Gillian asked.

Charles turned to look. "There's one standing by the wall on the left, the other three walked through the wall. Four just left, like this was some watch-stander's duty post and we witnessed a changing of the guard."

"What's behind that wall?" Gillian asked.

Bill went through his drawings and notes. "Nothing, this facing wall continues on to the left a few feet." Bill aimed his flashlight. "There's an opening into a space where the new water main was brought in, and all the lines feed off that." Bill looked for a path in the furniture piles and junk to work his way toward the opening. Gillian followed with Charles behind.

The path was like a maze, twisting and turning but eventually Bill led everyone to the opening in the wall and shined his light inside. More piles of junk filled the space. "See the water main?" Bill illuminated the far wall. A large pipe came through and several other pipes were connected, appearing more like an afterthought that led up into the ceiling.

"So they were walking into here from the hall?" Gillian asked. "Why?"

"Well there must have been an opening there before," Bill said. His flashlight revealed something odd where the hall would have been. "Hold on," he said, stepping out to shine the light along the wall and then arcing back. "I never noticed that before, it must be an optical illusion, probably because of the pipes or piles of debris."

Charles did the same with his flashlight. "I don't think that's an illusion...the wall is longer outside than it is inside the space."

"A room?" Gillian suggested.

"I've been down to the end of the hall many times and never noticed anything that would suggest a door or a room there," Bill said, stepping out and following another twisting path through the piles of junk back toward the hall. Gillian and Charles followed once more.

"Do we still have someone there?" Bill asked.

Charles pointed the SLS camera to the area where he had seen activity. There was nothing now, so he closed his eyes to sense if there was any other activity. "They're all gone. They were not happy we were down here making all this noise."

Bill shined his light along the wall. Plaster chunks were coming off near the west basement boundary wall, exposing very old bricks. He tapped his knuckles on the wall. "This all feels and sounds solid...like support structure." He kept moving further along the wall but his tapping sound changed and a large chunk of plaster fell, exposing a different kind of brick against a metal frame.

"Whoa, that's different," Gillian said.

"Yeah, that looks like a filled in door frame," Charles added.

"A holding cell?" Gillian wondered.

"I don't know. That would seem awfully small," Bill said as he stepped up to take a closer look at the bricks. The mortar was rotted away. Gillian stepped closer and gave a gentle push. One of the bricks fell into the dark space with a reverberating, scattering clunk sound. They could see in the light of the flashlight all the dust particles being sucked into the hole.

Gillian turned to Bill with a smirk. "Oops?"

"This is a wetwall," Bill stated. "You can tell with the negative pressure pulling in the air. Cool air in the basement is being pulled up through the wetwalls likely to holes or vents in the attic by escaping warmer air up there. They were typically used for plumbing, and to keep moisture from building up in the spaces it was all ventilated up and out."

Gillian's curiosity was growing regarding the hole in the wall and she aimed her flashlight inside. As she moved closer, she jumped back and gasped, startling Bill and Charles.

"What?" Bill said, moving to look into the hole with his light.

"I thought I saw something moving," Gillian answered, still shaking.

"I don't see anything, probably just dust in the light," Bill offered.

"If this is just a wetwall, why would there be a door, or military guards standing here like Charles said?" Gillian asked.

"A guard post or munitions locker or something?" Charles offered, then turned back toward the large basement room. "Shhh. Listen."

"I heard that too, sounded like furniture moving across the floor," Bill guessed.

"No listen, I'm hearing voices," Gillian whispered and pointed her flashlight back toward the path leading to the other end of the basement. All three stopped moving and listened to distant indistinct voices that gave them chills. They were like distant conversations in the dark.

"Activity is picking up again. I'm feeling a lot of activity that way." Charles pointed his light to the other side of the basement.

"On that side is the abandoned cistern and mechanical spaces where the box is located," Bill stated.

"The infamous 'Jack-in-the-box?'" Gillian asked.

"Yes," Bill confirmed.

"Isn't that also where Jeffrie Trace was killed?" Gillian continued.

Bill nodded and aimed his FLIR camera back along the narrow path back. Gillian stepped alongside. She pointed to the different colors showing up between the various pieces of debris and furniture along the back wall of the hall on the east side. "Why do you think that far wall would appear to be warmer?"

"You've used a FLIR before?" Bill asked surprised.

"I've had the occasion," Gillian said then shined her flashlight in the same direction. The air was feeling colder and thicker, and the light beam wasn't penetrating as far. Gillian felt the walls of the basement were closing in, and tried her best to repress her urge to run out in a panic.

Bill led the way back, taking time to check out other spaces off the large room, before heading toward the mechanical rooms. He stopped at the intersection to the short hall that led to the stairs. Other than the flashlights, the stairwell had only a faint hint of light that gave the doorway an odd, haunting glow. Bill checked the camera and digital audio recorder set up there and then continued on ahead down the hall past the mechanical rooms.

Gillian paused at the hall intersection and glanced at the doorway to the stairs; she thought she may have seen something from the corner of her eye, almost like the black outline of a hand on the wall, but with everything happening and all the odd noises, her nerves were on edge and she couldn't be sure. She pointed her flashlight and saw nothing.

Charles stepped up from behind and also peeked toward the stairs. "Ms. Gillian, did you see something?"

Gillian shook her head, "Seems like I always do, and yet, never quite."

"Jillie?"

Gillian turned to Charles, her mouth and eyes wide, "Tell me—"

Charles nodded, staying quiet to see if he could hear anything more.

Bill turned and shined his light back at them. "I just heard something."

"We did too," Gillian whispered, trying to hear more.

"That sounded child-like," Bill whispered back though his voice still carried into the depths of the larger room they just left. Their voices echoed and bounced from every direction.

119

Bill stepped back and picked up the digital recorder next to the camera on the floor. He rewound the recording a few seconds and hit play. *"Ms. Gillian, did you see something?"* Charles said.

"Seems like I always do, and yet, never quite," Gillian's voice followed.

"Jillie?"

"There!" Bill couldn't hold his excitement.

"That was clear," Gillian gasped.

"Shhh," Charles shushed everyone and pointed his light behind Bill down the other hall. "I'm hearing more voices. Almost like an argument.

Gillian couldn't stop rubbing her arms and Bill noticed. He asked in a whisper, "Are you all right?"

"Every hair on my body is sticking straight out, and I feel like it's freezing cold here all of the sudden," Gillian answered quietly.

"Continue on?" Bill asked.

Gillian nodded, "How much is left?"

"Just a few more spaces down this hall."

Gillian nodded again. "Continuing on."

Charles took point again, keeping Gillian in the middle, and led them all the way to the end of the east basement boundary wall. There were some large open rooms to the left that were piled up with very old equipment that had been used to manufacture prison shoes and clothing. At the end to the right was another room where the top of a very large brick cistern could be seen. Broken hospital beds and torn mattresses were piled all around.

Leading back, Bill paused at the entrance to the furnace and boiler room and motioned for them to listen. "Rustling noises and voices," Bill said in a hush.

Gillian stood next to Bill and peered inside, shining her flashlight around. The room was actually rather large and she recognized from the photos the replacement furnace and the older boiler not far away. There were pipes of all sizes throughout the ceiling and along much of the walls, emanating from the furnace and boiler. Everything in the room was covered in grimy black soot.

"Soot from the furnace?" Gillian asked.

"More likely coal dust. This whole room just always seems covered with it," Bill said.

Scanning the room, she stopped on a very large metallic box on the far wall, "That is—"

"The box? Yes," Bill answered with a sense of reverence.

Gillian pressed past Bill and entered, shining her flashlight all around. Bill and Charles followed close behind. She went straight for the metal box for an examination. She could see the top would have been operated by a pulley system attached to the ceiling and hinged at the wall, but all that was now gone, and the lid was tack-welded in a couple spots to the base along the front edge. Gillian gave Bill a glance and pointed at the side door to the box with a bit of confusion.

"The top and side were closed during coal loading, cutting down on dust and spillage. Then during use, the lid would be lifted and the side panel opened to shovel coal into the boiler." Bill used his flashlight to point out the various parts.

Gillian was curious about scuff marks on the floor around the side opening. "So this part swings out for access?"

"Right, but as you can see the top has been welded, and the lip goes over the top of the side door, so the side door is sealed up tight as well," Bill again explained along with his flashlight for emphasis.

Gillian knelt down for a closer look. Something wasn't right, but she couldn't put her finger on her thoughts yet. She filed the inconsistency in her mind for future reference—there were just so many questions. With everything welded how could Stacy get out this way? Everything appeared solid, except for a small rough cut hole in the side door. She shined her LED in but it all appeared pitch black inside.

"This always gives me the creeps, and even more so now in person down here," Charles said, as he pointed his flashlight up onto a wall across from the metal box. The rhyme was scrawled in red paint on the dirty white plastered wall above a long, cluttered work bench.

Gillian noticed something there and shined her flashlight on the wall. After a few seconds she reached into her pocket, pulled out a smaller UV flashlight. When she pointed the light to the wall and looked through the clear orange plastic filter more partially obscured letters glowed beneath the painted letters. She held the flashlight up for Bill and Charles. They could make out the same rhyme with some misspelled words.

"Gillian, is that what I think it is?" Bill asked.

"Looks like someone tried to wash it all off at some point, but that is blood residue," Gillian's answer was cold.

Charles motioned toward the back wall with a shush. "Voices."

Bill turned and rummaged through his cargo pockets. Digging through extra batteries, he pulled out one more small digital audio recorder, turned it on and set it on the box lid.

Gillian scanned more of the room with her UV light. There were traces of bio-fluids all around the room with a particularly large area on the floor next to the box and a floor drain. She pointed it out to Bill and he nodded. "The spot from the video," she answered to herself.

Without warning something swished by her face and landed on the floor with a metallic clang and rattle before rolling to a stop. Gillian stepped back and gasped.

Bill and Charles both turned their lights to a tin can on the floor.

"Get. Out."

Gillian turned back past the box with her regular flashlight towards the direction she believed she heard a clear voice. Another object flew past her shoulder, bouncing across the cluttered bench with a distinct wooden sound. She was certain something in the darkness had moved across the room. She tried to follow the shape. "I've got movement," Gillian hissed and tried to stay calm and quiet.

"Charles are you picking anything up with all this activity?" Bill asked as he checked the piece of wood on the bench that had been tossed.

"This is very confusing. I feel like there's a lot of tension and curiosity. Like there're a lot of waiting entities here," Charles answered.

"You. Are. Scaring. Him," a voice growled in the darkness.

"Did you hear that?" Gillian asked, as she trained her flashlight toward the far back wall next to a large wooden tool cabinet.

"Not good," Bill answered. "Remember Jeffrie's video." Bill stepped next to Gillian. Her eyes were wide and he turned to see the shadow from behind the cabinet—a head and shoulders of someone peeking around from the other side. Bill turned his digital camera as fast as he could as the shadow slid back out of view.

"Did you see—"

"Yes," Bill answered before letting Gillian finish.

Gillian took a cautious step forward while trying to fend off the intense chills over her entire body. "It's all right. We're not here to hurt you. Please come out," she said then waited for a response.

There were noises coming from all directions in the room as though they were surrounded. Charles scanned the room with his flashlight.

Gillian took another small step closer to the cabinet. "You need to come out. We're here to help you," Gillian pleaded again. The room felt colder and the air was thicker again, making it hard to breathe. She dropped her dust mask down and saw her breath in the light of her flashlight.

"Gillian this space is particularly bad with asbestos," Bill reminded her.

"...carrots..."

Gillian turned to Bill with her eyes wide. "Did you hear that?"

"I heard something, like a child, but I couldn't make it all out."

"I heard something about 'carrots.' Does that make any sense?"

Bill nodded. "I have several EVP's from over the years, but they've never made any sense."

Gillian took another step toward the cabinet, but Bill pulled back on her arm. "I don't think you want to get any closer."

Gillian turned to see the shadow peeking out from behind the cabinet then ducking back again. "There's someone there," she insisted. "Please come out. Are you Jack? Are you Tommy? Someone else? It's okay now. You're not in trouble, we just need you to come out so we can help you."

"Stop. Scaring. Him," a voice in the darkness growled as though from all directions at once.

Again something flew past Gillian, this time landing on the box with the loud metallic thud and clang. Charles was quick to illuminate the object with his flashlight. "This is getting dangerous; that was a brick," he announced.

Gillian took another step to see past the cabinet with her flashlight. There was no one there. She shined her light all around the area looking for a way out but there was none. "Where'd he go? How?" Gillian checked the wall and the sides of the cabinet for openings but found nothing.

"There's nothing back there. There's literally nowhere to go. I've been back in this corner before. We were seeing a shadow-figure. I'm just hoping I got some clear footage on camera," Bill said.

Gillian turned around and saw Charles was standing next to the box; the shadow figure's head was poking out from the other side of the box. She pointed but the shadow darted out of sight. She hurried past Bill and Charles shining her light but there was no one there.

"Gillian," Bill called out. "There's no one down here. We are literally chasing shadows."

"Charles, you said you felt like there were a lot of entities here waiting. Waiting for what?" Gillian asked in frustration.

Charles nodded. "It feels like they are all waiting for something very bad to happen."

The sound of something metallic bouncing off the back wall and rolling around on the floor echoed in the dark.

"Gillian, there's no one down here. Let's go," Bill pleaded.

"...ter carrots..."

Gillian turned to Bill. She could see by the look in his eyes he heard the child-like voice again too, but he was shaking his head. "Let's go now before someone gets hurt. The activity is getting too dangerous," Bill suggested. Gillian looked to Charles for support but he was nodding in agreement with Bill.

Bill picked up the digital recorder from the top of the metallic box and headed for the doorway. Gillian and Charles followed.

"Jillie—" a frail small voice called out.

"Don't. Belong. Here," another voice in the darkness of the room could be heard from behind them as they walked out.

***

Chapter 7
Lives Remembered

Crime scene photos from 1966 and 2014 were scattered from the dining room to the living room couch where Gillian was sitting in yoga pants and a long, over-sized t-shirt. Clippings and photos covered nearly every surface including her lap, the coffee table and floor. She felt only a little guilty that she had left the Stilles Asylum without so much of a good-bye when they had left the building the day before, after their investigation and search. There was so much weighing on her mind and she had been unable to sleep the entire night. She had ignored her phone messages all day from both Trent and Bill, trying to work out what had happened. She needed to process it all without distraction, and everything felt like a distraction.

Most of her time had been spent simply staring at the spread of photos and reports, feeling desperate to get a handle on the events, not only from 1966 and 2014 but also the day before. Bill's photos of paranormal entities, or shadow-figures and unexplained shapes from years past at the Stilles Asylum, gave her chills and goose bumps. She felt as though the very foundation of her years of experience as a detective, a student of science and practitioner of logic, was being shaken to its core.

"How can this be real?"

Don't let this shake your foundation. You're stronger than this.

"But I know what I saw. I know what I smelled. I know what I felt." Gillian reached down to a sore spot just above her ankle, and for the first time realized there was the hint of a bruise.

There is always a simple explanation. You will work this out, just have faith in yourself. I do. This is in no way any kind of mental set back. You can get through this. Think of this as just another challenge to be conquered.

"Well that may be all well and good, but this could end up being a major paradigm shift in my belief system."

Shifts in belief can be a good thing.

"I'm just not certain I can handle the end results of this kind of shift."

You will be fine.

Gillian sat and stared out across the array of photos and reports a few more minutes before realizing the tapping she had been hearing and ignoring was from her front door. She recognized the shadow through the door's glazed side window. "Trent."

"Gillian." Trent held two paper cups of coffee from his favorite deli. "Cream, two sugars." He handed one to Gillian.

Still foggy, Gillian replied, "Uh, thanks. I'm sorry, come in."

"Are you all right? Bill called and asked me to check on you. He said he'd left several messages and so did I. You left without saying a word." Trent noticed all the photos, news clippings and reports. He followed Gillian to her dining room, stepping carefully.

She pulled out one of the chairs and offered Trent a seat. "I'm sorry, I had a lot to think about," she said, and sat across the table taking a sip of coffee. "Thanks, this actually hits the spot."

"Thought it might. Bill mentioned what happened to you yesterday inside the Stilles. Again, are you all right?"

Gillian sat lost in a moment of thought, realizing that even on a warm summer Sunday afternoon, this coffee was exactly what she needed, and might even help clear her mind. "Oh, I'm sorry. Yes I'm fine."

"Stop apologizing; I'm concerned." Gillian followed Trent's glance over the living room, feeling a little embarrassed. "I can't image what you went through. I've been inside the Stilles a few times, seen and heard a few things, but never—"

Gillian pulled up her pant leg enough to show the new bruise just above her ankle.

Trent's eyes grew wide. "Holy crap!"

"Yeah. But we couldn't find anyone there. Just shadows. Nothing and no one tangible," Gillian said, sounding as though she was still trying to convince herself.

"That's what Bill and Charles were saying last night too." Trent stared at the spread of evidence and shook his head. "I've seen this before. I watched someone tear himself up over this—"

"I'm fine. Really. This is just me. Processing."

"Obsessing—"

"Processing," Gillian pressed. "I just need some time on this."

"To process."

"Yes. To process." Gillian scowled.

"Okay then. Take all the time you need. Don't worry about coming in the next few days. I'll let everyone know you're just taking some time to recoup from the weekend. No big deal."

Gillian nodded and took another sip of coffee. "Okay, no big deal."

"Right. To process."

"Yes. To process."

"And call Bill, please. So he'll stop bugging me to check on you."

Gillian took another sip of coffee and nodded once more. "I'll call Bill."

***

As Gillian parked, she saw Bill standing in his office door at the barn. She grabbed her shoulder bag and headed straight over.

"I'm sure glad you're able to come by today. I was getting concerned yesterday when you didn't answer my calls," Bill said, showing Gillian into the office.

"Like I said yesterday, I had a lot to go over in my head."

Charles was sitting at a small table by the main console. He stood, taking off his headphones to greet her. "Ms. Gillian." His deep voice resonated through the office space.

Gillian had forgotten how large he was; the headphones seemed ridiculously small on his head. She realized she was staring so she lifted her leg up onto a stool to reveal her bruise.

"Oh my God, you weren't kidding," Bill reacted and grabbed a digital camera from his desk. "Can I?" He pointed at the darkening bruise. Gillian nodded.

"Are you okay?" Charles asked with visible concern.

"It's a little tender, but otherwise I'm fine."

"This is astounding evidence." Bill took pictures from several different angles and distances, even pulling up a small black and white measured stick for scale.

"But how are you doing?" Charles pressed.

Gillian took in a deep breath and was slow to release. "I don't know where to begin." She shook her head. "I know what I experienced. I know what I saw. I know what I felt and smelled. But I have no explanation that satisfies my detective, scientific or logical mind. I have a million questions and as many doubts. I truly feel I'm diving into uncharted waters here."

"Well, welcome to the waters, we'll try to keep you from going under," Charles chuckled.

"We're all trying to figure this out," Bill reiterated.

"Well you said yesterday something about having some incredible evidence," Gillian said.

"Oh my God," Bill stammered. "I've never seen the Stilles Asylum so active on the recorders. We've got audio, EVP, video with motion and partial to full-body apparitions, FLIR, SLS camera capture, you name it we've got it."

"Jack?"

"Definitely shadow figures, but as you so eloquently pointed out, I don't know for sure who," Bill answered.

"Anything not listed as paranormal?" Gillian asked with noted concern.

Bill and Charles glanced at each other, and both shook their heads. "Everything we've captured appears to be unexplained or other-worldly at best," Bill said.

"You sound disappointed. This is what you've been telling me this whole time," Gillian scolded. "You're telling me you've got proof of the world of the paranormal that I have been so skeptical about."

"Sure, but—"

"Ms. Gillian, sometimes you don't have to be a medium to feel when someone is going through a dramatic life-change and shift in their beliefs," Charles consoled.

"I appreciate that, so show me what you've found," Gillian said with regenerated determination.

Bill glanced at Charles, then back to Gillian with a grin. "Thought you'd never ask."

***

Gillian pulled up a chair next to Bill at his main console, with Charles sitting on the other side. Two very large monitors filled the bulk of the console wall.

Bill took a moment to explain while he set up the views on the monitors. "What I'm able to do now in this world of digital recorders, is place all the files into a system that syncs all the time clocks at once." Bill used the cursor on the screen to point out the various files.

We had twenty digital cameras set up throughout the building, four on each of the floors as we headed up to start in the attic and one for each of the four staircase landings. Along with each of those cameras we placed digital audio recorders as well. Charles also placed a couple of FLIR cameras on the first and second floors and I have also included all of our hand-held cameras, Charles' SLS camera, and of course the entry hall cameras—all are time stamped."

"Why do you have digital audio recorders along with the video cameras? They're all digital what's the point?" Gillian asked.

"Great question. The digital cameras do record audio but the separate digital audio devices are set to record at a higher bit rate for a higher resolution," Bill explained.

"Ah," Gillian nodded.

"So if you watch the left monitor you can see all the different files in a linear timeline. On the right monitor are the video files; on the left, the associated digital audio file shows as a wave file under each of the videos so we can see all cameras at once synced to the timeline, or if I need to I can click on individual views to pull up front and center for closer inspection. I can scroll forwards or backwards to specific times and all audio and video files are synchronized," Bill continued.

Gillian nodded. "I am impressed."

"Okay, so I think I want to go over the visuals first," Bill said, and moved the cursor. Various digital cameras and audio devices popped up on the right screen with activities speeding along as he scrolled forward.

"So we can see exactly when Charles started each of the cameras," Gillian stated.

"Exactly. So if you remember Charles started ahead of us, but we passed him on the third floor and he caught back up with us on the fourth floor when we reached the attic stairs." Bill explained.

"Yes," Gillian acknowledged.

"Look, here on the second floor," Bill gestured with the cursor. The video views were arranged by floor. Gillian glanced at the screen and saw herself on the fourth floor with Bill and Charles.

Back to the camera view that Bill was highlighting with his cursor, there was some kind of movement in the main corridor near the elevator shaft.

"Does that look like someone limping?" Gillian asked.

Bill brought the image to full screen while scrolling back a couple of seconds. "We think it looks like someone on crutches. If you look closely, you can see one leg and the other appears to be missing."

"But as he goes past the main hall I can see through him to the window at the end of the hall, as well as the wall near the elevator shaft." Gillian stated. The hairs on her neck stood up, and a chill danced across her shoulders and down her back.

"That man is wearing a World War I uniform," Charles added.

Gillian glanced at Bill, "Residual or intelligent?"

"My guess would be residual. But wait, there's more." Bill reduced the view and clicked on another from the first floor, scrolling back a few seconds. "At the same time there is this."

Gillian could see what appeared to be a shadow figure peeking from around the corner near the western edge of the hall, and an antique wheelchair further down the hall rolled out into the main corridor, stopping halfway, before returning.

She rubbed at the back of her neck in an attempt to stop the tingling. "Residual or—"

"Definitely intelligent," Bill answered with reserved excitement. He scrolled the timeline forward several minutes. "Here we are coming down from the attic." Bill highlighted the view from one of the cameras, and then pointed to another from the same floor. A shadow figure stepped out from the children's playroom and then back. Bill brought the view to full screen.

"Intelligent," Gillian stated.

Both Charles and Bill nodded.

"Jack?"

"He's keeping his distance—I think so, but there's no proof." Bill he reduced the view before scrolling further along.

"We continued to investigate the fourth floor then moved down to the third floor," Bill said. They watched as Charles turned off the cameras one by one. Bill then highlighted another view of the second floor's main corridor and there appeared to be a nurse pushing an antique-style wheelchair with someone who appeared to have no legs. Other than being able to see through them, they both looked quite solid and real.

"The wheelchair looks to be pre-World War I, and the nursing uniform looks to be late nineteenth century," Charles noted.

"Residual—" Gillian guessed again.

"That would be my opinion," Bill replied. "That would be very consistent with how the Stilles was being used during the Spanish-American War in 1898. The garrison was starting to be used as a military hospital and rehabilitation facility. The first floor was specifically used for medical purposes, surgeries and such, while the second floor was used for recovery. The rest remained barracks. In 1918 during World War I, the whole facility was turned into a military hospital and recovery rehab facility."

"So there appears to be a great deal of military paranormal activity energy here," Gillian offered.

"I have seen evidence of that through the years, but again, not to this extent and so intense. This is just phenomenal evidence," Bill explained.

"But we didn't notice any of this while we were searching," Gillian said with concern.

"Not uncommon. Although we were getting audio hits throughout our searches, and we'll go over those in a few minutes. But first," Bill said while he scrolled forward more. They watched as Charles picked up the cameras on the third floor, turning them off again, one by one. Bill highlighted another view from the second floor, this time from the FLIR camera. Two short, cold objects appeared to move very fast across the secondary corridor from one side to the elevator shaft. Bill brought the file to full-view and backed up a few seconds to run again.

"Those appear very cold on the spectrum, when we walked past that camera a few seconds earlier, you could see we showed up as very bright hot," Gillian explained.

"We were pretty hot still from the attic, but yes it's hard to explain objects that are moving across the corridor being that cold on the spectrum," Bill replied.

"Residual?" Gillian asked.

"Unsure. Possibly," Bill shrugged. "They could also be classified like a shadow figure."

"Intelligent—"

"Shadow figures are usually classified as intelligent haunt,"

Charles answered.

"There is one notable sound capture from the first floor just before we left the second floor," Bill offered, then pulled up an audio file and reran with the volume up. There was a very long but distant sounding scream that echoed through the hall.

Gillian's mouth dropped. "I don't remember hearing that."

"None of us did. That was picked up on one of the digital audio recorders near what used to be the surgical room in 1918," Bill answered.

"Residual?"

"Likely. The sound was recorded as an EVP," Charles answered.

Bill continued to scroll through the timeline to Charles picking up cameras on the second floor. "If you'll notice we're moving on down the stairs back to the first floor." Bill pointed to the row of hand-held cameras, then stopped, backed up and pulled Gillian's up to main view. "Watch as you are walking down the stairs behind me, you swing the camera a bit while you're turning onto the first landing. Your camera radically points up for a second and you caught this."

Gillian's eyes grew wide as there was a shadow figure standing at the top of the stairs behind her in a corner, and for a brief second there appeared to be a single red eye shining in a dark humanoid shape. "That's a person!" Gillian exclaimed.

Both Bill and Charles shook their heads.

"Ms. Gillian, I was coming onto the staircase landing just above that not two seconds later, and there was no one there," Charles said with a tone of disappointment. Bill pointed to Charles' camera view at the same point in the timeline.

"Then how do you explain eye-shine?" Gillian asked. "Just like what I saw down in the basement later." Gillian's hope of someone physical hiding in the building was fading.

"I've got dozens of photos and video examples of shadow figures with one, two and even more eyes shining back in the camera IR light as well as in regular lighting."

"Ms. Gillian, the only thing I can tell you is I caught a whiff of some awful stink as I walked past that corner, and honestly thought Bill had cut one," Charles chuckled in an attempt to lighten up the tension.

"Oh, so does that happen often?" Gillian asked with a smirk, looking directly at Bill.

Bill gave a sheepish nod and they all chuckled as he changed the monitor view back and scrolled forward more, quickly changing the subject. "Okay, now here we are again searching through the first floor, and if you notice your camera view and mine, we both pass that wheelchair we saw earlier. Notice it's not just sitting there in the doorway, it's tucked around the corner up against a stack of bed frames."

Gillian was getting that familiar feeling across her neck and arms again. "That would imply someone or something pulled it out, then pushed it back in and then around the corner. You were saying earlier—intelligent right?"

"Poltergeist; physical manipulation of objects, and definitely intelligent," Bill nodded.

"And what were you getting through all this, Charles?" Gillian asked.

Charles shook his head. "I was mostly dealing with a very fanatic, angry old man who just kept screaming into my face throughout the first part of the day."

"What about?" Bill asked.

"Honestly I'm not completely sure, but he may have been trying to tell us there was no Jillie."

"The famed Jillie who's supposed to be Jack's sister?" Bill asked. "He was saying there was no Jillie? You didn't mention that before."

"There was a lot going on, and honestly I was having difficulty understanding the message of this particular entity. He appeared so incredibly agitated and angry. Kept saying things like, 'Stop Jillie nonsense' or 'stop got them.' It was all very jumbled and didn't make a whole lot of sense. Even later that evening—"

"Whoa, wait. This thing followed you home?" Bill asked with concern.

"They can do that?" Gillian asked, as the tingle down her spine grew. She couldn't help but remember the shadow in her bedroom a few nights earlier and wondered if it was something that followed her home from the Stilles.

Charles nodded. "It happens, but I'm getting better at forcing them to leave me alone. This one was so insistent, yet still so jumbled up before he finally left. Kept saying things like, 'Got them all' and 'come for her.' I'm thinking all the talk about Jack's sister, Jillie, is just another part of the urban legend and not so much fact."

"I still wonder if this entity is simply being triggered by Gillian's name?" Bill wondered out loud.

"We've all heard someone calling Jillie's name. Remember down in the basement after lunch?" Gillian asked.

"Sure, but again your name could be just a trigger," Bill suggested.

"Jillie, not Gillian. Nobody calls me Jillie."

"All I'm saying, there's no actual evidence that Jillie existed, even according to your own notes and records, Bill. Jillie is just as much a mystery as Jack," Charles continued.

"I have corroboration that Jack existed, and that he often talked about his sister," Bill stated.

"But, as you've stated before too, you have no corroboration that Jillie existed—no one ever saw her," Gillian said. "So who is Jillie?"

"Admittedly, all the EVPs I have regarding Jillie don't make a whole lot of sense and we picked up more in the after-lunch segments," Bill said as he scrolled forward.

"Please continue," Gillian said.

"Here's where Charles set up the camera and digital audio recorder on the stairs leading down to the basement, and we walked out. Now listen here," Bill suggested as he brought the remaining audio recorder volumes up. There was a wash of distant noises, shuffling sounds, and muffled conversations echoing throughout the first floor. Then after several minutes without warning all the sounds stopped.

Gillian scowled. "What happened? Did the recorders just stop?"

Bill shook his head. "Listen." He turned the volume up. The background hissing noise increased, but Gillian could hear other noises now—like wind in the distance, and the low rumble of a large truck passing on the street below. "It's like everyone, all the entities just stopped. It continues like that until you hear us reenter the building to go down into the basement. And oh, by the way, watch this." Bill centered the camera on the staircase to the basement, as a dark shadow passed and the camera was knocked down a couple steps. The only noise was of the camera falling. "Our shadow figure didn't like having a camera there on the steps, apparently."

"I guess not," Gillian mocked.

"Now for the good stuff," Bill said with a gleam in his eye.

"Wait, what we saw before wasn't good?" Gillian asked.

134

Bill scrolled on through the timeline. "Just wait. As you'll remember we followed Charles down to the basement. Gillian, your camera view is not as helpful...you really need to remember to aim at more than just the floor."

"Hey, I did pretty good upstairs. It was dark going down into that basement; I was trying to watch where I was walking. I kept getting my pants caught on something," Gillian defended.

"Charles, this is where you were picking up some activities at the end of the room, at the far end," Bill stated.

"Yes. Very strange. All I can figure was I was seeing some type of changing of the guard ceremony, and they were very unhappy that we were down there making noise. I got the feeling they thought we were being extremely disrespectful of their activities," Charles explained.

"I can't really see anything from your camera—it looks almost like a FLIR. Were you able to see anything?" Gillian asked.

"He had the SLS camera but wasn't pointing it down the hall at first," Bill replied.

"I forgot, sorry. But yes I was seeing men in antique uniforms from at least a couple different eras, late 19th century and World War I," Charles explained. "Some were coming from the wall as others were going into the wall there, while two switched places outside of the wall in that short hallway."

"Yeah that's all coming up shortly. Notice your camera, Gillian, this is when you were feeling as though someone was pulling your pants leg and touching your shoulder," Bill said. pointing the cursor over at her camera view, moving wildly in all directions.

"And that awful smell," Gillian added.

"Listen, you heard this with your ears and we caught this on the camera recorder," Bill increased the volume for her camera.

"Leave. Now. You. Don't. Belong. Here," a voice said low with an edge of anger.

Gillian squirmed from the memory of that voice in her ear, as her camera view spun and Bill slowed down the frame. For only a few frames her camera caught a dark humanoid shape and what appeared to be a red glaring eye.

Bill stopped the video. "There it is again. The shadow figure and a glowing red eye."

Gillian almost felt sick to her stomach at the sight; the memory of the whole incident was still very fresh. "I was so startled. I'm sorry I screamed and fell. I hope I didn't hurt your camera. Then that thing grabbed my leg and started dragging me!"

"Looks like the camera landed on you as you fell back, but if you look at my camera view," Bill switched the screen. "Here's where I turned and called out your name. I was startled as well, but I tried to catch anything I could with my camera."

The jerky motion of the camera made clear imagery of the dark shape hard to discern.

"It's quite interesting that while I was being dragged away by whatever that thing is, it let go the instant you yelled my name." Gillian pointed to the screen. "What was that on Charles' camera at that same moment...looks like some kind of stick-figure?"

Bill paused and pulled up Charles camera view. "That's the SLS camera. The SLS uses technology developed for video games—it's able to see the human body and replicate movements and how it sees people or entities." Bill took his cursor and pointed out the figure on the screen. "This is one of the entities Charles was seeing in that short hall."

"And let me tell you, he was not happy with all the commotion," Charles added.

Bill continued to scroll forward through the video. "Here's after we inspected the wall and found the bricked up doorway. Activities started to pick up and if you listen here, you can start to hear voices in the distance." Bill turned up the volume once again. They could all hear the sounds of voices as though in conversation, if not arguing, but words were not clear. There was an echoing throughout the large room that distorted the sounds.

"I'm going to fast forward a bit further. This is when you and Charles stopped at the hall leading to the staircase up, where you thought you saw something."

Bill resumed playing the video as Charles asked, *"Gillian, did you see something?"*

In the video they could see Gillian shake her head, *"Seems like I always do, and yet, never quite."*

"Jillie?"

Gillian turned to Charles, her mouth and eyes wide. "Tell me—"

Charles nodded.

Bill's flashlight shined back at them. "I just heard something,"

Bill's voice said off-camera.

"We did too," Gillian whispered.

"That sounded child-like," Bill whispered back.

Bill paused the video again. "I'm really thinking your name is acting as a trigger here."

"That voice sounded so frail, out of breath—so child-like," Gillian reiterated.

"I'm going to scroll forward some more, wait until you hear this." Bill forwarded several minutes. "Here we are in the furnace room." He started the video when he was asking, *"Gillian, is that what I think it is?"*

"Looks like someone tried to wash it all off at some point, but that is blood residue," Gillian replied.

Gillian's shaky camera captured Charles as he motioned toward the back wall with a shush, "Voices."

Gillian's camera showed Bill rummaging through his various cargo pockets. Digging through extra batteries he pulled out one more small digital audio recorder, turned it on and set it on the box lid. The audio file started playing at that point, adding to the overall sound of the video playing.

The SLS camera video feed went dark and another digital video started as Charles switched cameras. *From Charles' video camera Gillian could be seen turning and scanning more of the room with her UV light. There were traces of bio-fluids all around the room, and a particularly large area on the floor. She pointed it out to Bill and he nodded. "The spot from the video," she whispered.*

Without warning something swished by her face and landed on the floor with a metallic clang and rattle as the object rolled to a stop. Startled, Gillian stepped back and gasped.

Bill paused the video. "You can see from my camera view, whatever that was just missed your face," he said, then resumed the video.

Gillian's camera had caught Bill and Charles as they aimed their lights to a tin can on the floor.

"Get. Out," a fourth voice clearly said.

Bill paused. "We all heard that." He started the video again.

Charles' camera focused on Gillian who turned back past the box. She was shining her regular flashlight in the direction of a clear voice, and another object flew by her shoulder, bouncing across a cluttered bench with a distinct wooden sound.

Bill paused again. "That looked like a leg of a chair or something," he commented and resumed the video as Gillian hissed, *"I've got movement."*

"Charles are you picking up anything with all this activity?" Bill asked.

"This is very confusing. I feel like there is a lot of tension and curiosity. Like there are a lot of entities here, waiting," Charles answered.

"You. Are. Scaring. Him," a fourth voice growled.

"Did you hear that?" Gillian asked, as she trained her flashlight and camera view toward the far back wall near a large wooden tool cabinet.

Bill paused again saying, "And yes we ALL heard that voice," then restarted the video.

"Not good," Bill said. "Remember Jeffrie's video."

From Charles' camera Bill was seen stepping next to Gillian then turning to see a shadow of head and shoulders peeking from behind the cabinet.

Bill quickly turned his hand-held digital camera to document the shadow as it slid back out of view. The video was shaky but there was a distinct shadowy humanoid shape before it vanished.

"Did you see—?" Gillian asked.

"Yes," Bill answered

Gillian took cautious steps forward. "It's all right. We're not here to hurt you. Please come out." The digital audio recorder picked up noises from all directions in the room, and Charles' camera panned as he scanned the room with his flashlight.

Gillian's shaky camera moved as she took another small step closer to the cabinet. "You need to come out. We're here to help you," she pleaded again.

Bill's camera caught Gillian dropping her mask and her breath appeared in the glow of her flashlight.

"Gillian this space is particularly bad with asbestos," Bill said.

"...carrots..." another voice spoke.

Bill paused the video. "I ran an analysis of that voice through my audio program because I had such a good sample. This is what I got." He played the enhanced audio file. *"...I have ... carrots for. You..."*

Gillian shook her head. "That just makes no sense to me."

Bill nodded and resumed the video. *Bill's camera showed Gillian turn to Bill with her eyes wide.* "Did you hear that?"

"I heard something, like a child, but I couldn't make it all out."

"I heard something about 'carrots.' Does that make any sense?"

"I have several EVPs from over the years, but they've never made any sense," *Bill answered.*

Gillian took another step toward the cabinet. Both Bill and Charles' cameras showed Bill pull on Gillian's arm, and say, "I don't think you want to get any closer."

Gillian's shaky camera captured a shadow peeking out from behind the cabinet then ducking back again. "There's someone there," *she said.* "Please come out. Are you Jack? Are you Tommy? Someone else? It's okay now. You're not in trouble, we just need you to come out so we can help you."

"Stop. Scaring. Him," *a voice growled.*

Bill paused the video. "Again, we all heard this."

"That voice sends chills down my back," Gillian admitted.

Bill resumed the video, *Charles' camera showed something fly past Gillian, landing on the box with the loud thud and clang. Charles was quick to illuminate a brick with his flashlight and camera.* "This is getting dangerous," *he announced.*

Gillian's camera showed her taking another step to film behind the cabinet, but there was no one there. Her light and camera searched for a way out, but there was none. "Where'd he go? How?"

Bill's camera showed Gillian checking the wall and the sides of the cabinet for openings, but she was unable to find anything.

"There's nothing back there. There's literally nowhere to go. I've been back in this corner before. We were seeing a shadow figure. I'm just hoping I got some clear footage on camera," *Bill said.*

Gillian's camera turned back towards Charles who stood next to the box. A shadow figure appeared again from behind the box. Her camera caught the shadow as it darted down and out of sight. She hurried past Bill and Charles to the other side, shining her light, but no one was there.

Bill paused and rewound the file a couple seconds before running it in slow motion. There was a dark shape of a head and shoulders but no details. "That was definitely a shadow figure." He resumed the video at speed.

"Gillian," Bill called out. "There's no one down here. We are literally chasing shadows."

"Charles, you said you felt like there were a lot of entities here waiting. Waiting for what?" Gillian asked.

Charles nodded. "It feels like they are all waiting for something very bad to happen."

There was the sound of something metallic bouncing off the back wall and rolling around on the floor.

"Gillian, there's no one down here. Let's go," Bill pleaded.

"...ter carrots..."

Bill paused the video again. "I enhanced that beautiful piece of audio as well," he said with excitement before playing it.

"I. Found. Mister Carrots. For you."

Gillian scowled. "What does that mean?"

Bill shook his head. "I have no idea, but that was about the clearest version of that voice on that subject I have ever caught."

Bill resumed the videos, Charles' camera showed Gillian turn to Bill as he was shaking his head. "Let's go now before someone gets hurt. The activity is getting too dangerous," Bill said. Gillian turned to Charles for support and the disappointment showed on her face. Charles' camera showed Bill pick up the digital recorder from the top of the metallic box and head for the doorway. Gillian and Charles followed behind.

"Jillie—" a frail small voice called out.

"Don't. Be... ...ere," another voice was buried in the distance.

Bill paused again. "Unfortunately I had just turned off the digital audio recorder, so those last voices were only caught on Charles' camera. The only other audio I was able to get is iffy at best," Bill said and played another enhanced audio file:

"Jillie. Don't. Leave—" the first frail sounding voice could be heard, then a second gruff voice broke in over the top, "Don't. Belong. Here."

Charles noticed Gillian was shaking so he fetched a pitcher of iced tea.

"Oh, thank you," Gillian said.

"Oh man, I'm such a horrible host," Bill scolded himself.

"Gotcha covered, my friend," Charles answered, pouring them all some tea. "Are you going to be all right, Ms. Gillian?" he asked. His voice calmed her.

Gillian nodded and took a sip of the iced tea. "This is all so much to process. Just when I think I may have found some evidence of a physical person hiding there, then no. And the voices in the dark. The cryptic messages. What or who is a Mister Carrots?"

Bill took a sip of his drink. "I have no idea. More research is needed to try and piece this all together."

"That hole in the wall," Charles said as well. "That whole ceremony thing has me really scratching my head. I'll have to dig through my resources and see if I can find anything on that."

"Speaking of research and resources, I recently got a favorable reply from one of the survivors of the Stilles Asylum, Mrs. Dorthy Bridges," Bill announced. "I've been trying to get an interview with her for years."

"And?" Gillian asked.

"Well I was able to track her down through some other survivor sources and have been in contact with her granddaughter, Jesse Turner. Mrs. Bridges has had a recent change of heart and has granted me an interview this Wednesday. I know Charles you have other plans and are unavailable, but Gillian would you like to come along?"

"Sure, where?"

"It's a bit of a drive. She lives outside of Portland."

"Oregon," Gillian stated as if to make a point.

"Only three hours away," Bill argued.

"Okay. Yes. I'd like that very much."

***

The drive down the I5 corridor was beautiful and Gillian was fairly certain Bill was keeping the conversation light knowing they were about to have a heavy conversation with a survivor of the Stilles Asylum.

After exiting the freeway and a short drive through downtown Portland, they ended up in a residential area with nicely groomed homes built in similar design around the late fifties, early sixties. Bill spotted the address and parked in the street alongside the other cars of the neighborhood.

A younger woman of color stepped out from the front door and

141

greeted them. "I'm Jesse."

"I'm Bill Hartfield, and this is my associate Gillian McClary." They all shook hands.

"My grandmother is on the patio in the back if you will follow me please. I'll be honest, I think I'm more nervous about this meeting than she is. She is insisting now that she needs to talk to you, so I hope you are ready."

"We are indeed ready, and grateful to have this opportunity," Bill replied with graciousness.

Gillian noticed the numerous family photos throughout the modest but well-kept home. Though the furnishings were dated, everything was in very nice condition. They continued on through the kitchen and out a back door leading to a beautiful flower garden, with shade trees lining the back fence. The woman was sitting in a garden chair next to a small table with a pitcher and glasses.

"Grandmother, they're here. This is Mr. Hartfield and his associate Ms. McClary."

"I'm very happy to finally meet you in person, Mrs. Bridges. Please just call me Bill." Bill offered his hand. Mrs. Bridges nodded and took his hand for a brief shake.

"Please call me Gillian," Gillian said as she too took Mrs. Bridges hand for a brief clasp greeting. Gillian noted that Mrs. Bridges appeared to be in her late eighties or more. The wrinkles in her dark brown skin were deep and weathered.

"Please call me Dorthy," the woman requested with a modest smile, and gestured to the other two seats near her table.

Jesse stepped from the back of the house with a fourth chair and started to sit too, but Dorthy gave her grand-daughter a hard glare.

"Grandma, I want to hear this too. You don't ever talk about your younger years," Jesse protested.

"Sweetheart, there are things in this world about my life..." she shook her head with a furrowed brow. "Things you don't never need to know 'bout."

"But you can tell them? Total strangers?" Jesse questioned with respect. Gillian was impressed with the young woman's respectful restraint.

"Sweetheart, please go inside. I'll call for you if we need anything."

Jesse stood and wiped at some moisture on her cheek, gave Bill and Gillian a concerned glance, then with reluctance walked back inside.

Dorthy waited without looking for the back screen door to close and latch, before leaning forward toward Bill and Gillian. "Maybe someday after I'm gone, if you're so inclined you can tell her what we talk about today," she said softly.

"Dorthy, you have nothing to be ashamed about regarding anything that happened at the Stilles," Gillian assured.

"My dear I'm not ashamed of anything in my life. I just don't know that I could stand to see the pain and horror on her face if she ever knew."

They all paused and allowed those words to carry their weight a moment before Bill broke the silence. "Would you mind if I recorded this session? I'd really like to capture all this in your words and expressions."

Dorthy paused in thought a moment before nodding. Bill pulled out a small digital camera connected to a short stand, set it on the small table, pointed it and started recording. The auto-focus and auto-audio leveling took over the rest.

"Where would you like me to start?" Dorthy asked.

"Wherever you're most comfortable, Dorthy. What do you remember of the Stilles?" Bill began.

"Ah. My first memories," she answered then gazed off toward her garden almost as though in a trance. "I remember a woman going to the store, leaving me home alone. I was I believe four years old. After three days, the Sheriff came by to get me and took me to the Stilles," she stated without emotion.

"Father? Grandparents?" Gillian asked.

"Never knew him, and never knew of any grandparents. That would have been around 1951. I was quickly introduced to the ways of the Stilles by the monster of the night. I later realized his name was actually Frank."

"Frank Mills," Gillian softly uttered.

"Frank was an abuser of the worst kind," Dorthy continued, again without emotion. Gillian recognized the coping method. "He had a particular taste for the youngest of us, coming in the night to take us to the basement. I learned fast to try to hide from him as much as I could, but he was ruthless and relentless."

"Didn't the staff know? Didn't they try to stop him?" Gillian asked.

Dorthy gave Gillian a knowing glance. "Of course they knew. They all knew and were too afraid of him to do anything. When he finally disappeared we all thought there would be some relief, but Ruphord was well-schooled by his mentor, and took over the abuses and added tortures." Dorthy broke for a moment to take in a deep breath and a sip of ice tea. "With Ruphord—well, he expanded his abuses to nearly everyone of all ages and gender, and a lot more children began to disappear."

Gillian noted the first signs of distress on Dorthy's face. "If you need to take a moment," Gillian offered, but Dorthy shook her head.

"Do you know anything about the stories of Jack-in-the-Box?" Bill asked.

Dorthy took another sip and nodded. "I was there the day he and his sister arrived," she answered.

"Sister? Jack had a sister?" Bill locked eyes with Gillian.

"Yes. I was there when she was murdered by the new monster in the house," she answered.

"Please, can you tell me?" Bill asked trying not to sound too excited for the new revelation.

Dorthy nodded again. "Let me think, that would have had to have been a Sunday because shoe and clothing production were shut down for the day and that only happened on Sundays. It was my turn to try and find and steal any late harvest apples from the orchard out of the cold storage across from the furnace room in the basement. I would have been, I believe nine years old at that point." Dorthy gazed off toward the garden again before continuing. Gillian noted that Dorthy seemed to gain her strength from her garden, again another recognized coping method. "A distraction was created; an over-flowed toilet and spill, up on the fourth floor for Ruphord to go clean up. I was trying to get into the cold storage room, but it was unexpectedly locked, when I heard children screaming and shouting. Ruphord was bringing them down the stairs. I couldn't go up the stairs to get away, and I was running out of time to hide anywhere else, so I ran into the furnace room and hid under the workbench behind some boxes."

"I could see Ruphord was carrying two small children, lifted up by their arms; a little boy and a smaller little girl. The little boy was screaming out her name, Jillie—and she was just—screaming.

Ruphord flung the little girl out toward the far wall against some wooden crates and she just landed like a sack of coal. He turned his attention to the little boy calling him Jack and then saying that old rhyme about Jack-in-the-box as he put the boy into the old coal box and closed the lid. The boy kept screaming about returning Mr. Carrots and the little girl's name, Jillie—"

"Wait a second," Gillian interrupted. "I'm sorry, you said he was screaming to return what?"

"Ruphord would torment the boy with a small patchwork stuffed rabbit doll called Mr. Carrots, but no one understood the meaning of that except me. I was too afraid to say anything. I didn't see, but apparently Ruphord had taken the doll from the little girl."

"Then what happened?" Bill asked.

"After he locked the little boy, Jack, in the old coal box, he started on the little girl," Dorthy paused again for another sip of ice tea and glanced off. "I know too well what she went through, and what should never happen to anyone especially that age. He put her onto the table across from the bench and tore off her little white coat and her pretty blue dress with the white dots. She fought and kicked and screamed like I never heard anyone scream before. Then—" Dorthy paused again.

"Then?" Gillian asked really not wanting to continue with what she was certain she already knew.

"Then? Then after what seemed like forever, the little girl stopped. Stopped kicking, stopped fighting, stopped screaming. Jack kept screaming her name over and over—Jillie. I just hid there under the workbench, I couldn't run, I couldn't help closing my eyes but that didn't make any of it go away."

"What happened to her?" Bill asked.

Dorthy nodded and continued. "Ruphord had made it quite clear what happened to children or anyone for that matter that crossed him or made him unhappy. They ended up in the furnace, and that's exactly what he did with that little girl. I watched as he tossed her in like so-much trash. He picked up all her clothes and her pretty little black-buckled shoes, little white hat and coat and threw them in as well, but he kept the patchwork rabbit doll to torture Jack with for years after."

Gillian wiped at the streams pouring down her cheeks, holding her hand over her mouth. Even when she thought she knew the worst that could have possibly happened, what Dorthy described was almost more than she could bear. "And you didn't dare say anything or he would know you had witnessed him," Gillian choked on her own words.

"Ms. Gillian, I've spent the bulk of my entire life trying to forget that moment, along with all the other horrendous things I witnessed and lived through there, but never could. I have no idea how he found me, but after Mr. Hartfield contacted me about my time at the Stilles, and after some long hard thought…I realized something. I realized that life is a precious thing…that no matter how short on this planet, it only really exists if there's someone to love you and remember you when you're gone. And that little girl, that precious little life needed to be remembered, if for no other reason than for proof she existed. Ruphord tried to deny her very existence."

"So Jack had a little sister named Jillie," Bill restated.

"And Ruphord would deny that every time Jack would say anything, perpetuating the notion that Jack was simply crazy," Dorthy added.

"So Jillie is real and Mr. Carrots was her doll," Gillian summarized. The recordings were all beginning to make sense now. "But what about Jack?"

"Jack ended up in the box most times. Ruphord saw to that," Dorthy declared. "Everyone wondered how it was he lived being in that box so much of the time. We often swore we could hear him in those solid brick walls, but that would be crazy now wouldn't it?" Dorthy gave Bill a smirk.

Bill nodded. "Were you there when Ruphord was killed?"

Dorthy poured herself some more ice tea and swirled the ice cubes in the glass. "No. I would have enjoyed that, but I managed to successfully escape when I was about thirteen."

"Successfully? How many times did you try?" Gillian asked.

"I don't remember. Just that they would send the Sheriff and the dogs after me every time I tried. There was no allowing a little black girl to escape from the Stilles Asylum and embarrass them all. That wouldn't look good. But one day I finally got far enough away that they stopped searching. Took me three days to reach Tacoma. I managed to catch a freight train south and almost made it to Oregon, but was forced out by some hobos that decided they wanted me for their entertainment. I hid in a barn outside of Vancouver during a

146

fierce windstorm and was discovered by a farmer's wife. She was my angel on earth, my first real mother—Angie. Angie and Ralph Struasburg. They took me in, kept me safe and eventually adopted me, told all their friends and neighbors I was actually family from back east, and they never explained how I was black. She gave me my name, Dorthy, because of how she found me in the barn that day."

"Your name? You didn't have a name before?" Bill asked.

"I never knew my original name, or even if I ever had one before I arrived at the Stilles. While I was there, I was called by many names that I would rather not repeat, or remember until my true mother rescued me," Dorthy answered, staring off once more.

"That must have made for some interesting family conversations," Bill suggested.

"My mother never allowed those conversations to even start," Dorthy stated. "Eventually I graduated high school equivalency after being home-schooled, and met and married my late husband, Earl, in 1969. He worked at a shipping company on the Portland waterfront. Eventually became a manager and retired before he passed away six years ago. We had one daughter we named Angie, Jesse's mother, named in honor and memory of my mother. My daughter passed away two years ago from cancer. Jesse lives here with me now, and helps me around the house, but I know she and her fiancé will want to move on with their own lives soon enough. I'll likely move into a retirement home." Dorthy stared off toward her gardens again as though lost in her own thoughts.

Dorthy's words hung for everyone to reflect upon—a life story expressed in a matter of minutes, from tragedy to triumph. Gillian sat and wiped at tears, while she admired the woman's strength and endurance.

Bill broke the silence, "I'd like to thank you for your time, Dorthy. If you'd like I can make a copy of this interview for you to destroy or pass on to your granddaughter at your discretion."

Dorthy never looked back, but nodded. Gillian noted a tear track tracing down Dorthy's cheek when she and Bill stood to leave. Dorthy gave Gillian's hand a pat, when Gillian squeezed her shoulder. They thanked Jesse on their way to the car.

The ride home was a long, quiet reflection of the lives remembered that day.

***

Chapter 8
Hell's Portal

Gillian decided to give the Stilles Asylum investigation a few days break to try and remind herself why she had left Frederick, Massachusetts for a small town on the opposite coast. Port Latch was small but offered plenty for a detective to stay busy or for taking time off. Gillian decided on taking some time off to pick up all the photos and newspaper articles scattered around her house, placing them back in order, gathered in corresponding groups so the next person who desired to go through the case file and supporting evidence would have a clearer picture from the start.

After weeks of digging, she was no closer than Joe was four years earlier and was possibly worse off, as she now doubted her own belief structure. Science and logic had been tested to the limits, strained, twisted, crumpled and collapsed in a heap around her. She pulled up digital still-printouts taken from videos by Bill years earlier and just days ago. Shadow figures, faded images of apparitions, and other unexplained imagery that further clouded her judgment, shaking her faith of years of training. As much as she wanted to believe there was someone physically responsible for everything she had experienced, she was unable to back anything with evidence. Her own personal experiences did more to disprove her belief system as she glanced at the fading bruise around her ankle.

For some people a paradigm shift in belief might be considered a form of enlightenment, but for Gillian she felt pain and a twinge of terror. She was being forced to face the possibility that her worst nightmares were true. Life after death was not a fairy tale of passing through the pearly gates and living in eternal peace and tranquility. In fact, her deceased family might be living out eternity by the side of the road where they perished, in an afterlife of damnation no matter the lives lived of guilt or innocence.

From the mountain of documentation, affidavits, written and

recorded testimonies sitting in front of her, there appeared to be no relief or justice for the innocent. The Stilles Asylum had proven to be a prison of horrors for innocent children of all ages and mental and physical capacities; tortured, abused, beaten, starved, left for dead and outright murdered for hundreds of unfortunate residents. A horrible nightmare where only a few lived to escape. A travesty to be buried and in time forgotten by the living, and yet their voices and shadows remain behind in the dark recesses of an old building for all eternity. Hell on earth.

Gillian sat back on her couch wiping at the moisture on her cheeks, and laid her head back closing her eyes. She felt a sense of calm with the passing scent she long recognized as Daniel's cologne. Many times she thought the couch was in need of deep cleaning, because she often caught the scent of his cologne while sitting there. She took another deep breath through her nose in search of another chance of the scent, but now there was none. Still, she felt the familiar calm of reassurance she received in Daniel's arms so long ago. He always managed to know when Gillian needed assurance and clarity of thought and administered the required dose of hugs for the desired effect.

In that instant of calm collection, there was a moment of clarity. *How did Stacy get out through the coal-chute, if the box is welded shut?* Gillian sat up and glanced down at a photo sitting on her lap. The photo was a video capture from Jeffrie's assistant Dylan Roe's camera view moments before Jeffrie's murder. She could see from the light of Jeffrie's camera screen pointed forward, the corner of the metal box with the side door. The shot was grainy from the IR imagery but something wasn't lining up.

Gillian thumbed through several other still shots and found one from her video angle Bill had been so nice to print out for her of an establishing view of the furnace room and the coal box in full view. The metal box side door appeared to not be in the same place.

That must be an illusion, Gillian thought as she looked at Dylan's camera shot again much closer. His angle in the room appeared nearly identical but the picture size was different. Still the side door appeared to be in a different location, and there was an area that appeared to be darker than the surrounding sides of the box. The way the light from Jeffrie's camera glinted off the metal, the side door appeared to be slid just to one side.

Gillian thumbed through more crime scene photos and found another angle with Jeffrie's body and the box in view in the background. This time with full flash lighting the side door was appearing to be in the position that Gillian's video capture showed; closed, and closer to the front corner. She re-examined the video still from Dylan's camera view, but with her phone camera, and enlarged the view. The door was further away from the front side corner, and a darker area was exposed. "The side door slides open!"

Gillian hit Bill's number on speed-dial, but her phone started ringing with an incoming call, "Detective McClary," she answered without checking the number.

"Gillian, it's Bill. Got a moment? I've got news—"

"I was just trying to call you. The coal-box side door slides to the side. That's how Stacy got out through the coal-chute," Gillian blurted out.

"The coal-box side door? I was calling to tell you I just got the floor plans in today. That walled up basement door is an opening to a stairwell," Bill stated.

"Stairwell? Up to where?"

"Down!" Bill corrected. "Do you have time to—"

"I'll be right there!"

                                   ***

When Gillian walked into Bill's barn office she could see that both Bill and Charles had been busy rearranging the space. There was a large table in the middle of the room covered with antique-style structural drawings and more strategically placed on some of the walls.

Bill rushed over to meet Gillian at the door and guided her attention to the large table. "You've got to see this!"

"I have to show you this too," Gillian said pulling some of the photos out from her shoulder bag.

"Look," Bill pointed, too excited with his own finding to see what Gillian was holding.

Gillian could see he was pointing at a drawing of the first floor of the Stilles but something seemed off. "That's not right. That drawing is backward or something."

"Mirrored actually," Bill corrected. "This is the structural drawings for the Hamilton C. Hayward Garrison built in 1899 outside of Baltimore."

"Fort Hayward. I've heard of it, but I've never been there," Gillian marveled at how small the world often seemed.

"These are copies of the actual blueprints for that building that were taken from the prints for the Stilles built ten years earlier, and according to records, were 'mirrored' to better fit the topography. These blueprints are the closest I can find to the Stilles, because the Stilles' blueprints were apparently destroyed by water damage at some point. There were a few minor changes, including some additional floors, but indications from all the construction records show everything up to the fourth floor is identical...including—" Bill paused for dramatic suspense and turned toward the wall behind him and pointed. "The subbasement, or better identified as the garrisons' armory."

Charles was finished tacking down the corners and did his best 'gameshow display' gesture to accent Bill's introduction. "If you will take notice here on this other structural drawing, you can see the main basement level is identical to the Stilles, only in mirror image as well." Charles stated with the tone of a game show host. "And here is the location of the bricked up stairwell down to the lower level armory." Charles pointed to the location.

Gillian stepped up for a closer look. "How did you get your hands on these? This looks really old."

"Again, they are scans of the originals and this took several years of research and pestering the archive custodians to locate and finally get these sent out." Bill stepped up to the sub-basement drawings and pointed. "Check this out. Here is the cistern, clear down to this lower level. I often wondered why they would need a cistern that large inside the building...right?"

Gillian nodded, trying to follow along in Bill's excitement.

"It wasn't completely for building use, like the boilers for steam heat, or cooking, showers and toilets, but more for fire suppression in case of a fire in the armory," Bill's voice was pitching with exuberance. "Look here," he pointed again to another structural drawing back on the large table, pulling the large photocopy out from under the first floor drawings and sliding it on top. "Here is an elevation of the armory level—check out the distance between the lower level and the basement level. That's ten feet, and the storage vaults all have ten feet between them. That's all for blast protection and the open span down the middle of the building is steel-beam reinforced—absolutely incredible. And here on the cistern is a bank of fire water mains leading to the various vaults. That's all cutting-edge fire suppression for 1888."

Gillian looked back at the overhead view and pointed to something else she didn't recognize. "What's this? Looks like some kind of train tracks?"

Bill's excitement grew even further, "That is another new surprise. The 'Powder-Block' building out by the well-house was not anything like my previous research suggested, at least if I am to believe these drawings are exact duplicates of the Stilles. The storage was not under that building, but that was where supplies were delivered and brought out for distribution, keeping those activities safely and securely away from the main garrison. These drawings show an underground rail system for small railcarts, about three feet wide by about six to eight feet long, moved by a pulley system to and from the lower armory level. See here?" Bill pointed to a spot on the drawing. "Here is where the tunnel meets in the armory."

"So you're saying there may be another way in and out of the Stilles?" Gillian asked.

"Well, I don't know about that, actually. Maybe into the armory level, but the drawings show only the one passageway in or out through the bricked up door frame. The rail system passage was not designed for foot traffic," Bill said scratching at the back of his head as he glanced around at the different drawings.

"What about wetwalls? Is there any way to cross over into those? Maybe something Dorthy said was more true than crazy after all?" Gillian suggested.

"What do you mean?"

"She said they all thought Jack was in the walls. Maybe he actually was?"

"Well that's another interesting feature I noticed here. Remember all those chimneys all around the roof line on top of the building?" Bill asked, and Gillian nodded. "I often wondered about this. Did you ever see any fireplaces in the building?"

Gillian thought a moment, then shook her head slow in thought. "Now that you mention that, no."

"Right. The building was heated by steam radiators from the

boiler system. Turns out, most of those chimneys go straight to the armory level for ventilation, a few are wetwall ventilation for the rest of the building, but I haven't seen any place where they cross over. They all seem separate."

Gillian glanced around the room and shook her head. "We've got to do some more investigation inside the Stilles and that outbuilding," she said and handed Bill the photos.

"Oh right. The box side door? It slides, you say?" Bill asked as he looked over the photos.

"That's how the little girl got out of the building through the box," Gillian stated.

"Right, Stacy, the girl you mentioned."

"Did I mention her name? Crap!" Gillian scowled. "I hope I can trust in your confidence in keeping that between us?"

"Absolutely," Charles said holding his right hand up as though swearing on a bible in court. Bill nodded in agreement.

***

Gillian was always amazed at how well Bill knew his large collection of video and still photos from the Stilles Asylum. In a matter of minutes he had several dozen different versions of videos and photos from over the years that showed the metal box and the side door.

"I can't believe I never noticed that before," Bill said with disgust, shaking his head. "Without a doubt, I can see differences in the placement of that side door. And on this one," Bill pointed to a video shot on his large monitor, "an obvious dark area indicating an opening."

"I know what you mean. When we were down there, I looked at that side door and it looked solid, and well-connected to the rest of the box. I realize now what I was having some thoughts about, but couldn't put my finger on it at the time," Gillian said.

"What was that?" Charles asked.

"There were scrape marks on the floor close to the box, but not how one would expect if the door only opened outward. I blinded myself to believe the side door could only open in one way, instead of allowing the evidence to lead me to the actual conclusion," Gillian said shaking her head. "Poor detective work on my part."

"Don't beat yourself up too much," Charles consoled. "There was a lot going on at the time, and you blame yourself for far more than you should."

Gillian caught the look between Bill and Charles after his comment, and gave both a hard glance. "Is there something more here you're not telling me?"

Bill squirmed in his chair as Charles gave him a knowing glance.

"What?" Gillian asked.

Bill nodded to Charles. "Yeah, maybe now is as good a time as any?"

"What!" Gillian now demanded.

Charles cleared his throat and pulled his chair closer to Gillian at Bill's video desk. "I found out a few more things regarding my recent encounter at the Stilles," Charles paused a moment.

"Go on?" Gillian pressed.

"The angry old man that was pestering me. We were thinking he was talking about the little girl, Jack's sister. But so much of what I was getting was so jumbled at first. Eventually I managed to get some time with the entity, to get him to calm down. You see, sometimes an entity can come across as angry when they are really just frustrated or excited. In this case a little of both," Charles explained.

"I'm not following," Gillian said, feeling a bit frustrated.

"I started getting some different imagery from the entity, confectionery imagery, candies…specifically candy beans, along with a wheelchair and a pipe. Some entities will speak in feelings, emotions or imagery, and he was trying to show me something like pictures, and I found that every time I attempted to put it all together with Jack's sister at the Stilles, this old man grew more agitated. But when I brought up imagery of you, he kept giving me candy, beans, wheelchair and a gentleman's pipe," Charles continued. "I think this is all something meant for you, Ms. Gillian."

"Me? That would be impossible. Why me? I don't—" Gillian stopped and put her hand to her mouth, tears began welling up in her eyes.

"It's okay, Gillian. Only you can tell me what this all means," Charles prompted and took her other hand in his.

Gillian took a moment to clear her throat and wipe at her cheek. "Only two people ever called me Jillie; Daniel in private. I was his

155

'Little-Jillie.'"

"And the other?" Charles pressed.

"Daniel's grandfather, Walter. He overheard Daniel calling me Jillie at our wedding. He always called me Daniel's Jillie-bean after that. It was a loving play off the candy; always saying I was so sweet. Right up to the last time I ever saw him alive...right after Kristin was born."

"Can you tell me a little more about Walter?" Charles asked.

Gillian nodded. "Everyone thought of him as a grumpy old man, hard of hearing, but I could tell he heard people just fine, and I think he knew I was onto his game; he just liked to annoy people. I'm not really sure just how much he really needed the wheelchair either. It was our little secret," Gillian started to smile then gasped again. "I just realized, he always carried a very ornate pipe inside his sweater or coat pocket, but I never saw him smoke; he wasn't allowed. He was usually on his oxygen."

"I believe we can say we know now who this message has been for," Charles said.

"What message? I don't understand? Why now?" Gillian asked.

Charles paused a moment. "I think he's been trying to give you this message for a very long time, but hasn't been able to get through. At least until I came along. Remember when I said I often attract entities because I can sense them? He attached himself to me the moment we met."

"So what is the message? I don't understand," Gillian asked again.

Charles looked hard at Gillian. "Stop. Stop blaming yourself. This is not your fault. You did not kill your family."

Gillian's eyes began to burn, barely able to keep them open, nor stop the tears rolling down her cheeks.

"He says, I've got them. He got them, Jillie-bean. He got your family. He was there to guide them to a better place," Charles continued. "They're not stuck alongside of that road. The only one reliving that horrible event that night is—you."

Gillian put her head down and began to openly weep, and both Charles and Bill put their arms on her shoulders to console her as best they could, handing her a tissue.

"His continued message is, I'm coming for you when your time comes. They'll all be waiting for you at that appointed time," Charles spoke soft and reassuring. "This grumpy old man in a wheelchair and pipe calling you Jillie-bean has been desperately trying to tell you for years to stop blaming yourself. He's been desperately trying to get you out of that dark place you've been hiding in. Also, that they all are often checking in on you, but you haven't been willing to believe your own senses."

Gillian looked up wiping at her eyes, "I don't understand. How am I not believing my senses?"

Bill took Gillian's hand, "Often a spirit entity can be sensed by many different factors. Sometimes something from the corner of your eye, a shadow, or a familiar smell, sometimes—"

"Smell?" Gillian interrupted. "The other night when I came home I thought I smelled tobacco like a pipe, but I just thought it was something coming from the house, a previous tenant. I would have never thought it to be Walter's pipe, I never saw him smoke it, let alone smelled it. Sometimes I can smell Daniel's cologne, but I've always just thought that was simply permeated within the couch cushions after all the years."

"Do you feel comfort in those experiences?" Charles asked.

"Well I thought Daniel's cologne bottle might have broken in the box sitting in the living room once. I was comforted to find out the bottle wasn't broken, but yes, I do feel a sense of comfort," Gillian admitted.

"I would suggest that Daniel may be visiting on some of those occasions," Bill offered.

"What about Kristin? I miss her so much too. I've never felt or seen anything from her?" Gillian said. Again she noted a glance between Bill and Charles. "What?"

Bill turned to his computer console and pulled up a file, "Remember that day we first met at the Stilles and I uploaded the Jeffrie Trace files?"

Gillian nodded, "When we discovered the body down the well."

"Exactly, remember I set up the digital audio recorder. I picked something up on the recorder. I wasn't sure if I should have you hear this, but Charles thinks you should," Bill said and clicked on the audio file:

The file started with some hissing then, *"I didn't realize we're going to be officially on the record here today?"* Gillian could be heard saying.

"Oh no. That's not for us. That's to capture any EVP's while we're

out here. I've had a few in the past out here where I wasn't expecting any activity, and found them quite by accident. Again, I want to take advantage of my time here. " Bill could be heard saying.

"Well I enjoy having lunch here, " Gillian could be heard saying, then another voice was heard in the background. It sounded like a child but was unintelligible.

Bill paused the file, then clicked on another file, "this is the cleaned up and enhanced version."

Bill ran the file: it started with very loud background hissing, then a child's voice, like a little girl, *"I like sitting here with you, Mommy."*

Gillian's eyes grew wide. That was a voice she knew oh too well, and one that she thought she would never hear again for the rest of her life. There was no mistaking that little girls voice, the Maryland accent, intonation, everything about it was, "Kristin!" Gillian burst into tears once more.

Charles gave Gillian a few moments, "They've all been reaching out to you, but you've been buried deep in a dark place of guilt and blame. It took the stubborn tenacity of a grumpy old man to finally get through. He wasn't going to let me alone until I figured this out."

Gillian half chuckled through her sobs in agreement, "That's Walter." She stood up, took a deep breath and walked out the door. Startled, Bill started to follow but Charles gestured to stop, "Give her a moment, and let me?"

Bill nodded.

After a few moments Charles stepped outside to find Gillian standing at the fence overlooking the training arena staring out across the large grassy area, and stepped alongside without a word.

After a few more moments Gillian turned, "Thank you."

"You're welcome. I'm thinking your psychologist friend would say this was a serious breakthrough moment, don't you agree?" Charles offered.

Gillian smiled and shook her head. "I don't have a psychologist friend. She's just—"

"I know," Charles interrupted. "I saw who she was the moment we met. Sometimes our best counsel comes from within."

"Yes, but sometimes it's good to open up to those around you on the outside looking in too. Something I don't believe I have ever allowed since that day."

Charles nodded, gazing out across the training arena. "Even from beyond."

***

Monday, July 15th, 2019

Gillian thought she was early enough that next morning to be first to arrive at the Stilles Asylum, but Bill and Charles were already standing by the Powder-Block building as she pulled up to park. She grabbed a couple of strong LED flashlights and a new dust mask. She dressed for the occasion in her old hiking clothes and shoes, expecting to be rummaging around in very dirty places, and could see that Bill and Charles had done the same in old worn jeans and long sleeved shirts. Charles looked particularly ready for action in his overalls and ball-cap.

"Morning," Charles greeted with a wide smile.

"Morning," Gillian answered. "Getting an early start?"

Bill fidgeted with the door latch. "I don't think this thing is actually locked. Are we allowed inside?"

Gillian stepped up to see, "I'm here now if there are any questions of permission. Besides, Trent and the facility guys are on their way with the keys, so we've got a few minutes to look around here before we check on the coal box side door."

Bill opened the large barn-style door and stepped in. "Great. From what I see, nothing has changed." Besides light coming from the large door there were only splashes of light coming through upper non-boarded windows and he took his LED and shined around the darker spaces covered with various boxes of junk and broken furniture. Stepping closer to the middle of the building, he pointed his LED to the floor. "Here's where they filled in the storage access, or at least that's what I was told. This should be access to a loading area, see?" Bill pointed his LED up above to show the remnants of a block and tackle system for lifting heavy loads.

Gillian and Charles continued to roam around the space, when she noticed some dark smudging on the concrete flooring and led under a table piled with junk around it. "That seems out of place," she commented.

Charles took little effort to slide the table back a bit to expose an

159

opening in the floor, partially covered by the remnants of a large wooden door. He leaned over the opening and aimed his LED straight down. "That goes a long way down."

Gillian leaned over and shined her light down too. "Looks like metal ladder rungs on the side there leading down."

Bill stepped up and peered down as well. "I've never seen this before."

"That dark smudge on the floor…" Gillian began.

"Looks like coal dust residue, "Bill answered.

Charles pulled the wooden door out of the way exposing more of the opening and the space below. About twenty feet down, they could see several old-style broken and emptied wooden crates, and a set of rails with a small railcart. sitting sideways to the tracks in a small room about twenty feet square. The tracks led off toward the Stilles' main facility through an opening in the wall below that was not much larger than the railcart. The part of the floor that was sealed appeared to be the original loading and unloading access opening, and the smaller side access appeared to be for climbing in and out of the space via the metal rung ladder on the inner space wall.

Gillian then realized a change in the breeze coming from the opening, and an awful smell as though something had died. "That's interesting." She backed away, waving the air from her face.

"Probably a dead raccoon, dog or something. I really can't imagine anything else that could have fit through that first opening. Probably fell in, unable to climb out and died from starvation or something," Bill suggested.

"So this leads to the lower level below the basement over there," Gillian said and pointed toward the main facility.

Bill pulled out his cellphone and opened up a photo folder. "I have pictures of those drawings. See, here are the blueprints for this building and the connection to the Stilles."

"That's got to be two hundred-fifty to maybe three hundred feet. Do you think that's still a viable shaft open all the way?" Gillian asked.

Bill shrugged. "Hard to say. They built this place like—well, like a fort."

"Go figure," Charles' deep voice rumbled when he chuckled.

Gillian stepped back toward the main door opening. "Trent and the facilities guys just pulled up. Let's check that coal-box side door."

***

Trent handed Gillian keys to the facility locks. "I brought a pole to prop up the door on the coal chute outside here like we discussed last night and some really strong LED lights too."

"Great, I'll call you on the radio when we get down into place," Gillian said on her way to unlock the fence.

"I still don't think that little girl could have lifted that heavy lid by herself," Trent added, shaking his head.

"The answer is in there somewhere," Gillian said as she led the way to the back door with Bill and Charles in tow. She made quick work of the lock and got the doors open without delay, mask on and LED shining down the hall. Gillian was on a mission and was not about to be intimidated by any noises or other distractions.

Charles was fighting to keep up with Gillian as she dashed for the staircase to the basement, but he caught up with her at the top of the landing. "Ms. Gillian, please. Let me take the lead down."

Gillian could see the concern in his eyes and Bill too. "Okay, but I have one goal today. I want to know how that little girl got out through that coal chute. I need to see that side door."

"I understand. I'll get us down there. I just want us all to be safe. We all know what has and can happen down there." Charles took the lead down the stairs with cautious steps.

"We're not here to scare anyone, "Bill called out as a precaution. "We're just trying to understand some things."

Charles was quick with his LED to scan the bottom of the stairs and the short corridor to the right, then continued to the left to the main cross hall. Again he scanned around the corner to the right before turning to the left to lead on to the furnace room on the right.

"GET. OUT."

They all paused and glanced at each other. "I heard that clear," Gillian whispered. "We keep going."

"We are not hear to hurt anyone or scare anyone," Bill called out once more.

Charles reached the furnace room and set out a large LED

161

portable floodlight, filling the room with light as Gillian and Bill entered.

They all gasped and turned at the sound of something metallic clanging on the floor just past the coal box, and Bill set up another LED portable flood light, pointing to a tin can still rolling across the floor.

"We're not here to scare you, or hurt you. We just need some answers," Gillian called out, as she knelt down by the coal box side door for an examination.

The door had all the appearances of being well-connected to the cast iron box at the hinges for the door. A small rough-cut hole allowed a couple fingers inside for a grip and Gillian to slide it aside revealing a narrow opening.

Gillian shined her LED but had a limited view. She started to examine the top and Charles took her queue and used a pry bar under the welded metal and padlock. After a few tries the lid was freed and Bill and Charles lifted it up and propped it open.

Gillian knelt down and pointed her light to the back of the box. She could see a sliver of daylight from the opening above in the back. She pulled her radio from her belt and called out, "Trent. We're in, can you shine your light down?"

"Copy that," Trent's voice crackled. A shaft of brilliant light filtered down to the back of the box, and for a moment Gillian thought she saw movement.

"I just saw something moving, was that you?" Trent's voice called over the radio.

Gillian was trying to reposition herself for a better view squatted down, and heard something crunching under her feet. Bill and Charles shined their lights and they were all taken aback to see the floor littered with small animal bones as well as a thick layer of coal dust and dirt.

"Uh, negative. I think I saw that too," Gillian answered back on the radio.

"Could be a raccoon or other animal," Bill offered, pointing at all the bones. "I'd be real careful. They can carry rabies."

"Well, if it was an animal, it went somewhere back in that corner. I've got to see," Gillian argued.

"Please, Ms. Gillian. Let me," Charles said.

"This is my investigation now. I can see this is exactly how Stacy got out of here. I just need to figure out how," Gillian answered.

"Gillian, we're all in this together now. We can help," Bill pleaded.

"JILLIE!"

They all stopped and looked off in different directions.

"I heard that loud and clear," Gillian said pointing her LED toward the back of the coal box.

"Me too, but that sounded like it was coming from behind me," Bill said, shining his light toward the back corner of the furnace room.

"I heard it from behind me," Charles turned towards the door to the hall.

Gillian stayed close to the floor and scooted back to where she thought she had heard the voice. Even with her light everything seemed dark, covered in black muck or coal dust. Remnants of the coal that had been deposited over the years still remained toward the back of the chute and down in a hole in the floor. Portions of the brick had crumbled. The hole was barely more than eighteen to twenty-four inches wide. "There's definitely a hole in the floor," Gillian reported.

"Definitely be careful of critters," Bill pressed. "Don't get bit."

Gillian got close enough to peek up the chute, and waved her hand out for Trent to see.

"I'm seeing your hand now," Trent called hollered down.

"Copy that," Gillian replied, then turned toward the hole. There were sounds coming from the small opening. Scuffling, shuffling and something that sounded like voices again. Gillian could feel the hairs on her arm and back of her neck standing straight out.

Bill and Charles watched. "Everything all right?" Charles asked.

"I'm hearing sounds and what seems like voices. Are you getting anything? Feelings? Anyone reaching out to you?"

"Yes, but they don't seem to be making a whole lot of sense," Charles answered.

"What do you mean?" Bill asked.

"Well, Walter has been back pestering me again. Seems very anxious. Keeps repeating for Jillie-bean to 'stop.' But I thought we went through all this messaging already. Walter keeps saying, 'he's broken, fractured, dangerous.'"

"He who?" Gillian pressed.

163

"Not clear, but I just got this very strong in my face by Walter, 'STOP, they're not like the others.'"

Gillian scooted back from the back of the box and stood to exit the side door opening. "Well, that doesn't seem very helpful."

"He's pretty insistent," Charles affirmed.

"Well, what seems obvious to me now, is we need to get down to the lower level. Something's down there."

"You think there's something more than just an animal?" Bill asked.

"I have to know. Shadows, animals either one, I need to put this all to rest," Gillian argued pulling out her radio. "Trent, did we ever get that asbestos report?"

"Roger that. The basement was all cleared of asbestos from the last report done back in 1993—only the pipe insulation wrappings had asbestos. Upstairs the asbestos was reported in the flooring, ceiling tiles and again pipe and wall insulation," Trent responded over the radio.

"Copy that. How soon can we have the guys come down and open up that doorway to the lower level?" Gillian asked then waited a rather long unexpected pause. "Trent? Did you copy my last?"

"Uh, I copied." Trent paused again. "That is going to be an issue."

"I'm not sure I copy that," Gillian replied.

"Yeah well, the guys don't want to go into the facility, let alone go down to the basement," Trent answered.

"I guess I'm no longer their 'favorite?'"

"No…they just don't want to find any more dead bodies," Trent answered.

"Tell them I promise no more bodies."

"No good. They're shaking their heads, and—now they're getting in their truck," Trent said as the radio crackle paused again. "And— leaving. They are actually driving away, and—waving."

Gillian turned to Bill and Charles. "Looks like it's up to us."

Charles pulled the long pry-bar and lowered the coal-box lid. "Shouldn't take too long," he said with a grin holding the pry-bar up.

Gillian held up the radio. "Roger that, we're heading to the door now, we'll take care of it ourselves."

"Are you sure about this?" Trent asked.

"Roger that, we're sure. We'll stay close on radio," Gillian replied.

"Roger that, standing by."

***

Bill set up a couple LED flood lights for the hall and part of the large room, while Charles and Gillian were examining the exposed brick inside the metal door frame. Charles raised the pry bar and Gillian shook her head while pulling at a brick. The mortar was brittle and loose and the brick fell to the floor. Charles gestured her to step back as he gripped the wall's opening and pulled. A large chunk of the wall tumbled forward and other pieces fell back into the cavity with a loud echoing of thuds and crashes.

The sudden change in air pressure pulled the dust into the cavity as more pieces of the wall continued to fall away and drop to the floor. Charles took the pry bar and cleared the remaining chunks around the metal door frame, and swept at the pieces on the floor with his large boots to clear a path.

Gillian took her LED to illuminate the cavity—a landing with a couple feet to the right leading toward the west boundary basement wall, and to the left a couple feet to steps leading down. The steps and landing were made up of a combination of natural and cut stone, reminding Gillian of an ancient castle.

"Like some kind of portal to hell," Bill suggested.

"Ms. Gillian, please," Charles asked and Gillian allowed Charles to take the lead down the steps, sweeping aside the thick spider webs.

"Pholcus phalangioides, or Cellar Spiders. Common in western Washington outbuildings, basements, under outdoor furniture or other undisturbed areas where they build tangled webs. Basically harmless," Bill announced as he grabbed one of the LED floods and followed from behind with the light up over their heads.

"We just called them daddy long-legs, back east," Gillian said.

"Well they still creep me out," Charles complained.

The staircase was about four feet wide and fairly steep. Charles reached the bottom and made a quick sweep with his flashlight then made room for Gillian and Bill. "Be mindful of the awful—"

"Oh MY GOD, THAT SMELL," Bill choked out, trying not to breathe or puke. His voice reverberated from all around like an echo chamber.

165

Gillian was familiar with this type of odor; death and decayed flesh, but still had a hard time keeping her composure.

Charles took a portable LED flood light and set it on a ledge in the wall at the end of the staircase lighting up a large portion of that area. The ceiling was arched rough-cut stone work down to the walls, where two rows of large arched storage areas on either side of a long, wide aisle that seemed to disappear into the darkness.

Charles glanced around the end of the staircase wall to the left to see stack of broken wooden crates and an old turn-of-the-last-century hand cart.

Gillian turned to the right with her light to see around the staircase wall on the other side. "There's the railcart system."

Bill stepped out around her and the corner, his footsteps sounded like he was walking on fall leaves and brittle twigs. "Just like the drawings showed. See? There's the loading and unloading wench and block-tackle overhead, along with the wench and cable system to pull the railcarts back and forth from the outbuilding." Bill walked over and aimed his light into the tunnel. The light seemed to be swallowed up by the darkness in the depths of the tunnel. "And surprisingly devoid of webs."

"Watch your steps." Gillian pointed to the floor with her flashlight. The floor was covered in animal bones and a dark black muck.

"Looks to be small animals, rats, squirrels, maybe some cats and dogs," Charles suggested, pointing his flashlight at some larger animal skulls on a pile of bones. Every word and sound echoed throughout the space.

"But all scattered, not together. These animals have been eaten and the bones scattered," Gillian said, tracing her flashlight around the floor.

"Well I guess that explains the smell." Bill worked his way along one side of the long arched hall. He stepped up to the first arched wall with a metal door and tried the latch, but the door would not budge; however, there was an inspection hatch that opened and Bill shined his light inside.

"Bill be careful, I'm sensing them again. The guards, they're not happy with your approach to that door," Charles warned.

Bill turned from the door, eyes wide. "They're not all animal bones."

"I get it now. They're guarding HIM. That's Ruphord!" Charles exclaimed.

Gillian and Charles walked with care to the door and peered inside. In the center of the very long arched storage vault was a wooden crate and sitting on top was a human skull with a single twisted upper front tooth.

"That explains that part of the mystery," Gillian said softly to keep the echoing to a minimum.

Charles took his time examining the situation inside the vault. "There are three guards posted around the skull. They are keeping Ruphord here in that place. They are punishing him," Charles explained, then turned to look at the railcart tunnel. "And that's why the spirit at the well house is scared and hiding out there. He is afraid he will be punished too." Charles turned and closed the inspection window. "We should not disturb them; this is sacred grounds to them."

"Well I'm not certain that will be possible. We've found human remains...that makes this a crime scene," Gillian explained.

"From 1966, isn't there a time limit or something, or maybe location related? Inside there, right? We're still allowed out here with you right?" Bill asked. He wasn't ready to be pushed out of this new discovery at the Stilles Asylum—this never-before-seen space below the basement.

Gillian shined her light around the long room again. There were several more vaults still open where the doors were gone. "I suppose we can continue to search, since we haven't technically disturbed anything inside that room. I'm still looking for whatever came down here through that opening in the coal box."

"Okay, that's what I'm talking about," Bill said, trying not to sound too excited, since there were human remains discovered just inside the one vault.

Gillian walked down the middle of the main hall trying to get her bright LED flashlight to shine to the far end but the light seemed to be engulfed by the darkness of the space. Charles and Bill took opposite sides looking into the storage vaults. They were all roughly eight feet tall, arched and about as wide, thirty feet deep and roughly ten feet between arches.

Charles stepped a few feet into one then called, "Ms. Gillian."

"Find something?" Gillian stepped up to the entrance. She could see something against the back wall of the vault that Charles was lighting up with his flashlight.

"Another someone," Charles' deep voice echoed out of the vault.

Gillian and Bill approached to see a skeleton wearing a military style jacket with peace symbol patches. The body appeared to be broken and chopped into several places with blood stains all over, and then put back together in a seated position against the wall, the skull balanced on top.

"I recognize the patch on the shoulder; Army 5th Special Forces Group Airborne; Vietnam era between 1964 to 1971," Charles explained.

"J Billings," Gillian read off the name tag on the jacket. "He's on my list of missing." All three stood and stared a few moments in silent reverence.

"I'm sorry, gentlemen. There's no way around this now, I have to follow protocol and officially call this an active crime scene. You will need to leave," Gillian explained and pulled out her radio. "Trent, do you copy?"

"Trent here, I copy."

"We have human remains down here in this lower level."

***

Chapter 9
Monsters in the Dark

Trent stood on the lower stone floor, adjusting his mask which didn't stop the horrendously putrid smell of death and decay. Taking shallow breathes through his mouth, he held on as best he could and approached Gillian. "At least it's cooler down here."

Deputy Burelli followed, losing his late morning coffee into his mask, and pulling the mess away from his face in embarrassment.

"Try not to breathe too much through your nose," Gillian suggested.

"The Sheriff's office is sending a deputy over shortly, same with the State Police. They didn't sound to be in much of a hurry though," Trent reported.

"The M.E?" Gillian asked.

"Tony is up in Pouslbo on another case. He'll be here as soon as possible. So—what have you found?" Trent shone his flashlight around the cavernous space.

"We've likely found Ruphord's remains in that closed vault." Gillian pointed her flashlight on the closed door. "And possible remains of J. Billings, one of the original missing cases over in that vault." Gillian moved her flashlight to the second vault.

"Chief, where do you want me to put these portable LEDs?" Burelli asked, holding his hand over his mouth.

Trent shook his head. "Deputy, it's bad down here, but pull yourself together and place them around here for now, okay? Also make sure your body cam's on."

Burelli nodded and positioned a portable LED flood light but it barely illuminated the gruesome animal bones covering the stone floor.

"Are we allowed to continue the search or do we wait?" Gillian asked.

"This is our jurisdiction, our case until some other higher agency says otherwise," Trent replied. "Do you believe there's someone else down here?"

"Well, we both saw some movement at the coal chute. I haven't been able to identify what that could have been, so I'm not sure if we're talking a who or a what yet," Gillian said.

"Roger that. Deputy—be on alert, we're going to check all spaces for someone or something alive down here," Trent ordered.

"Alive—down here?" Deputy Burelli shook his head in disbelief.

The sound of crunching and cracking animal bones echoed with every step as they approached the next vault shining their flashlights all around. Deputy Burelli took a couple cautious steps inside then paused. "I've got clothing and—yes, a human skull, and torso skeletal remains, uh—possibly two."

Gillian stepped across the long hall to the vault directly across and shined her light inside the open door. "Two—no three bodies, maybe more, but I definitely count three skulls in here," she replied coldly. She was trying to keep calm although every hair on her body was now standing straight out. There were seventeen cases of missing people that had been loosely blamed on the Stilles Asylum facility, but never any evidence—until now.

Trent stepped over to the next vault down the row and peered inside with his flashlight. "This is just weird, four more partially clothed skeletal remains propped up against the sides of the vault." Trent whispered, trying to avoid the obnoxious echoes.

"Clothing era, is it antique or modern?" Gillian asked.

Trent turned back for another glance, "Oh yeah, that's too modern, looks late nineteen-sixties, seventies maybe."

Although they were getting closer to the far end of the long hall, and what should be the bottom half of the cistern, Gillian noted everything was still dark and foreboding with no discernible details. "We're going to have to do a complete full-on forensic investigation of this entire space, but for now let's see if we can get a preliminary body count." Gillian continued to the next vault before pausing. She once more aimed her flashlight towards the far end. "Did you hear that?"

Trent turned to Deputy Burelli and motioned him to set another floodlight which again did little to improve the view of the space.

"It's like some horror movie dungeon scene," Burelli said under his breath.

"I think I heard something moving, is that what you heard?" Trent asked.

Gillian nodded as she continued on to the next vault. "This is incredible. Four, maybe more skeletal remains all propped up along the sides."

"This is beginning to remind me of the catacombs of Paris, with all the bodies we're finding down here." Trent shook his head with disbelief.

"Two more here," Deputy Burelli announced before moving on to the next vault.

Trent leapfrogged on to the next one past Deputy Burelli. "Looks like three more here."

Gillian moved onto the next vault on her side of the hall. All the bones on the floor were blackening, as were the floor and walls. She wiped her finger across a stone and it came away covered in black dust. "Coal dust," she announced.

"Hey, how many cases of missing people from here do you have?" Deputy Burelli asked."

"Seventeen, why?" Gillian wondered.

"I've been keeping count and so far we've found nineteen bodies," Deputy Burelli answered.

Gillian scowled. "That can't be right, are you sure?"

Deputy Burelli checked the running tab on his cellphone. "Nineteen…that's not counting that first one you said was Ruphord."

The air felt just a little colder across Gillian's neck at the probability of more victims than known cases. She glanced around at the gruesome shadows and turned to the cistern at the end of the long hall then shone her light inside the last vault. At the far end was a large black pile of crushed coal and fallen stonework that reached clear to the upper left ceiling edge, across the entire backside and spread out on the floor out to the vault entrance. There was a hole in the back left ceiling. "The other end of the hole from the coal chute above," Gillian surmised. She stepped inside the vault to get a closer look into the hole, but could not get close enough without climbing up on the coal and stone debris pile.

Trent followed close behind. "Looks like that pile of coal and stone is nearly solid from years of damp conditions." He kicked at some coal and only a few pieces came loose.

"Okay, so something could crawl in and out through that hole into the coal box above. Some of the mystery is coming clear now," Gillian said.

"A small to medium-sized child could crawl through that opening, animals for sure, what are you thinking?" Trent asked.

"Hey guys, I keep hearing noises out here," Deputy Burelli called out from the vault doorway.

Gillian and Trent walked out of the vault and listened, shining their flashlights at the cistern. The stonework could be seen but covered in a thick layer of black coal dust, causing the light to appear to be absorbed with no reflections. "Gillian this is your call now. I don't see anything living down here. We've been hearing noises, but this whole lower level is nothing but an echo chamber of odd noises," Trent said.

Gillian shook her head. "I don't know anymore. I've spent the last several weeks chasing something that only appears to be dark shadows, with no substance."

"Sure, but one of those shadows left you with a sore spot and bruise on your ankle," Trent argued. "That's got to be something."

"LEAVE," a voice echoed into the cavernous hall.

Gillian's heart leaped straight to her throat and she felt as though an electrical current dashed across her back. "Did you—"

Trent's eyes were wide. "YES."

The distinct sound of metal striking stone echoed into the cavernous hall without warning. "GET. OUT," the unseen voice echoed from what appeared to be from all directions.

Deputy Burelli, pulled the safety strap off his service weapon and hovered his hand over the top while he leaned over and set out another small floodlight which only seemed to aggravate the odd shadows.

"Steady, Deputy," Trent ordered with a reassuring glance.

Gillian examined the cistern while standing a few feet away. There were odd shadows in the dusty blackness but no apparent place to hide. "We're officers from the Port Latch Police Department. We're not here to hurt you. We're here to help you," she called out, then listened, taking a step closer.

"Gillian, I don't think you should—" Trent warned as something metallic struck stone and echoed, repeating rhythmically every few seconds.

Gillian rubbed at the raised hairs on her arm and could see even through their masks from the others' expressions that they were feeling the same.

"Jillie?" A frail voice called out from somewhere. The echoes bounced from all directions.

"NO! They do not belong here," the first unseen voice argued.

"My name is Gillian. This is Chief Johnson and Deputy Burelli. Please come out. We're here to help—"

"JILLIE! I found Mr. Carrots for you," the frail voice echoed out from a distance.

Trent leaned toward Gillian and whispered, "Does any of this make any sense to you?"

Gillian whispered, "Yes, this absolutely does now." She turned toward the cistern. "Jack, it's time to come out now. Time to leave this place. Please come out," her voice echoed into the darkness with no response.

"Is this a ghost or someone for real?" Deputy Burelli asked trying to understand what was happening.

Gillian shook her head. "I honestly don't know anymore, but I'm going to try to help whoever or whatever is here. I just need them to come out so we can be sure what we're dealing with."

"The only way I know to get the legendary Jack to come out is by saying—" Deputy Burelli offered.

"No. That is an awful trigger," Gillian interrupted. "That would be aggressive. I don't want to show aggression."

They waited for any response but only heard the occasional tap of metal on stone. After several minutes of listening, Trent leaned toward Gillian. "You know it may be the only way to get him out here, ghost or not."

Gillian shook her head again. "Please, Jack, Tommy, whoever is here with us. Please come out. We just want to help you," Gillian pleaded and again waited for several minutes. Her mind raced reviewing her negotiation skills for people in distress, showing signs of PTSD or suicidal to make sure she wasn't missing anything.

Gillian turned to Trent and Deputy Burelli standing a few feet back from her. "All right, but I will say the rhyme. Maybe if I recite it nicely he'll simply come out. Just don't act aggressive."

Trent nodded and glanced at Deputy Burelli to assure him as well. "No aggression here."

Gillian stared at the black dusty cistern wall. "Jack, please come out? Jack? Jack-in-the-box, shut up tight. Down in the dark, without any light. Jack-in-the-box, oh so still. Won't you come out—"

"Yes. I. Will," the growl of an angry voice echoed from all directions, followed by another distinct louder clang of metal on stone.

From the left side of the cistern, a black shadow figure stepped from the darkness with only the sound of metal dragging across stone.

Deputy Burelli instinctively squared up and pulled his service weapon to a safe ready. Trent unlocked his service weapon and laid his hand across the top at the ready.

Gillian held her hand out back toward them. "Don't move. Steady."

The black shadow figure took another ragged step into the light. Gillian could see a short figure, adolescent in size but with bare feet that seemed too large, and his left hand was out of proportion as well, and seemed larger than it should. His right hand was behind his back. He was wearing torn and tattered pants that only came down to just below the knees, and a torn and tattered shirt with no sleeves. Everything was absolutely covered in pitch black coal dust and muck, from the sparse hair on his head, to his spindly arms and legs, down to his bare feet. Only his blood-shot eyes seemed to glow from the surrounding blackness.

When the figure looked at Gillian his gaunt features changed from childlike to strained anger, with the same intense glare from her earlier encounter. She felt as though electricity was shooting across her shoulders and down her spine. She drew in a long, deep breath in an attempt to calm herself.

"You don't belong here," the figure spoke with an intense fierceness, his glare jumping back and forth from Gillian to the two other men.

"I just want to help you," Gillian offered.

"You are scaring him," the figure continued, and with a slow deliberate motion pulled his right hand around from behind his back with the sound of a metal fire axe dragging across the stone. Upon sight of the axe Trent and Deputy Burelli pulled their service weapons to bear, along with their flashlights shining directing into the face of the dark figure.

"No, don't shoot," Gillian ordered. "Lower your weapons and

174

lights, you're hurting his eyes." Gillian could see the figure squinting in pain from the bright flashlights.

"That's the missing murder weapon, Gillian. You know how fast he is with that—" Trent announced.

"I understand," Gillian interrupted, concentrating on the dark figure.

"Jillie? I have Mr. Carrots for you," the figure's features changed again to childlike and he pulled a ragged piece of cloth from a pocket and held it out toward Gillian. She could see what appeared to be an old patchwork doll with long ears and little stuffing, covered in black coal dust.

"NO! THEY LIE!" The figure's features changed in an instant back to a fierce glare toward Deputy Burelli and Trent. "YOU. ARE. SCARING. HIM," the figure growled.

Gillian was starting to recognize the personalities. "No Tommy. We're here to help you. We want to help you," Gillian said with a soft and assuring tone. "It's time to leave this place. We can help you. Just put the axe down." Gillian took another cautious step forward but stopped short when the figure snapped his glare back to her.

"You. Cannot. Help," the figure argued, but his tone had softened. "You do not belong. HERE."

"Neither do you now. It's time to leave. Let me help you. Please, Tommy, let me speak to Jack," Gillian pleaded her case.

The man's features softened, "Jillie?"

"My name is Gillian—"

"My name—is Jack Thomp—. My name is Jack Thom—," he repeated, but Gillian could see he was struggling with the words. "I am six years old and my sister Jillie is four. My mommy said— Mommy told me she will be back—to, back to take me—she promised—my name is Jack," the man tried again, as his eyes appeared to show a look of confusion and pain.

Trent and Deputy Burelli watched only one thing during Gillian's exchanges. Each time the voice was fierce and angry, the axe head rose off the floor a few inches, and when the voice was childlike, the axe lowered back down.

"Gillian, watch the axe," Trent whispered.

"JILLIE!" The figure's features softened. "Jillie I have Mr. Carrots."

"NO! NOT JILLIE," the voice and facial features changed back, anger glaring from his eyes and the axe rising.

"Please, Tommy. I only want to help you and Jack. Please put the axe down. Nobody wants to hurt you or scare Jack." Gillian took another step closer. "Hand me the axe."

Trent and Deputy Burelli both tensed up but attempted to remain calm. All three noticed his face looked old and more gaunt, his eyes fading in fierceness and sinking deeper into the sockets. His expression changed to that of frightened confusion.

"Who are—you?" His frail voice sounded ancient, labored and cracked.

Gillian felt off guard for a moment. There was another entity in this fractured person.

"Who's that?" Trent whispered.

She shook her head, "I'm not sure. This is definitely a clear case of dissociative identity disorder. We're talking to at least three different personalities now."

"Can you—help me?" the figure gasped with the frail tone of a dying old man.

"Yes. I'm here. We're all here to help you. Please put the axe down," Gillian asked.

The frail figure looked at Gillian with confusion, shaking his head, "I don't understand."

"I'm here to help you. You can leave this awful place now, but you need to trust me," Gillian continued to plead.

The man shook his head, "I belong—here. I didn't—I didn't protect. I didn't protect—Jillie. I—I have Mr. Carrots now—for Jillie," the man spoke in a labored hush. Gillian could see from the flashlight's glow a glint on the tracks of tears now running down his blackened cheeks as his face changed to that of deep, tormented pain. "My fault—the furnace—all my—fault."

Gillian's mind was racing. These three personalities appeared to be all fractures of the one, and this last one seemed to be corroborating Dorthy's story. Jillie was killed and thrown in the furnace while Jack helplessly watched from the hole in the side of the coal-box. Gillian felt a queasy pain in her gut.

The figure's features changed again, his glaring eyes darting from Gillian to the officers and back. "YOU. ARE. HURTING. HIM! I. PROTECT!"

176

"Yes. Yes you do, Tommy. You have for many years. You need to let go now… I'm here to protect you and everyone else now. You can trust me. You need to believe me—I want to help you." Gillian half-stepped with her hands out, palms up to help give more assurance. She could see the axe lowering, the man's facial features were softening. If she could only reach him through dialog and get him to drop the axe, but Gillian could not help but feel she was running out of time. She watched his eyes darting back and forth from the officers to her and back. He was becoming more frantic, desperate, unhinged. "Tommy, you need to look at me. Keep your eyes on me. I'm going to help you."

In an instant, the facial features changed again. "NO! YOU. ARE. SCARING. HIM!" The axe rose off the floor. "YOU CANNOT HELP US. YOU DO NOT BELONG HERE! WE BELONG HERE! LEAVE! NOW!"

"Tommy, listen to me. You don't belong here. Neither does Jack. Neither of you ever belonged here. Jack can't blame himself for what happened to Jillie. You can't blame yourself for what happened to Jack. Jack survived. You survived the only way you knew how. You can't blame yourself for—for surviving," Gillian paused as her words struck a deep personal nerve. There was a sudden clarity in what she was saying. Through all the years and countless times she had told herself and others in her career those very same words but never truly allowed those words to sink in, she finally understood. "We—we can't blame ourselves—for surviving." Gillian gave a quick glance back toward Trent and Deputy Burelli to see them both giving her a curious look. "You don't belong here, you never did. Please—please, let me help you." The dark figures' glare toward Gillian softened, and for a brief moment she thought she was breaking through, making that connection that could finally deescalate the situation.

"NO—NO! I BELONG HERE!" He grew agitated once again, and his gaze darted back to Deputy Burelli and Trent before taking an unsteady step toward Gillian, raising the axe to shoulder height in an instant.

Three seconds was all the time required. Three short seconds that felt like an eternity for Gillian as she attempted to scream out, "NO! DON'T SHOOT!" But she was unable to get the words out before hearing the first explosion piercing her ears with incredible stabbing

177

pain, drowning out her voice and watching the first bullet shatter the axe handle just below the axe head. Gillian marveled at how the axe head appeared to defy gravity, holding its place mid-air.

She attempted to reach out toward the figure, but her body felt paralyzed, frozen in place, as she witnessed the next bullet hit his chest, tearing through the frail tissue, vital organs and exiting the back, trailing flesh and bone fragments. She struggled in her formation of those three simple words and motion, as each of the next four bullets hit their mark, one after the other with deliberate purpose, tearing flesh and bones at center mass and exiting through the back. The dark figure floated backwards, knocked off his feet, defying gravity as he hovered above the floor.

Her last word pushed hard from her lungs but was still drowned out by the ringing explosion of the final 9mm round, which resonated through the cavernous chamber. In those three seconds Gillian felt a desperate need to discover what more she could have done, what in her years of training did she miss, what action could she have taken to change an outcome that ended within an eternity— three seconds long.

She dropped to her knees next to the frail figure on the floor and watched his features change from glaring anger to childlike wonder. His tiny voice whispered, "Jillie, can we...go...home now?"

Tears streamed down Gillian's face as she watched his features change to that of a gaunt old man with a look of saddened confusion, exhaling his last breath with a cold dead stare. She reached over with a soft tender touch and closed his eyes.

***

Sunday, Sept 22nd 2019

Gillian sat at the picnic table outside the Stilles Asylum and enjoyed the shift in the seasonal temperature as well as the passing shower that cooled the September Sunday afternoon. The occasional sun breaking through lit up each droplet of water on the grass like scattered diamonds. The umbrella came in handy for the few stray drops as Charles parked his large dually truck. Bill stepped out from the passenger side and noticed another picnic table with umbrella. "New addition?"

Gillian waved. "Hey Bill, Charles. Yes, and there'll be a few more next summer."

"Hey, Ms. Gillian," Charles said as he sat. Bill set up a small camcorder on a tabletop stand pointed to the back of the Stilles Asylum along with a digital audio recorder.

"Just in case?" Gillian asked.

"Always," Bill grinned.

"I'd like to thank you two gentlemen for meeting with me here today," Gillian started.

"Of course," Bill replied. "We've hardly heard from you over the last, what, ten weeks since—"

"Is everything okay, Ms. Gillian?" Charles asked with concern.

Gillian nodded. "Yes, yes. I'm fine. I just wanted to give you two the latest update before I go public with a formal press conference tomorrow."

"That sounds serious," Bill said.

"Well you guys have so much invested in the outcome, and I've not been able to keep you in the loop during the formal investigation," Gillian explained.

"We understand…protocol," Charles said.

"Yeah, exactly," Bill agreed.

Gillian pulled up a large folder with paperwork. "We've received testing results on a few things finally. First off…the body found in the well."

"Is it who we thought?" Bill asked.

"The DNA results came back after testing a known cousin of Frank Mills against the bones found and there was a six percent match—"

"Wow that's a great percentage for cousins," Charles stated.

Gillian nodded. "Exactly. The State PD, Sheriff's Office and FBI have signed off on a positive identification. And, there were cut marks on bone fragments that match striations on the axe head found in the lower basement."

"So do they have a suspect?" Bill asked.

"Due to your research and vast interviews with survivors of the Stilles, the FBI and State Police along with the Port Latch Police Department have signed off on Ruphord being the best suspect for the murder of Frank Mills," Gillian said with visible pride.

"Nice job." Charles nudged Bill with his elbow.

"What about the skull in the locked vault?" Bill asked.

Gillian nodded and pulled out another piece of documentation. "Since the vault door is one piece of corroded metal and can't be opened without great effort, and with Charles' recommendation not to disturb the sacred space, they have concluded along with Bill's extensive research and eye witness accounts, that the skull appears to be Ruphord's, and will remain sealed."

Charles turned to Bill again. "Wow! That's a surprise. I expected that once the state took over the internal investigation, because of the shooting, they would tear the place apart."

"Don't get me wrong here. Between the FBI and the State Police, their combined forensic teams searched every inch of that place, top to bottom," Gillian explained. "Long after clearing Deputy Burelli for the shooting."

"And Trent as well…right?" Bill asked.

"Trent only fired one shot, shattering the axe handle. Deputy Burelli fired all the other shots, but was shown to be justified, due to Jack's actions with the axe," Gillian explained.

"How do you feel about that?" Charles asked.

"I wish none of that had happened, but Deputy Burelli was rightfully concerned for everyone's safety. He did the right thing. I just wish I could have had more time."

"What about Jack? Were they able to identify him?" Bill asked.

Gillian pulled yet another thicker set of documents from the folder. "Unfortunately, there is no background on record of Jack or his sister prior to your witness account from Dorthy. Both agencies are even a little sketchy on his age. The best the M.E. and the forensic lab with the FBI could determine was that the subject was approximately 66 to 72 years old. If all the eyewitness accounts are correct, they all corroborate that Jack showed up at the Stilles Asylum in 1956 at the age of six, so then the numbers fit their best estimate. 1950 to present time is 69 years."

"Well I suppose that could still be considered circumstantial, that this is the same man that was that little boy, right?" Bill asked.

Gillian nodded. "Yes, but there's another interesting side note that almost nails everything together—the small ragged doll, Mr. Carrots, held onto by the subject was tested for DNA, and there was a surprise found."

Charles and Bill exchanged excited glances. "Go on," they said together.

"There were two strong examples of DNA on the doll, the first example was of the old man we believe to be Jack."

"And the other?" Bill couldn't wait.

"The other DNA sample was determined to be female and is a fifty percent match," Gillian answered with her best reserved exuberance.

"His sister, Jillie," Charles said with a tone of reverence.

"This corroborated Dorthy's story, and with DNA proved he, indeed, had a sister," Gillian stated. "There's so much more. Remember Dorthy saying they all started to believe Jack was in the walls. Well that was very much the case. The forensic teams did extensive searches in the wetwalls and elevator shaft. They found DNA matches to Jack all over the place, and his autopsy report showed evidence of his activities climbing all through that building, even clear out to the Powder Block building. He had thick calluses covering his hands, feet, elbows, knees, shoulders and scarring all over his body from crawling through tight spaces. He was disease-ridden, and his growth was likely stunted by the horrid conditions he lived in, but he still appeared to be very strong. A fast climber with a very strong grip." Gillian pulled out a copy of the autopsy report.

"That's incredible. I don't understand how he could have lived so long," Bill said, shaking his head in disbelief.

"The M.E. said he didn't have much longer to live; his lungs were nearly non-functional due to the coal dust. He was dying of CWP, better known as Black Lung Disease along with significant signs of mesothelioma. He had maybe only a few months left at best."

"But how did he live? That just doesn't make any sense," Charles asked.

"That is still very much a mystery, but the large amount of animal bones throughout the lower level, along with teeth marks on some of the victims' bones, indicate he lived off rodents and some larger animals as well as cannibalism when available. He also had access to fresh water from a small opening in the cistern in the back. The well was not completely shut off from the cistern. There's an overflow that runs down through a drain in the stone flooring," Gillian explained.

"You know I often thought the lack of rats, mice or squirrels were due to the strong presence of the paranormal in the building. Even though Martin said Ruphord would try to feed his captives with dead rats, I never thought that someone would really do that. I feel a bit ashamed for missing that," Bill said.

Charles patted Bill on the back. "Easy mistake."

"Thanks, pal," Bill smirked. "Did they find anything else of interest in the building?"

Gillian pulled out another set of documents. "There were two more holes at the coal chute, one leading up the wall further to more wetwall access, and another to the east side that led down to a space behind the cistern where they found Jack's makeshift nests. They also found evidence of at least four other 'kill-zones' outside of the furnace room, including the end of the tunnel at the Powder Block, with large amounts of bio-material cross-matched to several of the victims."

"The police never noticed that before?" Charles asked.

"The police never had a reason to do any thorough searches. There was never any witnesses to any assaults, just people reported missing," Gillian explained. "Besides, the people making the reports were not exactly willing to be overly helpful to the police."

"What about the opening by the cistern where he walked out?" Bill asked. "Even Trent's vest camera showed Jack appearing out of the wall."

"There was an opening to a path around the side of the cistern that was obscured by all the black coal dust," Gillian explained. "I got a chance to go back later after the place was better lit, and the opening is much more obvious."

"Was there any evidence from the furnace?" Charles asked with concern.

Once again Gillian pulled more documents. "Again, the stories from the survivor interviews have been corroborated. There was significant bio-material, including bone fragments and teeth, to indicate the furnace had been used extensively to cremate bodies, mostly smaller children. It's like all the horror stories have come true."

"That's just crazy," Bill said shaking his head. "I suppose now you feel this all debunks the paranormal stuff we investigated and documented, right? After all, you were right; this was a person—not a shadow."

Gillian shook her head and reached across the table to Bill's hand.

"I admit that finding a living person behind this mystery has restored my faith in science. But you've shown me there is more to this universe, and several of the forensic teams asked about the shadow figures and the voices as well as the objects moved and thrown that they witnessed for themselves. I don't disbelieve what I witnessed here at the Stilles. Instead I have a better appreciation of the world and beyond…thanks to both you and Charles."

"Thank you, Ms. Gillian," Charles nodded.

"So now what?" Bill asked.

Gillian scooped up the documents and put them back into her folder. "Thanks to your previous investigations, research, and interviews with survivors, this case has reached the governor. He is creating legislation to have the Stilles Garrison designated a historical landmark. The grounds will be made a park, and he is procuring funds to restore and create spaces within the building as a museum—"

"And I suppose, whitewash the awful history of the asylum?" Bill interrupted with a scowl.

Gillian shook her head. "Actually the opposite. He's looking to tell the story of the garrison and the asylum with all its horrible detail, and pay tribute to the survivors. But he's looking for an expert to take charge of the whole project."

Bill shook his head. "Where is he going to find someone like that?" Charles and Gillian both gave Bill a hard glance. Bill scowled back. "What?"

Gillian pulled out a large manila envelope with an official Washington state seal on the return address. "The Governor is hoping you'd be interested in the job. He seems to think I might have some influence on your decision."

Bill felt he needed to remind himself to close his mouth. "I would still have access to all the spaces to continue my paranormal research?"

"All the spaces except the lower basement which is being requested to be permanently off-limits, due to Ruphord's remains," Gillian explained. "But that, I'm sure, could be up to negotiations with the Governor and whomever takes the job."

Bill glanced over the proposal. "So that's what you're going to talk about in the press conference tomorrow?"

Gillian nodded. "That and formally closing the Jeffrie Trace murder case, along with nearly all the other cases found in the lower basement. The axe head blade striations match wounds inflicted on all twenty-two of the victims' skulls and other bones."

"Twenty-two?" Bill asked in shock. "Joe and I only had something like seventeen missing persons' cases with the Stilles Asylum."

"Well, that just means I have a few more mysteries to figure out now I guess," Gillian said with some reverence.

"That's just incredible, congratulations Ms. Gillian." Charles held out his hand for a fist bump.

"Yeah, we should celebrate. I have sirloin steaks and more salmon I could throw on the grill. Anyone interested?" Bill asked.

Gillian nodded. "That sounds perfect." Everyone took a moment to let the new celebratory plan sink in until Gillian broke the silence. "Is it just me, or does this place seem quieter now?"

Charles looked over his shoulder facing the back of the large building, "It does feel like a lot less chaotic. The energy feels lower. They're still watching us, but yes—quieter."

Bill turned to look as well. "I sure hope that's not a trend. I still have more questions to ask and responses to document from the other side."

Gillian shook her head. "I'm sure you'll have plenty of opportunities."

Charles glanced over the top of the picnic table next to Gillian. "Ms. Gillian, can I ask you something?"

"Sure, what?"

"You have a brightly-colored beach towel next to you on the bench, but we're nowhere near a beach. What's that for?"

Gillian looked over and gave the towel a pat with a smile. "Daniel and I bought this for Kristin on our last vacation together in Virginia Beach. It was her favorite keepsake from the trip. I brought the towel so she knows to sit next to me here on the bench."

Charles gave Gillian a knowing nod. "She knows, Ms. Gillian. She knows."

***

Something seemed off, but Gillian couldn't seem to put her finger on it. She adjusted the framed award from the Mayor, set in the middle of a cluster of other frames, including her Masters Degree, certifications and a couple of awards and citations from the Frederick PD, then stepped back. "Hmm," she muttered unsatisfied. She readjusted the frame a touch to the left and stepped back again, shaking her head still unsatisfied.

"Knock knock," Darla announced as she stepped into Gillian's small office. "Fresh coffee."

"Thank you, Darla," Gillian answered a bit distracted.

Darla poured coffee into Gillian's cup on her desk, and noticed for the first time the silver 5x8 picture frame that had always been face down, was now upright. "Oh, honey, that is a wonderful picture of your family," she praised, then was surprised to notice more on the wall. "Oh goodness, you've been busy."

Gillian nodded with a shy smile. "I finally unpacked my last two boxes."

"Well, you know what that means, right?" Darla asked, and Gillian shook her head and shrugged. "You've moved in. It's official now."

"And, about time too," Trent scoffed as he stepped into Gillian's tiny office with Deputy Burelli in tow. Both gave the wall a glance, and Trent adjusted the Mayor's award a touch to the right. "That was one hell of a press conference this morning. So nice of the Governor's office to send a representative with the historical landmark news. All while closing the Jeffrie Trace Case. Gillian, you were great," Trent praised.

"Well I was certainly surprised with the Mayor's award too," Gillian said.

"Yeah. It was all Chief could do to keep from letting the cat out of the bag for the last two weeks," Deputy Burelli tattled.

"Okay, okay, no need to completely rat me out," Trent laughed.

"I'm just glad this whole messed up year is about over," Darla confessed. "We can get back to normal now."

Bud pushed his way into the office. "Make way, Mayor coming through," he announced in his best official manor. "Gillian, I just got off the phone with the Director at the Veterans' Home next door to the Stilles. They are being authorized to set aside a small area in the Veteran's Cemetery to inter Jack's remains."

"Why would they do that?" Deputy Burelli asked.

Bud turned and scowled at the Deputy. "They believe that because of the awful things that happened to Jack throughout his life there at the Stilles, which they still see as an Army Garrison, they would like to try to make amends through this simple gesture. And, the stone cutters have donated a headstone and whatever you'd like to have put on it," Bud turned back to Gillian with excitement.

"I do have something I wrote up, but I'd like to get everyone's opinion first." Gillian pulled up a piece of paper with some hand-written notes.

"I'm sure whatever you decide to say will be fine, honey," Darla assured.

"Well, I still want to be sure. This could possibly end up misconstrued, so please let me know." Gillian raised the paper to read and show everyone the layout:

In Memory of Jack, Survivor of the Stilles Asylum for Disabled Children

And his sister Jillie

Jack-in-the-box, shut up tight. Down in the dark, without any light.

Jack-in-the-box, oh so still. May you both rest now in peace,

By God's Will.

There was not a dry eye except Deputy Burelli. "Ma'am I don't understand something," he said with visible concern.

"What is it?" Gillian asked.

"I mean no disrespect, and I'm certainly not an overly religious man, but I have some Christian beliefs. That man, if we can call him that, was a monster—"

"Deputy—" Bud scowled.

"No, no. Please, I want to hear him out," Gillian requested.

"Thank you, Ma'am. We now know the creature in that building killed twenty plus people with an axe. Chopped them to pieces propping their bodies up for display, and by forensic evidence likely ate a good portion of them as well. He attacked that little girl and even you, Ms. Gillian, both earlier this year and again just a couple months ago. If that isn't a monster I don't know what is, and I can't believe he's going anywhere but straight to hell for his actions in the eyes of God."

Gillian's office fell silent for a few moments hanging on the Deputy's words. Gillian nodded. "I can understand, and respect your

186

position, your opinion. But I believe the true monsters of the Stilles Asylum, the creators of this urban legend nightmare are Frank Mills for creating Ruphord, and Ruphord for creating Jack. Jack; a little boy that from all accounts and witnesses, helplessly watched his little sister being brutally murdered by a true monster, then tortured for years after by that same monster. Forced to live in conditions that are not humane in any respect. That fractured child survived the only way he was allowed to know for decades."

"From everything we've been able to piece together he only killed those who attacked him, threatened him. None of those people in my case files appeared to be particularly nice people. Even Jeffrie Trace was threatening bodily harm right before Jack killed him. Can we condone the actions, the murders Jack committed over the years? Absolutely not, but he survived the only way he was given to know."

"As for that little girl, Stacy. Jack got her out of the building the only way he knew, pushing, pulling, dragging her to the coal chute, pushing her out, because the other girls had chained up the only other way out. That one hundred and fifty pound cast iron coal chute lid was far too heavy for Stacy to lift on her own. Jack did that. He got her out, telling her she didn't belong there. He never attacked her."

"Jack told me the same thing, and tried to remove me from the building as well the only way he knew. I understand that now. And I don't fault you for your actions. You acted accordingly; you followed protocol. My only wish was that he would have given me a little more time to try to help."

"Jack may have become, as you say, a creature, a fractured human, but that does not make him the same as the hideous, vile monsters that created him. So, I don't believe; no, I refuse to believe he will be going to hell for his actions, because he had already been sentenced to a lifetime there, in that hell called the Stilles Asylum for Disabled Children—and I certainly hope that he's finally now been set free."

Deputy Burelli gave a slow nod. "Ma'am, I see your point."

Everyone else in the room sighed a collective, "Amen."

***

Epilogue

From the near blinding yet comforting white brilliance, a small figure formed, skipping closer and wearing her Sunday best— white hat, white gloves, white overcoat over a blue dress with white dots, white knee high socks and black leather buckled shoes. Her shoulder-length blonde hair was tied back with a pretty blue ribbon that matched her bright blue eyes. Softly humming a happy little tune known only to herself, she continued undaunted and quite excited in her task as she approached a large, deep and dark foreboding hole before her. She stopped, and with hands on her bent knees, leaned precariously over the edge of the blackness that utterly contrasted her surroundings, without fear or the slightest concern.

"Jack? Jack—" she called down into the darkness. "Jack, it's time. Time to come out." She waited a moment, then called out again. "Jack. You can come out now."

From the darkness a black, dirty little hand appeared, but as the hand reached into the light out of the shadows of the hole, the dirt fell away. Then another hand reached up to the edge. Finally a little blonde head popped out, and the little girl tugged on his white collared shirt in an effort to help.

"Come on Jack. It's time. We've all been waiting so long. Gramma and Grampa are so excited to finally meet you," the little girl spoke with energized excitement.

The little boy stepped out of the hole and straightened his bow tie, wiped at his Sunday best black pants, checking the shine on his shoes before pulling a ragged, long-eared patchwork doll from his back pocket, and a half-eaten candy bar from his front pocket and taking a bite. "I have Mr. Carrots for you, Jillie."

"Mr. Carrots," she squealed with excitement, tucking the patchwork rabbit under her chin and taking her brother's hand, leading him away from the dark hole. The little boy looked back for a moment, expecting to see something, but realized he couldn't remember what he was looking for. Now all that mattered was his

little sister was leading them into the comforting white brilliance—
home.

About the Author

Mark T. Bacome has an extensive creative background ranging from professional musician, graphic artist, published cartoonist and writer/director/producer of several thousand radio and television commercials. He has published four Sci-Fi books of a series, "Descendants," "Hereditary Evil," "Body of Souls," and "Birth of a Goddess," between 2012 and 2017 through Amazon Kindle. Mark has a degree in Computer Network Engineering and works as a contractor for the US Navy while living with his wife and daughter in Bremerton, Washington. "Jack-in-the-Box" is Marks first attempt at a genre other than Sci-Fi.

www.ingramcontent.com/pod-product-compliance
Lightning Source LLC
Chambersburg PA
CBHW020517120726
47904CB00003B/864